"Who are you? What do you want from me?"

"As I said, these are presents for you."

He held up the long, dark shapes. She began to back away from him, frightened of the man in the strange costume. What did he want? Was he going to rape her? Well, let him try, she thought. I won't give in. I'll fight.

"Please don't be afraid. Look."

He removed one sword from its scabbard, then the other, and held them out to her.

"Swords," she said. "Oh my God. I'm going to scream. You better get away from me. I'm—"

"Yes, the swords of the samurai."

Instinctively her arms closed to cover and protect her chest. Not me, oh God no, please God no—

The sword in Mitzu's left hand swept up in an arc . . .

THE
BUSHIDO CODE

a novel by

Robert St. Louis

FAWCETT GOLD MEDAL • NEW YORK

Acknowledgments

The idea for this novel was developed in collaboration with Lewis Chesler. The author expresses his gratitude.

For her strong support and intelligent advice, the author thanks Maureen Baron, a writer's dream of an editor.

THE BUSHIDO CODE

Copyright © 1981 Robert St. Louis

Published by Fawcett Gold Medal Books, a unit of CBS Publications, the Consumer Publishing Division of CBS Inc.

ISBN: 0-449-14438-0

Printed in the United States of America

First Fawcett Gold Medal printing: November 1981

10 9 8 7 6 5 4 3 2 1

For Swifty Hirsch,
without whom . . .

If I go to the sea
My body will float on the waves.
If duty calls me to the mountains
My shroud will be made of moss.
So I will die for the Emperor,
Far from the peace of my home.

—A samurai song

CELEBRATION

THE SUN rises hot in New Mexico. On a barren ivory mesa lying at the heart of the Jemez and Sangre de Cristo mountains, just outside the city of Los Alamos, the sun had been steadily beating for five hours before the crowds began to arrive. Some had come for the ceremony because the Army invited them, some in the name of obscurely felt patriotism, some out of sheer curiosity, and still others, if anyone had bothered to ask, for no particular reason they could explain.

They had started drifting out from the city around eleven in the morning—tourists, locals, and even a few Indians and Mexicans from the valley—and by noon they numbered more than three thousand. They held their positions calmly under a feather-clouded sky, packed in neat tight rows on bleachers erected only the day before. In the dry air, thick with dust, many had begun to sweat, touching their foreheads with the remains of Kleenex crumpled from the long drive into the mountains.

Across from the bleachers, on the edge of the open plain, the platform for official guests was filling up. Freshly painted regulation gray, the platform sported bright circles of red, white, and blue bunting, the colors blending into one as waves of heat rose from the arid ground. At the center of the platform, flanked by the unfurled flags of New Mexico and the United States, sat a wooden lectern, lined on either side by clusters of metal folding chairs, each with its hard Army-issue cushion. The spectators were prepared for discomfort and had brought their own cushions, along with jugs of juice and cans of beer. They knew the spectacle would be worth the discomfort.

Behind the platform, stretching over nearly eighty acres of scrub-covered desert, loomed the three hun-

7

dred buildings of the Los Alamos Scientific Laboratory, housing proton accelerators and atom smashers and all manner of equipment that hardly anyone present would ever understand. Still farther on the horizon hung the majestic purple-peaked caps of the Jemez range. The lab, one local old-timer was fond of telling tourists, was J. Robert Oppenheimer's idea, but the mountain range was God's, and only a fool had any trouble deciding who was the smarter of the two.

General George Britten stood on the ground below the platform, shielding his eyes as he scanned the sky. He was tall and silver-haired, and cut a dashing figure against the landscape. George "Horseshoe" Britten, they called him, and anyone who had read the morning papers could have identified him. It's going to be bright and clear, he thought, in another twenty minutes. Just in time. He made his way onto the platform and set his briefcase down by the lectern, watching as the remaining dignitaries came toward him from the laboratory's white-domed assembly hall. He felt strange being back after so many years, back where the original tests had been done, and even now there was something eerie about the place—the isolation, the emptiness. He glanced at the audience and squinted, so that his bushy eyebrows fell at right angles to his long narrow nose, and the sunlight, beating down on his face, turned his eyes into deep hollows. God, yes, it was strange, he thought, and listened to the buzz of the mountains' silence in his head.

Behind him the rest of the original Los Alamos crew mounted the platform. There were Oscar Berryman and his wife Marie, and Dick Farrell and Elmer Bly and, down at the end of the row, old Harry Sears. Wasn't it amazing? After thirty-five years Harry still had his childlike dimpled chin and his wife still gabbed in that crazy chattering whisper. For the briefest moment General George Britten wondered how much he himself had changed. But he was not normally inclined to such thoughts, and when the laboratory's public

8

relations woman appeared on the dais the reflective moment vanished as abruptly as it had come.

"General, Lieutenant Colby asked me to tell you that the planes are ready. We're ready to start."

He looked down at the woman. My oh my, sweetheart, you sure are pretty.

"You tell Lieutenant Colby," the general said, "that we'll wait just a little longer. This here sky's going to clear up, and we're going to have ourselves a beautiful day."

"Yes, sir."

As the woman turned away, a wide bank of cirrus clouds rolled from the face of the sun, and General Britten let his eyes play over the crowd. Tanned faces, string ties, garishly patterned blouses and slacks. General Britten thought that if he could take these people and weave their hopes into one voice, then he could convince anyone, and the United States Congress in particular, that the American people were as ready for war as they had ever been. All the political pundits were saying that the United States had lost its will. Vietnam, they said, has destroyed America's faith in its right to lead. Bunkum, thought General Britten. Hogwash. The United States of America was ready to lead the free world—in fact, had no choice but to lead. Because that was our destiny. "The strong do what they can," the general loved to say, quoting Thucydides, "and the weak do what they must."

The sky, as General Britten had predicted, cleared to reveal a burning orange-white sun, and the desert dust changed color before his eyes. The mountains gleamed even more brightly, each pointed peak like a cardboard cutout against the horizon. On the ground below the platform, newspaper photographers jostled each other for better angles, snapping continuously while television crews behind them aimed videotape cameras. The general felt himself stiffen and throw his shoulders back in a totally reflexive gesture. But he was unaware of his motives. Nor would any casual observer have concluded that the general's smoothing of his lapels

9

and fussing with the folds in his jacket had anything to do with the presence of cameras. But to General George Britten his uniform symbolized his purpose in the world and defined his life in some crucial way that even he did not understand.

The cameras clicked and churned, sweeping across the platform and out across the audience. While the general stared toward the crowd, many in turn stared at him. They were hot and wanted the ceremony to begin. They watched the general shaking hands, directing people to their seats, making room for an old, stooped man with a cane, and then bending down to whisper in his ear. They watched him signal a young woman in a yellow checked suit, and then take his seat next to the lectern. At the rear of the platform there seemed to be confusion as to who should sit where; the wind had blown away name tags taped to the metal folding chairs earlier in the day.

General Britten looked over his shoulder. It was time to begin. He raised his index finger and the young Army lieutenant at the end of the aisle stepped to the microphone.

"Ladies and gentlemen, please rise for the national anthem, which will be sung today by Victoria Hill."

The ample Miss Hill, who sang ballads in a downtown nightclub, strode to the microphone. With the briefest nod of her head, the conductor of the Army band began to play. *"O say can you see-e-e-e . . . by the dawn's early light . . ."* echoed across the mesa. Hands over their hearts, the three thousand sang in unison.

When the anthem was over, a short trim man in an Army uniform stepped to the lectern. He was dwarfed by the microphone stand and forced to stand on his toes. He delivered, in a flat, boring voice, a history of the Los Alamos laboratories, a history that was, in fact, anything but boring. But the audience had no patience for lectures. They had not driven miles to sit baking under a torrid sun and listen to the lieutenant extol the wonders of science. The lieutenant said technology could be put to good uses or bad, and the crowd

10

barely paid attention. The men in the audience toyed with their string ties and the women in lavender and puce pants suits fanned themselves. The lieutenant said moral choices belonged to the realm of statesmen, and that hard choices often had to be made. The crowd, now thoroughly restless, had stopped paying attention altogether.

If you don't finish mighty soon, boy, the general thought to himself, they're going to be sorely tempted to get up and leave.

". . . and so I am pleased to present to you a distinguished servant of our country. As a young man he served on General Eisenhower's staff in Europe. He was wounded, decorated, and awarded the Silver Star and the Purple Heart before returning home. At war's end he was here at Los Alamos, and he was until his retirement from the Army an adviser to the Joint Chiefs of Staff. Ladies and gentlemen, a man I'm sure you all recognize and join me in welcoming, our guest of honor today, General George Britten."

General Britten stepped to the lectern, adjusted the brim of his hat, and listened to the brief ripples of applause. Well, now, that isn't much of a welcome, he thought. The boy put 'em to sleep, so I'll just have to wake 'em up. He retrieved his speech from his briefcase, weighted the pages with two brass paperweights on the lectern, and pulled out his stopwatch. The medals on his left breast pocket reflected darts of sunlight as he moved.

The general was much respected among his colleagues as a public speaker, and he knew that to pause for the slightest beat before beginning to speak could change an audience's mood from restless to expectant, focusing their attention on him. He clicked his stopwatch, adjusted his mirrored aviator glasses on his nose, and again held up a finger to the young lieutenant standing near the mobile phone at the edge of the dais.

"Thank you, Lieutenant Kennedy. I am pleased to return to Los Alamos today, where thirty-five years ago we fought with and changed the course of history.

11

America is embarking on a difficult journey again, a new and perilous journey . . ."

The general's voice boomed richly over the crowd. While the young lieutenant's flat, Midwestern twang had sounded whiny and thin over the large speaker horns, General Britten's voice—full, deep, and slightly hoarse—took on a majestic roar. The general felt the dry air and dust bite into his throat. I've got to stop inhaling those damned cigars, he thought.

". . . and the essence of leadership is choice. We will make mistakes, but we must always choose. The people of the United States must choose whether to lead, or to follow. We must resolve to fight for our freedoms. As a great historian from the past said, 'The strong do what they can, and the weak do what they must.' Our battle is not only with those who would attempt world domination. It is with ourselves. Do we have the courage and the will to maintain a strong defense? When our moment in history comes again, as it came thirty-five years ago, will we be as prepared? Need I remind you that the price of liberty, ladies and gentlemen, is eternal vigilance?"

At this last phrase General Britten theatrically raised his hands. The wind was up, the flags sailed in full colors, and he heard the cameras click and saw zigzags of sunlight bounce from the flagpoles in the moment before the applause washed over him.

Now that's what I call applause, he thought. You woke 'em up, George, you really did.

Fifteen miles away, at an airbase on the far side of the Jemez range, four B-52 bombers prepared for takeoff. On the edge of the airstrip, where black bubbles rippled the tarmac, special effects director Loren Hutchins lit a Marlboro, wiped perspiration from his cheeks, and wished he were back in Los Angeles, working as usual at Twentieth-Century Fox, and not out here on this godforsaken desert. He had checked the explosive charges on the dummy bombs, and stood aside as the four pilots climbed into their planes.

"Now remember, gents," he said, "you've got to hit the timers before you jerk the harness, or you're gonna have one awful mess inside your planes."

The pilots nodded and one by one closed themselves in. Loren Hutchins crushed out his cigarette with his foot.

"Aw, damn," he said aloud, realizing he had coated his shoe with sticky black tar.

He turned and headed for the communications tower. Who had ordered him to do this gig? Probably one of those pipsqueak young executives looking to make friends at the Pentagon. What really annoyed him was spending two weeks planning an effect that was taking place on the other side of the mountain. He wouldn't even be able to see it close up. He would only see it on television when he got home.

At the radar tower Specialist 3rd Class Tyrone Williams waited to escort him up the steps.

"How much time?" Hutchins asked as the planes' engines chugged to life.

"He's seven minutes into the speech."

The air controller in the tower had been listening.

"That'll be seven minutes and eleven seconds," he said as Hutchins and Williams came into the room. And then, tonelessly into his headset, "Ready for take-off. At twelve thousand feet it's real smooth. Four knots."

The three men in the tower watched the planes roll to the edge of the airstrip, turn around, and one by one lift off and soar up, heading west. Brackish burning jet fuel and a dull thunder trailed behind them.

"Seven minutes and fifteen seconds to target," the controller said into his headset. "Absolutely right on the . . . *mark!*"

Specialist 3rd Class Williams turned to Loren Hutchins and said, "I guess you're finished now. I hope they work."

"Course they'll work," Hutchins said. "If your flyboys do like I told them. Now, can you get me out to the airport? I got a little boy at home with the flu."

13

"Just a minute," Williams said. He picked up the green radiophone, looked at the clicking digital clock on the console, and said, "They're on their way, Lieutenant Colby, sir. Six minutes and fifty-eight seconds to target."

Hurry up, Hutchins thought.

Williams set the phone down. "Okay, Mr. Hutchins, sir, let's get you on your way home."

". . . and a group of dedicated men, the leaders of our country and the armed forces, and the finest scientific minds in America. Men who wanted only one result, and that was to end a war. Our effort was given the name Project Y. Today we are going to see—"

In mid-sentence General Britten stole a glance at his ticking stopwatch. I've been talking too slow, he thought. Mentally he began editing his speech, cutting sentences and phrases from the last two paragraphs. He had less than a minute left to finish.

"—what the result of that effort looked like to those of us who proudly participated in Project Y. You will see here today what we saw thirty-five years ago, a simulation of the largest explosive device then known to mankind, two hundred kilotons of power, a triumph. A triumph of the intellect and courage of man—" he paused for a dramatic breath "—the conquering of nature in the name of peace."

A distant rumbling filled the sky, its reverberations already audible in the east. As the general's last phrase boomed across the mesa the noise, with what sounded like sudden force, grew louder. By the time the general removed his glasses the rumbling seemed to echo over the mountains, first as a series of alternating thunderclaps, and then a steadier roar, a consistent pounding like the sustained roll of a bass drum, an enormous orchestra of drums.

Almost as a single body, members of the audience craned their respective necks, palms above their eyes to block out the sun, searching the horizon. Even a few on the dais, although aware of what was coming, leaned back in their seats to study the sky.

General Britten, ignoring the approaching B-52 bombers that held everyone else entranced, took his seat. His mind had moved on to the reunions, and how they would help him. An opportunity for stirring up editorial writers and local Kiwanis and Lions clubs, for prodding his fellow observers on the platform to return to the public arena. Make speeches. Write letters to the editor. Organize and raise money for congressional campaigns. Get *our* people in.

But not even George "Horseshoe" Britten could ignore the lure of spectacle, and when the bombers banked into the valley, he could not help shifting in his seat and raising his head ever so slightly for a view of the entertainment.

Over the mountaintops the B-52s came into view. They dipped in vee formation across the cluster of laboratory buildings and, according to instructions, swooped close to the plateau and buzzed the crowd. Hats flew into the swirling dust. Candy wrappers whipped across the ground. The noise was ear-splitting.

And although the bottom of the vee was off-center, the crowd was clapping furiously, snapping Instamatics and Nikons and unspooling Super 8 along with the professionals. When the planes banked again into the sun, and regained formation, their engines spat out a high-pitched burst of sound like a screaming in the sky.

"Pick it up, fellas," said the message in the headsets of three pilots. "On vector 5 southwest, we're up and over." The voice coughed. "Walter, did you get any sleep last night? Are you fighting with Josie again? Because your tail's dragging and you're lousing up this beautiful formation. Get your ass in gear."

The vee, with the bottom suddenly straightened to perfection, swanned into the mountains, and the reverberating drumroll built to a torrential, unceasing whine, a mind-numbing, brain-shattering screech. The moment was both explosive and serene. It was more

15

like a series of quickly sketched drawings, rapidly registered images, than anything real. It was too real. And when the sleek instruments of aviation appeared practically vertical, when the vee formation seemed to be aiming directly for the sun, when the planes appeared to defy natural law and be on the verge of falling from the cloudless blue blanket of sky, a hush fell over the crowd. They stopped squinting. They stopped taking pictures. What neither the young lieutenant nor General Britten could accomplish, the pilots, in a display of sheer technical skill, had done. They had captured their audience's total attention.

A cheap trick, the general thought acidly, finally bestirring himself to lift his head fully and witness the demonstration. A cheap trick, but a truly wonderful one. Yes, he admitted to himself, the grandeur of aviation technology was quite magnificent, and the pilots deserved this silent accolade.

Now the planes were soaring above the mountains, just barely visible from the ground. At that distance they could have been mistaken for little Cessnas or hot-air balloons or even birds.

"All right, Walter, wake up," crackled the mission leader's voice. "We're gonna count down now, you know, like with numbers. Five, fellows, four . . . three . . . two . . . one . . . *bingo!*"

Without warning, just as had occurred thirty-five years ago, the bombers released their payloads. The simulated bombs tore piercingly through the air until, at nine thousand six hundred feet, their mock casings split apart, and a new explosion of sound ripped through the mountains. This was strictly show business, for originally there had been only two planes, one payload, and virtually no noise.

As the casings fell away an almost supernatural flash lit the sky, a pure white light, laser-like—it was the burning of magnesium in sequential charges. Dust from the mountaintops gathered in puffs, slowly for half a minute, then in mounting speed, and four wispy clouds of dust ascended above the light. There was

16

another flash, so vividly bright the entire horizon radiated a luminescent glow, and then the four bomb clouds grew taller, widening as they rose, until the tops of the columns of dust and smoke twisted over and into themselves, billowing and expanding all at once, as four identical shapes blotted out the sun and filled the western sky.

Four mushroom clouds, gray and terrifying. The horror and the power made visible.

"Very nice, fellows," said the mission leader's voice.

Well executed, General Britten thought, as he stood to leave the platform. He paused next to the flag at the top of the steps as the others gathered around to shake his hand. They stood together, just the four men, as the photographers focused and clicked off their last shots, and then they all headed for the assembly hall.

1

"DARLING, come look at this."

Nancy Nagata jangled a set of hanging chimes—tiny crystal elephants, plastic giraffes, tin lions—on the main floor of Hartman's Toy Emporium. High above her, stained-glass windows forming the ceiling depicted children at play, and all around the store excited squeals of discovery could be heard. At her feet sprawled a pink stuffed teddy bear, a foam duck that quacked when pulled along by its string, and piles of silken pillows.

She felt the baby kicking furiously inside her. She kept wondering: boy or girl? But while she wanted to know, the whole idea of a needle stuck straight into her abdomen made her wince. Why chance amniocentesis, and maybe a miscarriage, just to satisfy curiosity? She was terrified of medical procedures in general, and the doctors had agreed that she was in perfect health, and she would, in all likelihood, give birth to a perfectly healthy, perfectly normal baby. Besides, half the fun was *not* knowing, and not knowing meant that none of the toys she bought would be sexist. Her child was going to grow up with as few of those hang-ups as possible.

"Mitch, darling, come look, please, this is adorable."

Nancy rested against the counter to take the weight off her feet. Outside, the afternoon was warm and muggy, and she was glad to be in the air-conditioned store. She had found herself tiring easily this last month and had grown increasingly dependent on creature comforts in the humidity of San Francisco's summer.

From the building blocks and erector-set section of the store Mitzu Nagata walked toward his wife, and the mere sight of his smile, the lilt of his stride, and the beauty of his lithe figure flooded her with a peculiar happiness. I must be going a little crazy, she thought. I'm damn near giddy most of the time. Sometimes she thought it wasn't right for life to seem so endlessly romantic, that letting the birth of her first child so entirely absorb her attention was not sensible for a liberated, intelligent woman. Her friends refused to believe that she would abandon her architectural career for full-time motherhood. How *can* you? You'll be so *bored!*

But she had asked for, and received, an indefinite leave of absence from the drafting tables of Skidmore, Owings and Merrill, and had relinquished plans for the office building on which she was project manager to another. She had decided to devote at least the first six months to raising her child. If I get bored, I'll go back to work. Well, maybe I will, she thought, and maybe I won't, but one thing's for sure. I'm not going to berate myself for wanting to be a mother.

She thought she had a perfect life, and that nothing could ever be better than it was now.

"What've you got, Nan?" her husband said, sidling up to her and kissing her cheek.

She shook the chimes she was holding. The little sculpted animals sang out a sort of atonal melody.

"For above the crib, don't you think?"

"It's beautiful," Mitzu said.

His voice wasn't excited, but Nancy had grown accustomed to that. After two years of marriage, she prided herself on understanding her husband. Great effusions of emotion—of joy, of sadness, of pain—just weren't his way. She didn't doubt for a second that his feelings were as intense as hers. He just didn't express them: The Japanese temperament. People said Mitch was *too* laid-back, too hard to know, but she appreciated his placid, unruffled calm in the face of all storms. Living with Mitch, she thought, helped her tame what she considered the hysterical little girl who lived inside her head.

Mitzu put his hand on her cheek.

"How're you feeling, Nan? You look tired."

"I *am* a little tired," she said, "but I'll be okay as soon as we get home. Should we take the chimes?"

"Sure, let's, and what about these?"

In one hand he held the *Sesame Street* Big Bird, and from the other he dangled a padded plastic frame, designed for hanging over the edge of a crib. It had a clock that did not run, a pink telephone dial without a receiver, and rows of colored beads approximating an abacus.

"Why not?" Nancy said. "How often do we have a baby? And with all this stuff in the crib, the kid won't have time to cry."

They piled the purchases next to the cash register. Mitzu just looked at them, grinning to himself. His first child. When Nan had asked him whether he wanted a girl or a boy, he had pretended not to care. But the truth was he wanted a boy. He was not altogether certain why, but he figured it had something to do with boys being extensions of their fathers.

It also had something to do with his own parents, and with some unexplored hope to bestow on them a grandson. To them, and to their tradition, a male was of inestimably higher value.

"Your first?" said the clerk behind the register, a gangly young woman with a frizzy shock of red hair and round blue glasses in red frames.

Nancy nodded. "Any day now," she said.

"I'd love to have children," the clerk said in a weary voice. "But you know, what kind of world is this to bring children into? I mean, everything's so awful these days."

"The world is what you make of it," Mitzu said.

"I suppose so," the woman said.

Mitzu took one bag, Nancy took the other, and for a moment they stood there, looking pleased with each other. They were the happiest they had ever been.

On Market Street they passed a young boy selling flowers for one of the religious cults. Mitzu couldn't distinguish between the various cults, and he disapproved of all of them, but he bought a pink carnation and planted the stem in Nancy's blond hair. Every woman on the block smiled at Nancy as she passed, sensing the joy radiating from her.

"Oh, *stop*," she said to her husband as he adjusted the flower, unable to hide her pleasure at the gesture. "Do you think a toy store should have a clerk who thinks there's no future for children?"

"I'm sure the management doesn't know."

"Do you really have to go back to the office? We could spend the afternoon in bed."

Mitzu was ashamed to admit that he wanted to return to work. Ed Stone was after him for the marketing reports, and he had two appointments with potential clients, and . . . and . . . and, well, damnit, in another month or two the board might decide to name him an executive vice-president.

"Stone wants me on a tour of our installations soon," he said distractedly.

"Oh, Mitch, you *can't* go. You just can't. Not until after—"

"Don't be silly, Nan. Of course I won't leave until after he's born. And it'll only be a few days."

Nancy smiled. "That's the second time you've said that today. After *he's* born. I thought you didn't care one way or the other."

"I only use *he*," Mitzu said, laughing, "because I hate to say *it*."

The sky darkened, threatening rain, and as Mitzu walked he watched the sun turn red behind foggy clouds. In an instant, so fleeting Mitzu was not even aware it had passed, the sun became in his mind the Japanese national flag. In the next moment it was merely the sun.

A darkened sun, an overcast sky, the lights on Coit Tower—that had been Mitzu Nagata's first view of his adopted country. As he crossed Market Street to the parking garage, he ran the reels of memory like home movies in his mind. He saw himself as a four-year-old in an alien country, being lifted onto a cable car. He

21

heard the strains of a banjo, scratchy and thin over a tinny radio speaker, and a squawky voice singing, "Pardon me, boy, is that the Chattanooga Choo-Choo." Then as a six-year-old, watching his mother slip through the door late at night, tired from her work as a cook, while his father, who was unable to find work, sat waiting for her on the floor . . . at nine, helping his father stock the shelves of their store with packages of tea and spices and rice . . . at ten, delivering bags to Nob Hill on his bicycle, hearing taunts from children as he waited outside the kitchen door. *Slant-eye. Jap. Nip.*

The movies flickered past his mind's eye in seconds, each pain as fresh and searing, each picture as clear as his hand in front of him, as if life were one continuous film, forever carrying the slights of childhood. He recalled suddenly climbing down creaky steps to his parents' basement apartment, and the transformation of a dark cellar hole into a maze of screens and paper lamps and cheap straw mats. And he remembered, too, how they had come to this country with hope for a new life, hope that was soon battered into humiliation.

He felt a lump in his throat.

He wondered if these memories had kept him in San Francisco all his life. Or whether he had remained out of a sense of duty to his parents. Instead of a college in the East he had chosen Stanford, and to offers of jobs elsewhere he automatically said no. American General offered him a transfer to Boston, but he rejected the idea out of hand, and when Nancy had asked him why, no answer presented itself. He just knew he never even considered it.

"Mitch, the ticket." She tugged at his sleeve. The garage attendant held his hand out, waiting.

"Of course, darling, I don't know what I was thinking."

He glanced at the sky, which was growing still darker, so dark he could no longer distinguish the red circle of sun.

The attendant took his ticket and directed him to a space on the other side of the floor. Mitzu thought the place was lit very oddly, and then realized he was seeing shadows of clouds falling on the concrete walls. He looked over his shoulder and caught Nan's eye following him. For a complicated mind, he thought, she was remarkably simple in her love for him. They had met when she was on assignment from Skidmore, Owings at American General, supervising the company's new headquarters. Her previous assignment had been as part of the team for Transamerica's pyramid tower, and Mitzu had been present at a meeting when she presented plans for the American General Building. It was almost love at first sight—her blond hair with the texture of tapestry silk, her nervous, girlish laugh, the flash of her green eyes. She appealed to him as all well-crafted physical objects did. She was like the perfectly designed assemblage of tubes and pipes that occupied a corner of his desk. She was ideal. She was the apotheosis of form. His love for her, he thought, might be the only pure emotion he had ever known.

Pulling the Audi up to the sidewalk, Mitzu leaned across the seat to open the door. Nan lifted her heavy body with extreme care, and got in. As he drove he basked in the splendor of her glow and the life she carried inside her.

"Mitch, I've been thinking. Do you want to put a carpet down in the baby's room?"

Before Mitzu had a chance to answer, there was a sudden crackle of lightning, then a flood of rain, and it began to pour.

2

IF ONLY someone had taught them to read in high school. Or prep school. If only, Jill Britten thought, someone had exposed them to a fragment of history. The public and prep school graduates alike seemed to have the most unbelievable difficulty with mundane concepts. If you couldn't read, then you couldn't think, and if you couldn't think, then all was lost. I've only been out of high school fifteen years myself, she thought, but even when I was there it was going to hell in a handbasket.

Jill peered over the tops of her glasses and considered the twenty scrubbed faces in front of her. They're all so straight, she thought. What happened to the oddballs? Maybe there aren't any oddballs nowadays. On H Street outside, a truck lumbered by the building toward Pennsylvania Avenue, rattling the classroom windowpanes in their frames. The intense midsummer heat of the United States capital seemed to seep through the glass.

"On March 14, 1920," she continued, "the Japanese garrison at Nicolaevsk was annihilated, and the Japanese retreated, taking General Dietrichs with them. This, of course, ended Japan's participation in the war. And Japan had almost nothing to show for her loss of thousands of her men. In defeat, and in the country's failure to finish the war with substantial new territory, the country went through a terrible soul-searching. Again the ancient warrior code of Bushido made itself felt. The country experienced an incredible surge of nationalism, and even among the most forward-looking, there were calls to return the warrior class, the samurai, to their former glory." Jill paused, sighed, and said, "Next week, we'll take a look at where the new nationalism led. I'd appreciate your giving the text a little more attention than you did this week."

Before she had assigned the material for the next class, the students began packing their bags, in a hurry to evacuate the room. They want lunch, Jill thought. She knew from experience that holding the attention of an eleven-thirty class demanded all her theatrical powers. They didn't like summer school much anyway, and they were hungry, so you had to make your lectures stand up and sing. She was actually finding the teaching of undergraduates more fun than she had imagined. If only someone had taught them how to read.

As she packed her own briefcase and prepared to face the unbearable heat, Colin Stewart approached her desk. Colin was one of those engaging eager beavers, with ashblond hair and a toothy smile, who was destined for Capitol Hill fame once he finished school. For weeks he had been begging her to find him a job with her brother. Unfortunately, her brother had more young kids clamoring to work for him than he could handle.

Colin Stewart had also been attempting since June to lure Jill into joining him for a drink or a movie or a dinner, in the hope, she suspected, of getting her into bed. Colin had retreated only when she informed him that her boyfriend was an FBI agent with whom she was unequivocably in love.

"Professor Britten, I don't want to pester you, but I was just—"

"Yes, Colin, I asked the congressman and he's going to see what he can do for you. I gave you a recommendation as the brightest thing to come down the pike in years."

"I can't thank you enough, really. I really admire him, I really do. He's such a rare politician—"

"Yes, Colin, I know," Jill said patiently, wondering if the boy's vocabulary consisted of words other than "really." "He told me you'd be hearing from him very soon. You can expect an appointment to talk to him."

"Thanks very much," Colin Stewart said, turning to

leave, and then hesitating in the doorway. "Do you really have a boyfriend who's an FBI agent?"

"Yes, Colin, I do," she said, laughing. "And he promised he'd shoot you if you didn't stop making passes at me."

"Can't hurt a guy to try," Stewart said with mock insincerity.

"Colin, if you put one tenth of that energy into your career, then nothing could stop you from conquering the world. I'll see you next Wednesday."

"Here, let me help you," Stewart said, touching her arm. She was walking with some difficulty, having twisted her ankle in a touch football game with Alex over the weekend.

"I'll make it, Colin. Thanks anyway."

She picked up her briefcase and saw, stuck inside the top, the note Alex had left her that morning. "Razzle dazzle 'em," it said. Still, Colin was cute, he was probably pretty good in bed, and a brief fantasy of having sex with him lingered a little longer than she would have liked. She had just read in the *Post* that boys were at their sexual prime, their peak, at eighteen and nineteen, and women were at theirs at thirty-five. From adolescence on, it was uphill for women and downhill for men.

Colin held her arm as they went down the stairway, toward the H Street door. What makes civilization tick, she told herself, is the repression of sexual urges. But even thinking about Colin made her feel guilty. Well, faithfulness by its nature implied betrayal. You couldn't have one without thinking about the other.

On H Street the heat had abated just enough to make walking tolerable.

"Good-*bye,* Colin. See you Wednesday."

"Thanks, Jill, uh, I mean Professor Britten," he said quickly, then turned and trotted down Pennsylvania.

The little hustler, she thought to herself. Burt really ought to hire him.

Waves of heat rose from the sidewalk. In front of the White House a line of tourists waited for admittance, and a Mr. Softee ice cream truck was doing brisk business. Jill wished she had her bicycle, but with her ankle so swollen it would have been useless anyway. Cabs were so cheap in Washington that she was tempted to take them everywhere. Her apartment, her office, and her classes were all in one zone—a dollar and a half would get her to most of her daily stops. But today, she had too many stops to make.

When the light changed she headed across Pennsylvania. A book was waiting for her at Kramerbooks, where she would stop for coffee, and then on to American Express at Twentieth and M to pick up tickets for her trip to Milwaukee, where she was delivering an absurdly well-paid lecture on the portentous topic of "America and Japan: Two Cultures in Conflict." Then to the library, to start work on her book. The Milwaukee lecture could be edited and transformed into a first chapter. If I procrastinate one more day, I'll never start the damn thing, and if I don't start, I'll end up as one of those tenure vultures and spend all my time buttering up the department chairman instead of working.

As she rounded the corner toward the bookstore, limping on her bad ankle and cursing Alex for tackling her in what was supposed to be just a loose, fun game, she knew something was wrong. Now what the devil was it?

Oh God, no work this afternoon. She remembered she was meeting Alex and Burt for a late lunch. She gave in and hailed a cab.

Just ten blocks south, in the new J. Edgar Hoover Building at Tenth Street and Pennsylvania Avenue, Alex Burgess was coping not with the heat, but with the invasion of his office by Buck Weston. Buck, who was in charge of the word-sorting computers downstairs, had parked himself in front of Alex's desk with the apparent intention of remaining forever, or at least the rest of the afternoon. A pale, wiry little creature, Buck had overlarge eyes and an incessant series of nervous gestures—a tapping toe, a twitching finger, or a fingernail constantly clicking against his front tooth. Like a Rube Goldberg perpetual-motion machine, his body seemed forever caught in a spiraling excess of energy.

Alex who would have been more than willing, even anxious, to recommend Buck's banishment from the second floor, even from the Bureau itself, could not bring himself to order Buck from his office. *Poor fellow, he just needs friends. Problem is, he's crazy. Give me a panel of psychiatrists and in ten minutes they'll declare the man thoroughly deranged.*

"This little .22-caliber Hopkins," Buck was saying. "A real beauty. Pearl handle, 1873. Single barrel, one shot, one of the best derringers ever made. Hopkins made it himself. The ladies used derringers, you know, carried them in their purses. Now the one I bought Belle Matthews herself owned. She ran a whorehouse in Vicksburg and kept it up her sleeve. And Alex, you won't believe what else I found. A cap-and-ball job, a revolver, used by Sam Bass."

Buck Weston stood just over five feet tall, Alex thought this might explain why Buck collected guns. Compensating for being a shrimp. Buck brushed his cowlick back, waiting for Alex to demonstrate some interest in his latest purchases.

"Sam Bass," Alex said, trying to hold up his end of the conversation. "The bank robber."

Outside in the courtyard, just visible through Alex's window, three men on a scaffold were polishing the two-foot-high letters memorializing the late, great J. Edgar. *The Most Effective Weapon Against Crime Is* was all that was visible above the scaffolding. The building itself defined Washington monumentalism—a stark angular brick monolith set back from the avenue in a plaza, with a concourse running through at ground level and a sunken courtyard just below.

"And in the butt plate," Buck Weston continued, "he carved his name. S. Bass. I only paid two hundred bucks for it, Alex. With his *name* carved in it. It's worth six hundred if it's worth a nickel."

Why does he pick on me? Alex thought. To what do I owe these extended reports on his gun collection? Well, it's my own fault. If I had closed the door or picked up the phone, he would have gone away.

But politeness had been bred into Alex Burgess by his forceful father, who believed in strong doses of a bare hand across the backside. Even when Alex had played football for Notre Dame he was judged to be out of his element. You're too damn gentle, Burgess, the coach used to yell at him. Get in there and *murder* those sunzabitches.

Buck Weston, all appearances to the contrary, was essentially a good-hearted soul marred only by an excessive need for the attention of his fellow man.

On the other hand, Alex reminded himself, Buck was also marred by his gun collection. Not that gun collecting was a flaw, but what sort of man, especially one who tended computers for a living, spent his spare hours prowling auctions and hunt-club meeting rooms in search of guns? Alex collected not guns but books, particularly those relating to international laws dealing with war crimes, in which he was something of an expert, and on which he had published a few scholarly monographs. It was his scholarship on war crimes, and two articles he had written on the mind of the terrorist, that had attracted the attention of FBI Director William Webster, who had asked the Justice Department to lend Alex to the Bureau. Alex had tolerated the basic FBI three-month training at Quantico for the opportunity to pursue terrorists, assured by the Attorney General that he could return to Justice's Criminal Division whenever he wanted.

And there was Buck Weston with *his* obsession— cleaning and polishing, testing and firing his guns, and not least of all his fanatic goal of turning his eleven-year-old son into a pistol marksman. It's the height, Alex thought, falling back on his private theory that short men busied themselves proving their manhood. All of which explained why Alex was a lawyer and not a gun-toting FBI agent.

Weston's catalogue of recent additions to his collection continued—"sawed off, Alex, a beauty, it'll split you apart at fifteen paces"—while Alex turned another corner of his mind to professional headaches, like convincing the Director to carve a chunk out of the budget for more psychiatrists.

Still holding Weston's fevered eyes, though, he idly speculated on how many of the basement crime specialists harbored similar bizarre hobbies. Maybe they would all be happier chasing criminals on the street instead of working in labs or with computers.

"We need new IBM add-on units," Weston was saying, finally having arrived at the reason for his visit to Alex's office. "I could use a couple more terminals, too, and Texas Instruments is putting a new sorter on the market. There's just not enough memory in those units for the stuff we're expected to handle for you guys."

There's not enough memory anywhere, Alex thought, for what any of us are handling. If we had any more memory, we'd go nuts. But philosophical discussions about memory and pain were outside of Buck Weston's agenda. What Buck and the computer jocks downstairs needed were more computers, and you could hardly blame them. When you needed their best work, you got it, and catching bank robbers and terrorists was impossible without them.

Weston bent down to yank up his socks—they were always at his ankles from incessant jiggling—and continued elaborating his pitch for bigger and more expensive computers. Alex turned another corner of his mind to an upcoming House bill on the criminal liability of federal police officers. The Director was worried, and Alex expected a grilling on the subject from Burt Britten at lunch.

"Are you going to marry the general's daughter?" Buck asked suddenly. "The general's daughter and the congressman's sister. Hell, Alex, you'll end up pushing Webster out and taking over the Bureau yourself."

"When we set a date, Buck," Alex said with as much

impatience as he could communicate, "you'll be the first to know."

"You could do worse," Weston said.

Yes, you blithering tyrant, I could. Now please, please go away. The telephone rang. Thank God, whoever you are. It was Burt confirming lunch, and Alex dragged the call out as long as he could, eventually mumbling baldly at a dial tone until Buck Weston waved a nervous finger and departed.

"Thank you," Alex said to the dial tone, and reached for his jacket.

The first thing Burt Britten noticed as he crossed the south portals onto the House floor was that Tommy Langston had nodded off at his desk again. For two days Burt had been stopping on and off the floor to hear his fellow congressman debate the merits of federal water policies, an issue Burt's Massachusetts constituents cared almost nothing about. But water fascinated Burt. A free commodity that wasn't free. Without a dam, Western farmers didn't have water. Without irrigation, they didn't have crops. The bill under consideration had Langston's name on it, and there Tommy Langston was, drunk again in the middle of the day, dozing with his head in his hand and his tie all bunched up around his neck. Absentmindedly Burt began counting the number of drunks on the unusually crowded floor, and without effort tallied thirty-one. They survived for the same reasons as Tommy Langston. Because they campaigned like madmen, because they hired brilliant staffs, and because many of them resembled America's idea of what a congressman ought to look like. Tommy Langston's California constituents would elect him term after term because he bore a stunning likeness to half a dozen movie heroes of the past twenty years.

Although he would have heartily denied it, Burt Britten also had the sort of looks a Hollywood director wanted when he called Central Casting for a politician—a Kennedyesque grin with white dinner-plate teeth, a

31

hint of dimples, and an adequate sprinkling of premature gray in his crisp black hair. A mirror image of his father, in fact, although Burt would have denied that comparison, too. In the morning Burt looked thirty, young and aggressive. After a hard day, sallow and pale, he might be forty. The rest of the time he split the difference at thirty-five, which was his actual age. He was the fifth youngest member of the House, and considered by many to be one of the most able young legislators sent by Massachusetts to Washington in a long time.

He crossed the bright orange-and-blue carpeting to his desk and sat down. Jack Brokaw, a House institution for three decades, was sitting next to him, half-listening and scanning a sheaf of memos. Brokaw leaned toward Burt to whisper.

"Hey, Shorty," Brokaw said, "Tom Langston is soused."

"I noticed," Burt said. "Don't call me Shorty, Jack. You make me feel as if I'm a kid."

"You *are* a kid," Brokaw said engagingly. "Who's floor-managing for Tommy?"

"Carrothers," Burt whispered back. "It's all stitched up. Guaranteed to pass."

"Over my dead body," Brokaw said with a smile.

"There's nothing you can do now, Jack. It's closed to amendments."

"I got me a friend in the Speaker's office," Brokaw said, this time with a bigger smile. Brokaw's friend, as Burt knew, was the Speaker himself. "It'll be reopened tomorrow."

Burt liked Brokaw. Against his will, he liked the man. During the current term they had probably not voted the same way more than two or three times. In public they accused each other of undermining the strength of America's great democracy and the sacred rights of the individual and the glorious system of free enterprise, but in private Burt could not help liking the man. It was a funny thing. You could despise a man's politics, find a lot of what he stands for reprehensible, and still enjoy his company over a drink and laugh at his jokes.

Maybe that's what makes us politicians, Burt thought, although his friend Alex Burgess would have told him that's what makes us human.

The Speaker was standing now, and Burt prepared to vote. Al Carrothers of Oregon took his seat.

"Do I hear a motion to adjourn, a second to the motion, thank you, this body is adjourned until eleven o'clock tomorrow morning."

Burt turned and saw Brokaw lift his sleepy-lidded eyes. There was a cocky look on his face.

"Your friend in the Speaker's office," Burt said, "has some pretty good connections. Quick adjournment."

"Don't he, though?" Brokaw said, rising. "Take a walk with me, Burt."

Talk a walk with me meant Brokaw had something important to say. Burt looked at his watch, saw that he had twenty minutes before his lunch date with Jill and Alex, and followed Brokaw off the floor. Reporters gathered round them as they came through the door, asking why the water bill had not come up for a vote as scheduled. Brokaw brushed them off with pleas of ignorance, but the reporters understood that before any water bill was passed, Jack Brokaw's fingerprints would be on every section, subsection, and sentence. One wire-service man followed them right through the door leading to the hallway and the Members Only elevator.

"Congressman, did you have anything to do with the postponement of the vote? Just a plain yes or no."

Brokaw glared at the man for a second, then retrieved his bureaucratic grin.

"The Speaker made the decision," he said. "I'm just one of four hundred and thirty-five. I suggest you talk to the Speaker."

The Members Only elevator opened, and that was the end of the conversation.

Outside, on the west steps of the Capitol, Brokaw led Burt past the tourists. There were hundreds of them, as usual, every shape and size and nationality, photographing their families at every conceivable angle against the Capitol dome. The building's facade was peeling worse than ever, shedding dangerously large chunks of mortar.

"They ought to fix this quick," Burt said, "before some innocent lawyer from my district gets clobbered and blames me."

"Look at all the Japanese," Brokaw said *sotto voce*. "And Germans. After the war they couldn't afford to buy toothpicks, and now we're buying all our cars and televisions and cameras from them. Not to mention their steel."

They strolled around the dignified and also peeling statue of General Grant, toward President Garfield, who was guarding Maryland Avenue. Burt felt the heat creeping up his neck, and loosened his tie.

"Do you have any idea," Brokaw continued, "how much your father is stirring people up?"

"You mean that idiotic speech at Los Alamos."

"That's what I mean, Shorty. And he's going to give some testimony up here for the Pentagon, and I just happen to have a copy of his testimony, which has—ah, how shall I put it?—which somehow found its way out of the Pentagon."

"I don't get it, Jack. Don't you want to see a bigger nuclear defense budget?"

"You've been listening to too many of my speeches, Shorty. Sure I want those boys in khaki to have all the weapons they need. But they always want *more* than they need, and we just got to keep this budget down."

Burt glanced at his watch. Ten minutes to one.

"You in a hurry?" Brokaw asked.

"I'm meeting Jill and Alex for lunch."

"Well, anyway, I'm going to send over the general's testimony to you, and I want some of your staff people to check his numbers, okay? And if you should accidentally mention that I had anything to do with this, I'll be forced to ram that appropriations bill down your throat.

But you can leak things that I can't, so you see what you can do."

"Well, Jack, I don't want to fight with him in public, but I can do some leaking."

"Good. Now go to lunch and don't keep that pretty sister of yours waiting."

Motives, Burt was thinking as he took another bite of curried chicken salad. People have the strangest motives. Is Jack Brokaw out to embarrass my father, or is he really after the Defense budget? Or does he have other fish to fry?

"He's a cute kid," Jill was saying to Alex, expiating her imaginary sins. "But if he makes one more pass at me I'm calling his mother."

"You ought to be flattered," Alex said.

The Gandy Dancer, a restaurant in the shadow of the Capitol frequented by legislators and their staffs, hummed and buzzed with the peculiar intensity of people who take themselves seriously. Across from Burt, Jill, and Alex sat Senator Moynihan with two White House lobbyists. Behind the senator were two Labor Department lawyers and a Transportation Department speechwriter with his wife and young son.

"No more football games for me," Jill said, rubbing her ankle, "touch or otherwise. I'm getting too old for these things."

"Ancient," Alex said, tenderly brushing his hand across her neck. "At thirty-one, you're an old lady."

"Remember when we used to stay up all night and talk," Jill said, "and still manage to go to classes the next day anyway? Now if I don't get my eight hours, I'm wiped out."

Burt chuckled. "I'm still surviving on five."

Burt and Alex had known each other for fifteen years. It seemed to Alex they had graduated from law school only yesterday, and from college the day before that. The passage of fifteen years seemed improbable to Alex's supremely rational mind, but no more improbable, when he got right down to it, than the fact that he was going to marry Burt's kid sister.

"Did you see the general's little show in the *Post* this morning?" Burt asked.

"Wasn't it awful?" Jill said. "I don't understand him. I honestly don't. What does he think is going to be gained by all this America the Strong nonsense? And to celebrate Hiroshima as if it were one of our finest hours. I can't even talk to him anymore."

"He's coming up to the Hill to testify on the defense appropriations bill," Burt said.

"You're kidding," Jill said. "Why Dad?"

"Because the Pentagon can use him, that's why."

Alex sipped his water. "You have to give the general credit," he said. "He's damn good on the stump. One of these days they'll run him for Congress. Probably for your seat, Burt."

Burt groaned. "Wouldn't *that* be hell? I'd rather run against Attila the Hun."

"That Los Alamos thing," Jill said, "makes me sick. I mean, how can he use something so ugly, so sad, just to scare up support for the Defense Department?"

"The Defense Department," Alex said, "doesn't need any help. He's doing it because he likes being a star. He likes the attention. You know that. He's *your* father. He wants the Defense Department to let him testify so he can get his picture in the papers again."

"No, it's worse than that," Burt said. "It's not just his ego. He believes what he says. He thinks the country needs a good war to bring us all together again."

"Auden wrote that behind every peaceful eye, private massacres are taking place," Jill said, "and sometimes, I think he was right."

They paused to let that sink in, their eyes moving around the table, each thinking about their own private massacres.

"I love Dad," Jill said. "He's not a *bad* man, and he was a good father. Even you have to admit that, Burt."

Burt grimaced. "All right, he was a good father. But . . . but . . ."

The sentence was left unfinished. There was nothing more either of General George Britten's children could say.

"Hey, you two," Alex said, "don't get morose. Burt, when's Marge coming home?"

Burt's wife had taken their seven-year-old twin daughters to her parents' house in Maine for the month.

"Three weeks," Burt said distractedly. "Jill, you have to talk to Dad. He's going to make a fool of himself."

"I can't, Burt. I can't fight with him, and he won't listen to me."

"Hey, I'm supposed to get grilled here," Alex said, desperately trying to change the subject. "You're supposed to grill me about Justice's bill. Aren't you going to give me grief about how we're creating a police state?"

But neither Jill nor Burt had the energy to fight with Alex. They had fallen into the well of their private lives, a dark and dangerous place, into their childhood memories, and into their sense of loss at growing up and discovering that the father who had nurtured them, taught them to fight for what they believed in, was no longer the man they had known.

He was a stranger to them—a man who made saber-rattling speeches and got his picture in the newspaper.

Their conversation turned to the weather, the presidential election, the blandness of what passed for continental cuisine in Washington's singles bars and Capitol hangouts. The subject of their father was not raised again.

3

NO ONE moved on the ward. There was no sound except for the hush of the respirators and the steady *blip-blip-blip* of cardiac monitors. Thirty-five glowing Lucite boxes, connected to tubes, air pumps, and pulmonary monitors, went on humming mechanically as always, bathed in the glow of heat lamps to keep their occupants warm. In the Lucite boxes newborn babies slept—thirty-five babies whose chances of survival ranged from the very good to the utterly nonexistent. One of them, a Chicano, had been airlifted from Bakersfield two hours before without his parents. His lungs, clogged with fluid at birth, now sucked in and out almost normally. The dark boy in number seven, who had perhaps three times the hair on his head one would expect at birth, was sending out erratic brain waves, and would probably not live more than a year. A preemie girl, born five weeks early that morning, was yellow from jaundice, and jerked spasmodically in what must have been primal dreams of terror. She, however, was going to be just fine. She would go home and grow up and forget, other than in some remote corner of her consciousness, the day she had arrived in the world weighing four pounds and barely alive at all.

Gavin Lancaster, M.D., in the first year of his residency and his second week of the neonatal intensive care ward, concentrated on his notes from evening rounds. But he was not yet what his roommate called one of the fine young cannibals, those doctors who manage to exist on four hours' sleep with no visible signs of wear and tear. Gavin showed the strain. He had lost twelve pounds from his already thin frame, and his shallow eyes looked terminally bloodshot.

His notes were a mess. He checked and double-checked them, because Dr. Solar was a demon on rounds. Easy enough for him, Gavin thought. He gets *his* eight hours every night.

Gavin looked up from his perch at the center of the ward hallway as a janitor rolled a bucket into the corridor, swabbing the floor, and as a ward nurse, against all hospital rules, brought her boyfriend in for a tour. Gavin was occupying the nurse's chair, covering the phones as a favor. Once, in the middle of exams, she had typed his lab reports.

"We only get the worst," the nurse was saying in a muted voice. "We get your birth defects, your premature babies, your babies who really ain't got a prayer."

That's for sure, Gavin thought. That morning he had witnessed, for the shock of his life, another doctor methodically reduce a baby's dosage of powerful anticlotting drugs until the baby's heart began to slow. Tonight the baby had died, and the doctor had returned to write on the chart, under cause of death, "Congestive heart failure due to deformity." A mercy killing, unquestionably, but still, it was pretty hard to take. The baby would have grown up thoroughly retarded from brain damage, but in medical school no one had bothered to tell Gavin Lancaster that doctors let babies die all the time. At least not so casually. Not to mention the fact that it was against the law.

"See that cute little girl in number two," the nurse was saying to her boyfriend. "Her mother's a heroin addict. So's she."

The corridor split the ward down the middle. On either side, from waist level to the ceiling, the walls were double-insulated plate-glass windows. The bottom halves of the walls were painted in stripes of garish blues and reds, primarily to cheer up the parents.

As the nurse strapped a gown and face mask on her boyfriend, urging him into the ward for a closer look, Gavin for some reason thought of Michael Douglas in *Coma*. He had seen the movie recently on television. It stuck like a nightmare in his mind. Of course it could never happen that way, but the premise was too credible for comfort. Bodies and parts of bodies being sold like fenders and tailpipes.

Somewhere in the heart of the hospital—Gavin often thought of the building as a collection of organs—the air filtration system switched itself on, its hum sounding at several frequencies below the air conditioning, which Gavin could recognize in his sleep. But his sleep, he realized, was not much different these days from its opposite. Sometimes he was sure he was sleeping with his eyes open.

The nurse and her boyfriend, who was by now exceedingly pale, slouched back to the lounge, and the janitor wheeled his bucket through the swinging doors at the end of the corridor. Again the ward was silent. Gavin felt severe hunger pains, or maybe just a need for caffeine, and headed for the lounge himself. An electronic chime on the nurse's station phone stopped him. He walked back, punched a silver button, and wearily picked up the receiver.

"Dr. Lancaster, Three-A," he said, the timbre of his own voice surprising him in the stillness.

"Dr. Lancaster, this is Dr. Dillon," the woman's voice said. "Do you have—" She stopped. "Wait a minute, *Gavin* Lancaster."

"Yes," he said hesitantly. The voice sounded familiar.

"Gavin, it's Marybeth. I didn't know you were here. I thought you were in Sacramento."

They had shared a corpse in anatomy class at medical school before Gavin had gone off to Santa Barbara to become a psychiatrist. But Gavin had eventually decided he preferred saving children's bodies to saving their minds.

"Santa Barbara," he said. "I just got back a couple of weeks ago. What are *you* doing?"

"I'm working for the chief of ob-gyn, Harry Bellows. Look, have you got an opening up there? The charts say you're full."

"Yeah, we have a spot open. We lost a kid tonight."

"We're on our way."

The line went dead and Gavin scrambled to the

40

lounge for a cup of coffee. He figured he had five minutes at most to put some food in his belly before all hell broke loose. He made a sandwich of slightly stale Swiss cheese and dry French bread, and sunk into one of the tattered director's chairs. He closed his eyes and methodically began to chew. I'm going to get gas anyway, he thought, and all that aluminum hydroxide is lousy for my stomach lining.

And then, as he swallowed a gulp of the bitter coffee, all the mysterious questions he had faithfully avoided since his final year of medical school crept unwanted into his mind. Why this baby, and not another? This baby about whom he knew nothing, who had yet to travel from the third floor to the second, who had not asked to be born, and who might, but for one of nature's accidents, be pink-cheeked and healthy and sucking at its mother's breast.

Why life, and why death, and why, in God's name, should my hands, my skill, have anything to do with either?

He popped his eyes open, sipped the muddy coffee as though it were poison, and forgot those questions for the thousandth time.

"I didn't want to wake you, Harry, I really didn't."

"That's okay," Harry Bellows said to his assistant as he yawned into the phone. "Just fill me in."

"We've got him in neonatal intensive. It's one of the strangest constellations of deformities I've ever seen. It's just weird, Harry. The mother isn't on any drugs. She hasn't even taken aspirin for nine months. She doesn't drink and she doesn't smoke and except for some chronic back pain she's in perfect health."

Harry Bellows was roused out of his bed shortly past one o'clock. He hadn't been sleeping well anyway, what with all the dampness and his sinuses acting up the way they did every year. Under normal circumstances his assistant would not have awoken him, but somebody had to talk to the parents, and Marybeth Dillon found the task as odious and frightening as her first

41

day of surgery. There was the same fear of the unknown, a horror at trying to explain the inexplicable workings of the body. Harry understood that. He had been a young resident himself once, a long time ago, and he knew how awful you could feel at one o'clock in the morning when all the textbooks and all of your experience could not tell you what you needed to know. And so he told his wife to go back to sleep, and he drove across the Golden Gate Bridge through the murky rain. There was virtually no traffic, and even driving with his unusual care he made the trip in under twenty minutes. He was not an old man, or at sixty-one did not consider himself old, but he reflected the caution common to all people on intimate terms with their own mortality. He drove slowly in the rain.

His crepe soles squeaked on the hospital's marble floors. When he reached the main-floor landing he found Marybeth Dillon waiting for him under the luminous hospital sign.

"Harry, I'm really happy you came," she said, leading him toward the elevator.

"Tell me more about the baby," he said.

"His left arm is almost amputated. It reminds me of those thalidomide case histories. The brain cage is soft, and it's squeezed in. And something's going on in the circulatory system I don't even understand. I ordered a scan and it looks like two holes in the aorta, maybe three, like it was pressurized or something and exploded."

Harry Bellows received this information without emotion, removing his glasses and drying them on the lining of his tie. But he had a vague idea of what was wrong with this baby, and his knowledge, programmed as well as any computer, was sifting through its well-marked files. *Bands,* said the open file. Haven't seen a case in years. When was it, 1968? No, '69, just before Christmas. That poor woman. Two miscarriages and then . . .

"Size?" he asked.

"Three or four centimeters, each of them," she said,

42

"as far as we can tell. The scan isn't the best. They've put somebody new on radiology rotation."

The elevator reached the second floor and Harry Bellows waited, in his old-fashioned way, for Dr. Dillon to step out. The neonatal intensive care ward was no longer quiet, because word had spread on the hospital's sensitive gossip circuits, and a few of the more curious young doctors had slipped away from their work, or sleep, for a closer look at the baby in box number nine.

As Harry Bellows pushed through the swinging doors onto the ward, they saw him through the glass windows and backed away from the box. They stood aside as he and Dr. Dillon strapped on face masks and gowns and entered the quiet chamber.

"Good morning, gentlemen," Dr. Bellows said softly. "May we have some privacy, please?"

All of a sudden Harry wished that Len Horvath, chief of neonatology, were here, but Len was in Bermuda with his wife and son, taking a well-earned rest. Len is good at these things, he thought. Len can forget.

He stepped to the north side of the ward chamber. After a short chorus of "Good morning, Dr. Bellows," the young residents and interns padded quietly into the hall. None of them was anxious to account for being away from his station. Harry Bellows was thinking only of that other woman years ago—Christ, what was her name . . . miscarriages . . . bands . . . oh yes, Turner, Elizabeth Turner, she was a dancer—and what he had felt forced to do for the second time in his career. Tonight would be the third time. The idea made him sick, physically ill, and he touched his round, protruding stomach in nervous reaction.

"The chart, sir," Gavin Lancaster was saying.

"Yes, thanks, Doctor—" Bellows peered at the nameplate—"Dr. Lancaster. Thank you." He noticed Lancaster's washed-out face, the grim exhaustion. We work 'em too hard, he thought. We've got to stop working these kids to death. They work like slaves and then when they're done all they want to do is gouge the

43

patient or the insurance companies and amass piles of money in retribution.

Holding the clipboard in his hand, Harry peered through his half-moon spectacles to read the baby's vital-sign monitors. Gavin watched, listening again to the deep hum of the ventilating system, working hard to avoid staring at the baby, at . . . well, at whatever it was in number nine.

"What do you think, Harry?" Dr. Dillon asked.

"Just a minute."

Harry Bellows held his hand under the glowing lamp above the baby and warmed his palm. Habit, even though now it didn't matter. But he didn't want to shock the baby with a cold touch. He laid the clipboard down and lifted the Lucite cover, then reached down to touch the baby's chest.

Gavin Lancaster finally brought his eyes to rest on the gnarled body in the plastic box. The left arm was attached by the thinnest reed of flesh. The head was squashed out of shape, like a crushed grapefruit, and both eyes bulged from their sockets. Where the nose should have been were only two holes—no cartilage, no shape. And yet the thing—no, he said to himself, not a *thing*, a baby—the baby was breathing, and breathing quite well. Two weeks premature, but alive.

Dr. Bellows' hand touched the sleeping baby's chest. Wordlessly he signaled for Gavin's stethoscope. Gavin passed it toward the box, keeping his fingers steady only by a prodigious effort of will. Dr. Bellows listened, first to the heart, then the lungs, poking and tapping and feeling.

"Dr. Bellows, I put him on Ampicil—"

"Yes, I see, thank you," Harry said, interrupting. He closed the top of the plastic crib.

"Harry?" Marybeth Dillon laid a hand on his shoulder. "Are you all right?"

"I'm fine," he said. "It's bands. Were you there for the delivery?"

"No, it was Mark Steinfels."

"He'd never seen them before either, I guess. No, he

44

wouldn't have. He's only been on staff for—how long? A year?"

"Seven months, Harry. What *is* it, exactly?"

"Bands," he said. "Amniotic bands. The fluid doesn't stay liquid for some reason, we don't know why. And it turns into fibrous tissues and starts to wrap around . . ."

His voice drifted off. He wiped his brow on his sleeve. He was sweating.

"Well, anyway, that explains why she went into labor. But the heart. It's not part of this syndrome. The ruptured aorta, the brain cage. Those don't make sense."

He turned his back to the baby, as though he could make the boy disappear, as if by walking away he could pretend this baby had not been born. His eyes glanced at the chart. Very professional, he thought, very thorough. This young Dr. Lancaster saw respiratory distress and started antibiotics. Kanamycin. Ampicillin. He might have chosen Keflin, but no matter, he had reacted instantly and with clinical intelligence. There was only one problem, Harry thought. The drugs should never have been prescribed.

Now he had to figure out how to erase Dr. Lancaster's excellent decisions. He had to determine the best way to wipe out any evidence of their existence. Dear God, he said to himself, only you can make a life, and only you can take it. But you can't want this baby to live. You can't. No more than that Turner baby, was it a boy or a girl? A girl. Oh dear God in heaven, I am sorry.

"Dr. Lancaster, would you please get me a blank chart?"

"Sir? Dr. Bellows?"

"A blank *chart*, please."

"Yes, sir, right away, sir."

Dr. Dillon watched Gavin leave. She knew what Harry was doing.

"I'm glad it's not me, Harry," she said. "I'm glad I don't have to do it."

"Do you think *I* want to?" he said in a low mutter. "It's the only thing to do. But the soft cage, the heart

. . . they're not part of the syndrome usually. I know I've seen this before . . ."

Gavin Lancaster returned with a fresh chart and the file copies of the original.

"Dr. Bellows," Gavin said, handing him the carbons, "I thought you'd want the copies. They hadn't gone downstairs yet."

Underneath his imperturbable mask, Harry Bellows smiled, and Gavin thought he could see the old doctor's eyes relax a bit. I'm not going to stop you, Gavin wanted to say. I know you're doing what you have to do.

Somehow among the three of them that message communicated itself, circled three minds, and came to rest.

Harry Bellows tucked the carbons in his jacket pocket.

"Thank you, Dr. Lancaster. Would you make out a new chart, please? And you'll leave off any indication of respiratory problems, won't you?"

"Of course, Dr. Bellows."

"How long are you on tonight?"

"I just came on, sir. At ten."

"Then you'll be here when the . . . the convulsions start."

Gavin had no doubt as to what would happen. He would discontinue the antibiotics and the baby's fever would rise. Maybe there would be a brief bout of pneumonia, and then the baby would go into convulsions and die. It would take less than a day.

"Yes, sir, Dr. Bellows, I'll be here."

"Do you think you can take it? I'll be glad to ask that you're relieved if you want." Bellows' voice was intimate and reassuring.

"I think so."

"Have you ever seen this before?"

Gavin was uncertain whether Bellows meant the baby's condition, or the changing of a chart.

"No, Dr. Bellows, I haven't."

"It happens sometimes, and we have to make a

46

decision. If there's any trouble, I'll take responsibility." He paused. "But there won't be any trouble."

"No, I'm sure there won't be."

Gavin shifted his weight uneasily from one foot to the other as he wrote a new chart. "Boy baby," he copied from the top line. "Nagata." He filled in the parents' names, the time of birth, the time of admittance to intensive care. A description of the baby's condition. Admitting nurse. Vital signs.

"Dr. Bellows, what about the time stamp?"

"Just fill in the chart, please," Harry Bellows said. "And sign it."

Gavin signed the chart and Harry wordlessly lifted the clipboard from his hand. Gavin watched him step into the ward hallway and walk purposefully to the time clock at the nurse's station. With a key he opened the clock's burnished brown case, set the time back one hour and eleven minutes, and inserted the new chart under the stamp.

Click. Click.

All finished. Harry set the clock forward, checking the time against the digital numbers above the ward's swinging doors, and snapped the clock's case closed. A neat little forgery. Folding the original chart into his jacket pocket, he glanced toward the end of the hall where the ward nurse was watching, a white shadowy figure whose expression was hidden in shadows.

Harry stood there for a moment, a bank robber with one foot out of the vault, dimly aware, as he had been eleven years earlier, that not all secrets would be kept. Secrets, like promises. No, the nurses knew, too. They knew that not all babies were meant to live. Len Horvath has done this a hundred times, Bellows told himself. Len is a decent and humane doctor who believes, as we all do, in the sanctity of human life. Len believes . . .

So why, Harry asked himself, so why do I feel like a murderer?

His head was bowed as he shuffled back to the ward, his shoulders slumped forward, and his doubts clung to his body like a weighty shroud. He could have sworn he felt the nurse's glare boring into his back, faint pin-pricks like icicles tingling on his spine, but she had already disappeared into the lounge, unconcerned. She had seen it all before.

"Dr. Lancaster," he said, handing Gavin the newly stamped patient's chart. "You have Dr. Horvath's number in Bermuda."

"No, sir, I don't."

"Well, I can get it for you, if you want to call him. If it'll make you feel better."

"No, sir, that's okay, it's not necessary," Gavin said.

"Thanks very much," Harry Bellows said. He left his gown and mask at the nurse's station. Then, with Marybeth Dillon following a few paces behind, he pushed quickly through the swinging doors to the corridor.

"Do you want to talk to him now, Harry?"

"How's the mother?"

"She's still down in recovery."

"Okay, I'll see the father in a couple of minutes."

The elevator disgorged them onto the third floor. Harry Bellows shrugged his jacket onto his nurse's desk and, closing his office door behind him, fell exhausted into a battered old wing chair. Nagata, he said to himself. Born July 13, 1942, Choshi, Japan. But how long did he stay there, and when did he come to the United States? And where was he when—?

With his head flung back and his fingers tapping on the arm of the chair, Harry sorted through the files of his mind. Somewhere in those files was a batch of articles on the genetic effects of radiation, several case histories he had read in medical school, a series from *Lancet* in the late fifties, another series in the *New England Journal of Medicine* in the mid-sixties. But his mental equipment was on the fritz tonight, he was tired and on edge and his sinuses were running rivers into his throat, and the files just wouldn't pop open the way they used to. You're slipping, Harry. You've got to face up to it. You're getting old and you're slipping.

He sat up straight in the chair and saw Shirley first, his wife, in a round, gold-plated Serra frame on his desk, and Harry Jr., and Alicia and little Oliver. Crazy little Ollie. Who had been unplanned. Who was now the cutest little tyke in Marin County. Whom they had considered aborting. We're too old to have another kid. He'll be lonely. He'll be like an only child. How could we have ever thought of not having him?

Those clippings have to be somewhere, he thought. Or are they at home? He knelt down in front of the filing cabinet and dug into the bottom drawer. The filing cabinet was brand-new and a tag—"Inspected by number 26"—was still stuck in the frame of the drawer. Now let's see, did I put them under Aortal Defects or Radiation or . . . oh yes, now he remembered. Under *H*.

He was momentarily proud of himself as he thumbed through the papers, but the feeling evaporated when his hands clasped the section he was looking for. Blood thumped in his temples and in the veins near his occipital lobes when he started to read. Lesions, often gaps, in aortal tissue. Amniotic bands. Frangible tissue of the brain cage. Irreparable damage common. Survival: one to three years.

"Okay," he said aloud. "Okay, Harry, you'd better face the music and dance."

He stood, opened his office door, and signaled to Marybeth Dillon, who was outside talking to a tall, handsome Oriental man. Narrow eyes, not like the Chinese, flat cheekbones. A sleek-looking fellow. That's an expensive suit he's wearing.

As Mitzu Nagata came toward him, virtually radiating high-pitched anxiety, but outwardly solemn and calm, Harry caught the man's gaze. Behind that cool facade, in those dark eyes, Harry could decipher, as though breaking a code, the signs of fear and confusion, and of not knowing, of *What's wrong with our baby?* Harry Bellows had seen those signs so many times in his life.

"Mr. Nagata, I'm Dr. Bellows, won't you please sit down?"

He watched Mitzu sink into the couch, lowering himself like a flower closing its petals against a harsh season. Such dignity, Harry thought. Such reserve.

"Why haven't they let us see our boy?" Mitzu asked. His voice was deliberate and uninflected.

"Mr. Nagata, I'm sorry I've kept you waiting. I know how difficult this must be for you."

What terrible, useless words. Harry sat next to Mitzu on the couch and lightly touched his hand. Harry felt that every patient responded better to a physical presence. "The laying on of hands," straight from witch doctors and primitive shamans and faith healers. Mitzu Nagata, however, had no use for immediate intimacy, and at the meeting of flesh against flesh Harry could feel him recoil.

"Just tell me, please," Mitzu said, with what sounded to Harry like repressed anger. There was frost in the voice now, something cold and unpleasant, all of which Harry dismissed as a by-product of fear. "Just tell me, please, what's wrong."

Harry mentally rehearsed his repertoire of soothing phrases, his grab bag of reassuring words for patients *in extremis*. But none of the standard verities applied. Not for this man, Harry thought. This man wants the truth.

"Mr. Nagata, your son is in the neonatal intensive care unit. He was born with what I can only call crippling deformities."

Harry took a deep breath. Mitzu simply stared, not responding.

"The precise condition is what we call amniotic bands. I won't bother to explain how—"

"No," Mitzu said. "Please explain."

Harry, taken aback, began assembling new thoughts in his head. How to explain? He noticed a film of perspiration covering Mitzu's face. Not perspiration at all, really. Not sweat. More like a cold fever chill. More like dew.

"The amniotic fluid," Harry continued, "is what supports the baby's life in the uterus. And it's a cushion, if you like, an environment in which the baby can grow. In some rare cases, the fluid doesn't stay liquid. It starts to harden and fibrous bands develop around the baby. Mr. Nagata, medicine has no explanation for this. We just don't know the reason. But the bands wrap around the baby. They squeeze—" Harry leaned closer, wondering how to put this gently "—they squeeze the baby out of shape."

"How bad is it?" Mitzu asked.

"I'm sorry. It's very bad. And your baby has another problem, tiny holes in his aorta, which is one of the main arteries leading to—"

"Yes, I know what the aorta is. Can they be corrected?"

He doesn't need my answer, Harry thought. He knows.

"Mr. Nagata, if there were any chance at all—"

"Will he live?" Mitzu asked, being, Harry thought, very much the dispassionate inquisitor.

"Mr. Nagata, I'm sorry to say his chances of survival are not very good."

"But he *does* have a chance?"

Harry debated with himself for a fraction of a second. There was no point in building false hope.

"To be honest, I'm sorry, no, there's virtually no chance."

Harry expected tears, some sign of grief or sadness. But nothing spoke in those dark eyes, and there were no tears. Harry examined Mitzu as he would examine a patient, seeking some evidence that his words had been heard—a trembling hand, perhaps, a wince or a grimace or a quickening of breath. But there was nothing. Mitzu had clasped his hands across his chest and straightened, sitting upright, as though, Harry thought, to give himself backbone, to draw on his own physical strength. Harry understood that no man cried easily, men had been taught not to cry, but he waited a moment longer for the tears, or for the man to reach

51

out for reassurance. His own touch had been rejected once, and from experience he had learned not to offer it again.

"Mr. Nagata, I'd like to ask you some questions. But I imagine you'd like to be alone—"

"No, Dr. Bellows. Ask your questions, please."

The voice was chillingly clear and reasonable. Harry was horrified. People didn't behave that way. They didn't just sit there and take the news like a weather report.

"Mr. Nagata, the problems this baby has are not in themselves uncommon. But together in one child they're most unusual. Are you aware of ever having been exposed to significant amounts of radiation?"

Mitzu paled. The coolness left his gaze and his skin lightened. Blood rushed from the surface, as in a victim of shock. Harry felt oddly relieved. Unable to evoke any response, he had felt impotent. Now he no longer needed an answer to his question.

"I was six miles from the blast at Hiroshima in 1945. I was three years old. We came to the United States a year later. I have never suffered, as far as I know, any ill effects from the blast. None that I can remember."

"You're certain of that."

"As certain as I can be," Mitzu said.

"And your wife?"

"I met her here. She grew up in Connecticut."

"She's an American, you mean."

"So am *I*," Mitzu said.

"Yes, of course," Harry Bellows said, feeling foolish. "Mr. Nagata, I'd like to run some tests on you next week, if I may. Not here at the hospital. We're not really equipped for genetic work, but we can take the samples and send them out."

"You think there's something wrong with me."

Harry wrung his hands. "There is some evidence that the kind of radiation you were exposed to could have caused damage. I'd like to find out. For your sake."

"Fine," Mitzu said. "Can I see my boy now?"

"You really don't want to," Harry Bellows said. "He's not a—"

"Yes, I *do* want to. Can I see him now?"

Harry Bellows sighed to himself. They always wanted to see the baby, no matter how terrible, no matter how deformed. You could never convince them otherwise.

"Come with me," Harry said, and Mitzu stood to follow him out of the room.

Some meories are safely locked away, Mitzu thought. We adopt, often unconsciously, screens and filters of varying power to obliterate agonies with which our minds cannot cope. We assimilate the petty terrors of childhood, we banish them to the nether regions of our pysche, where no prying or force of will or brave desire can penetrate.

I was six miles from the blast at Hiroshima. I was three years old. I have never suffered . . . none that I can . . . I was six miles . . .

The elevator seemed to descend with the slowness of fog. Mitzu's own words stayed with him, a refrain. He had not spoken the words in many years—so many years, in fact, that he was amazed by his own ability to remember so accurately the location, the number of miles, his age. *Tasukete kune . . . tasukete . . . . help, please help.* I am an American, he would say to himself. I am an American first, and second I am Japanese. My parents live in the past. I live in the here and now.

He had not been to Japan for six years. His relatives had all come to the United States, or they were dead. His maternal uncle Kiyoshi had been buried in the blast. Kiyoshi, who had brought him toy soldiers and swords and regaled him with stories of the Amida the Merciful and of the samurai. His cousins from Kyoto had been visiting at Hiroshima, and had died hideous deaths from burns. When, by chance, Mitzu would see photographs of the family, he would remember them as ghosts, and he would think of the new Japan, of a world that had begun not in 1942, but in 1956, when his parents moved from the Japanese ghetto to their house across San Francisco Bay, when his father sold the store and began to teach. Soldier teacher, teacher soldier. Mitzu thought of his black friend Derek Novel, who had watched "Roots" on television, who had waited in line for Haley's autograph, who had traveled on his vacation to Virginia to find, in plantation archives, the names of his great-grandparents. Mitzu was both fascinated and repelled, for while his own history was well documented, he preferred to forget. His great-great-grandfather had entered Edo with the Emperor, when the name of the city was changed to Tokyo. His great-grandfather had been with Admiral Togo at the battle of Port Arthur. His grandfather had been an advisor to Emperor Yoshihito.

But the samurai were no longer. Japan had no use for her warrior class.

Now he was an American, and an executive, and a man of responsibility, and he neither wanted nor needed any disturbing memories. There was a light . . .

a light in the delta, the cool air, fire on the water . . . soldiers running . . .

"Mr. Nagata, you'll have to put a mask on. And a gown."

At the entrance to the nursery Mitzu allowed the nurse to strap a white gown around him and to fit the gauze mask over his cheeks. *How will I tell Nancy? What will I tell her?* He glanced around him, through the windows at the plastic boxes. *I'm sorry, no, virtually no chance.*

"In here, please," Harry Bellows was saying, guiding him through the door. Mitzu felt the hand on his shoulder, steadied himself, and strode forward. A rush of dizziness swept through him, an unsettling vertigo. He passed one box after another, looking to his left and then his right, appraising the gnarled newborn infants. *Which one is my boy?* In the diffused glow of the heating lamps all of them seemed the same, all babies, one indistinguishable from the other. He heard the beeping of the heart monitors, his eyes were assaulted by the blinking readout screens, and he was dimly aware of two figures buzzing far behind him, their voices a murmur from which he caught only snatches of conversation. "He wanted to see . . . Bellows says . . . didn't cry . . ." Again Mitzu felt an arm on his, actually sensed rather than felt, for Harry Bellows had only just reached out to him.

"Here, Mr. Nagata," Bellows said.

Mitzu stared at the impressive machinery of life and death—translucent plastic tubes and chrome pipes and vials of clear liquid. His eyes lowered to the figure in the plastic box, and at first he saw what seemed an indiscriminate array of white patches and tips of needles and tubes flowing toward the pink body. But the flesh was suppurated and the sight was horrible, a bulbous, barely human head, eyes jutting up, and the dangling limb . . . There were soldiers . . .

soldiers along the road, his mother bundling him into the car with her luncheon basket, they would pass the soldiers by the river and would see his father soon. The car meant a trip to his father, his father wore uniforms, and his mother would take them home and mend them, his father was in the city, fighting the war . . . in early morning

"Mr. Nagata, are you all right?"

"I'm fine, Dr. Bellows, thank you."

He stood, rooted like a tree. There's been a mistake. This baby is not mine.

But in the baby's pudgy, swollen face he saw his own, and the faces of his father and mother, and all the faces in the photographs. And Teruko, Uncle Kiyoshi, in early morning . . .

in early morning, the sun rising as they passed two roadblocks, then another. The soldiers apologized. "Shigata ga nai," it can't be helped. More soldiers, marching, counting off, "Ichni, ni . . . ichni, ni," one two, one two, heavy-soled boots smacking the dirt road. It was a dream, all

a dream. Already in the tiny baby's lungs disease was festering, and the even pumping of air was a mechanical illusion. Death was setting in.

His hands rested on the clear plastic box. Rivulets of sweat dripped down his arms onto the cuffs of his shirt. Wait, they can save him. An operation, surgery, whatever it would take.

"Dr. Bellows, you could operate, I mean there's plastic surgery, there's—"

"Mr. Nagata, I'm sorry," Harry Bellows said as soothingly as he could. "He couldn't sustain heart surgery. The lungs are too damaged."

No, not us. Not me. The lights in the room flickered. His mother was slowing . . .

the car, stopping behind the barricade as troops passed. She handed him a bowl of fish. Her hand lay on his head, her touch warm and perfumed, and she, too, was eating. The sound of airplanes, his mother looking toward the sky, and then a flash of light, bright yellow streaks like banners, a fire in the clouds, a frieze of soldiers against the riverbank, a sheet of sun and thunder . . . the light . . . the white light . . .

The lights flickered again.

"Take him upstairs," someone said.

The baby's hand reached up, reached out, Mitzu thought, for life. He lifted the top of the box. Someone, someone he did not turn to see, tried to stop him.

"You shouldn't—" said the whisper.

But whoever had spoken fell silent and Mitzu let his hand drop toward the baby. He stroked the outstretched fingers. An iron mask rose up in front of his face, a shining mask of the samurai, orange and red with a dragon's head horns. "May we die as in springtime," echoed the words of a poem heard years before, "the cherry tree flowers pure and bright." He tried to blot out the mask and the smell of blossoms, rich-scented, and the long-suppressed prayer before battle. But the memories ran on, the pictures of his past unfolding, try as he might to blacken the screen. The light on the heart monitor blinked, white light . . .

filling the sky, a canopy of white, and an army truck across the road. The ground seemed to shake from the sound. His mother, she was running now, pulling him,

56

dragging him. She picked him up, squeezed to her breast, and they were down under the barricade blocking the road. He saw over her shoulder, the sky to the north darkened, a burst of dust, then fuller, rising higher and higher, spreading in the canopy of white, a towering gray cloud of dust, a mushroom cloud, but it was so long ago . . .

So long ago. It has nothing to do with now.

His eyes misted as he held firm to the baby's pulsing hand, praying he would look down and that this, too, would be a dream, and his baby boy would smile and cry and be whole again. But when his vision cleared the distorted figure lay in its plastic cocoon.

To the doctors around Mitzu this baby was merely ugly. One of nature's accidents. But to Mitzu this was his flesh and blood, the baby boy he had wanted, the life he had watched grow in his wife's belly.

It could not be ugly to him.

"Mr. Nagata, please," said Harry Bellows.

"Yes, of course, I should talk with my wife."

He laid the baby's hand on the white cotton sheet, closed the lid of the plastic box, and turned to leave. After only a few steps he stopped, glanced over his shoulder, and allowed himself a final, anguished, silent shout. One cry of pain, surging through him like a needle in his flesh.

And then the pain was over, and he was numb.

4

THE NUMBERS didn't tally. The trouble with corporations, Ed Stone thought as he pored over his division's annual report, is that they believe in the ideal manager. Train a man, offer him responsibility, and he'll perform like a circus elephant. When we're good, they promote us and ask us to do something new, when they really ought to keep us doing what we do best.

The American General offices were almost deserted. When he was alone, without others to distract him, Ed Stone yearned to be an engineer again. He missed the excitement of making objects. He missed the excitement of being out in the field, gearing up a plant, and witnessing the miracle of nuclear power. But they had rewarded him with the presidency of his division, and all he did was shuffle paper. Paper, paper, and more paper. Reams of the stuff. For the fifteenth time in a single day he promised himself that the annual report of the Systems Division of American General Corporation would shine as a model of intelligence and efficiency. I'm no good at words, he kept telling himself. But, in fact, he was quite adept at words, and would produce a model report, and he would eventually become the corporate animal whose existence he doubted: the ideal manager.

He sat behind his desk, fidgeting with his pencil and examining stacks of memoranda, files, and computer printouts. I'm going to hit this on the mark if it takes all night. I'm going to compose these sentences over and over again until I can recite them backward, forward, and sideways, and, if necessary, in Arabic, French, and Italian—those languages in particular, because they were the ones his prime foreign customers spoke.

But his concentration wandered. He glanced up from his work and stared out at the moon-dappled San Francisco streets. On the dark horizon Transamerica's pyramid tower glowed like a Christmas ornament. Instantly he was reminded of Nancy Nagata. Awful, it was just awful what had happened to them. You could plow your way through the little things in life, the mundane daily details, and then, with no warning, this awful thing happens and all the rest seems insignificant. What could you say? Only idiotic platitudes. By temperament, Ed Stone was unemotional. Not the sort of man who raised his voice or pounded his fist to make a point. What good were words now? You'll have another child. This, too, shall pass. If there were other words, if he could ease Mitzu Nagata's pain, he would have spared no effort, because Mitch meant so much to him.

Among all the corporate success stories on his staff, the business school whiz kids and the accountants and the marketing people, Mitch Nagata was special. Like Stone himself, Mitzu respected the beauty of invention, the majesty of well-crafted machinery. In their early years with American General, when it was still a minor company called Wright Electronics, Stone had been Mitzu's mentor, working side by side in a lab to develop fail-safe shutdown systems for nuclear reactors. The territory was fertile then, uncharted, and together they had designed a solution they were certain was the best. Old Horace Wright had backed them, losing money, and only since the spate of near-catastrophes in the last two years had their work been recognized for its clean, ingenious simplicity within the brotherhood of engineers. Finally, Ed Stone and his protégé had been saluted and given the credit they had deserved for so long.

Stone filled his pipe. It was a Savinelli straight-grain, a birthday present from Mitch. He tamped the tobacco down, struck a match, and the sweet fragrance of Dunhill Special Mixture No. 5 blossomed around

59

him. He savored not only the taste of the tobacco, but also those years in the lab, regretting at the same time his passage to higher corporate office. They offered you promotions and you took them. More money. More prestige. But you lost the tantalizing prospect of invention. Stone knew, too, that his protégé, twenty years his junior, possessed the true discipline, and that he would, like a long-distance runner, overtake Stone as both an engineer and an executive. He'll have my job someday. Because Mitzu Nagata, he thought, brought more than technical skill to his work. He had a kind of madness, an obsession, a way of seeing that appealed to both the executives above him and the men in the lab.

The city lights were fading outside his window. I ought to go to the hospital. I should be near him in case he wants to talk. No, I'd just be in the way. Mitch wouldn't want me there.

Stone's attention returned to the papers on his desk and he concentrated on a summary of the year's developments. His program of reaching out to the division's customers. His refinements in the installations. A sales curve climbing faster than ever before. Nuclear power might be a shaky industry for a while, but it would come back, it would grow, it would be safe.

The intercom buzzed, its sound lingering in the air.

"Yes, Marie."

"Mr. Stone, I've checked with the hospital. Mr. Nagata is still there. Do you want to talk to him again?"

"No, Marie, not unless he calls in."

"Yes, sir, and I have the tour itineraries finished."

"Would you bring them in, please?"

She appeared in his doorway a moment later, incredibly efficient, he thought, even at the end of a ten-hour day.

"Mr. Stone, you should go home. You're tired."

"I've got to finish this tonight. But you go on yourself."

She laid the tour schedules on his desk and stood back, not leaving, as though waiting for another assignment.

"It's Mr. Nagata bothering you," she said. "You know, all the girls like him, too. He's so polite. But there's nothing any of us can do for him. You're not going to help anything sitting here worrying."

He smiled at her being so protective.

"Thanks, Marie. I just want to get this section done and then I'll pack up. You go on home, though."

"Yes, sir. See you in the morning."

The day was fairly well shot now, and he ought to quit, conserve his energy, and start again in the morning. But now he had a new worry. He had planned a series of trips for his senior officers—a combination of goodwill tours and inspections of all the facilities in the country with American General equipment. The tours were an opportunity for his executives to flex their public images, to meet and ingratiate themselves with the corporation's customers. To further Mitzu's career, Stone had allotted him the most important customers. Oh, there had been complaints about favoritism. Mudball-packing, they had called it in Stone's Georgia youth. But the chairman's office had approved the routes. The brass, too, had pegged Mitzu for a rise to the top. But Mitzu wouldn't be able to do this tour now, and Stone knew that corporations were hardhearted. A personal tragedy just didn't fit into the equations for promotion.

It's the randomness, he thought. That's what it is. All day he had been mulling over what disturbed him most about Mitzu's dying baby. And finally he understood. It was the randomness and lack of explanations. If there was anything in the world that gave Ed Stone comfort, it was logic, or science, the notion of a universe in which an order lay behind all events. But Mitch had told him that the doctors had offered no explanations, no reasons. Not a clue as to why his baby had been born that way. Surely they ought to be able to guess, Stone had responded. But no, the doctors knew nothing, Mitch had insisted. Not an idea, not a supposition. Which only added, Edward Stone thought, an extra burden to the sadness.

He jammed a stack of unread files into a drawer, lit his pipe again, and resigned himself to living with one more in a long list of life's inexplicable tragedies.

5

MITZU STARED into the misty night. His eyes looked out at the island in the middle of the Bay, the hulking mountain of Alcatraz. How long have I been here? An hour? Two? When he arrived the sun was still lingering on the horizon, and now stars peeped through the twilight. Looking up he saw Orion's buckle faintly gleaming, and the Little Dipper tipping its cup toward the ocean.

He turned and started walking across the Embarcadero, nervously jingling coins in his pocket. Tourists passed by him, but he noticed none of them. A woman in a crinkly white dress, tall and wobbling on high spike heels, broke into his path and nearly toppled him.

"Excuse me," she said, slurring her words. "Have you seen my husband?"

Without waiting for an answer, she lurched away. Mitzu shook his head and tried to collect his thoughts. But his mind was empty. He had no thoughts, only images: a baby in a plastic box, the sad stillness of Nancy's face against the pillow, and the blank, unknowing gazes of the ward nurses.

Less than twenty-four hours had passed since Nancy turned to him and said, "Now, Mitch, let's go now." She was in labor.

The rush to the hospital. The waiting. The delivery. More waiting. Then Dr. Bellows and "I'm sorry."

Mitzu arrived home to their empty apartment at three o'clock in the morning, and had fallen helplessly into bed. When he awoke that afternoon his body was bathed in sweat. He had dreamed horrible dreams, but their exact content escaped him. He had opened the mail, read the newspaper, eaten two pieces of toast, and loaded the dishwasher. Somehow he had even managed to brew a pot of coffee. He had brushed his teeth and showered and dressed, but for the life of him he could not place any of those events in time, in the sequence in which they actually occurred. He had talked on the telephone with Ed Stone, with his mother and father, and with Jill Britten.

Jill Britten? Her voice flitted through his consciousness, and then her face. Then she was gone.

"Hey, buster, you okay?"

He had walked directly into a fish stall and banged his head. A flash of pain dazed him. He saw stars, staggered a step, and regained his footing.

"You okay?" the man asked again, a red-faced giant in a porkpie hat.

"Yes, just wasn't watching where I was going."

"That was a pretty good knock you took."

"Thanks, I'll be all right."

Mitzu crossed the street and headed for the parking lot where he had left his car. In half an hour he was due at his parents' house, and it was unlike him to be even four or five minutes late. He had, until now, run his life with meticulous attention to detail, and however disoriented he might be, his inner clock went right on ticking and continued to direct him. As he walked his left hand was reaching for his keys, and his right hand was smoothing his tie across his chest and flaring the collar of his button-down shirt. He was a man who liked making small gestures with his hands, because the motions obliquely reminded him of his competence and strength.

Where had the day gone? He had driven to the hospital at about four o'clock. The doctors, he discovered, had told Nancy only that her baby was in intensive care, and she had no memory of Mitzu's speech the night before. So he described the baby to her. She cried. He held her, comforted her, told her they would have another boy, but she cried louder and louder until a nurse, roused by her sobs, fed her a sedative. She would sleep through the night, the nurse said.

He drove to the Embarcadero. He liked hearing the sounds of the Bay, seals calling to each other off Seal Rock, and the faraway rush of the ocean. He had been coming down here since his first years in San Francisco, when his father brought him to see the fishing boats. Now, whenever he had no place to go, when he wanted to be alone, he came down to the water. There used to be a Bible-quoting woman who paced back and forth, spouting imprecations of doom. On this evening she was nowhere in sight, but the souvenir hawkers and peddlers were out in force.

He made a new effort to sort out what he had done that day. At the edge of the parking lot he paused and repeated the gesture with his hands, and as his fingertips fluttered across his chest the newspaper clipping came back to him.

Yes, right here in his pocket. How *could* they? How could they publish such a picture? And these four men? How could they celebrate such an anniversary?

He took the photograph out, smoothed its ragged edges in the shadows of passing car lights, and held it up to his face. The dots that made up the image seemed to decompose and reassemble before his eyes. Suddenly his mouth was dry as if stuffed with straw. The light

in the delta, the cool air, soldiers running

His heartbeat thumped. A vein throbbed in his arm. His breath quickened. Some men hurried to a limousine in the lot, its engine chugging wisps of smoke that were caught, like lightning, in the beams of other cars. Mitzu felt sucked into an undertow, some unrecognizable force pulling him down.

He pulled out his keys, stepped into his car, and drove toward the bridge. He had a very specific reason for having dinner with his parents, and he did not want to be late.

The elder Nagata's house sat on a spit of land overlooking the Bay, situated so evening's mists of moonlight washed over every room. Inside, its two occupants

65

went about their business with no outward display of the tragedy so close to their lives. In her dressing area, an alcove off the master bedroom, Hiro Nagata straightened the blue mat on her makeup table and thought about her son. There wasn't much to be learned by asking him about his child. The truth seemed clear to her. She had suspected—no, not suspected, she had known, always known, that Mitzu could not have escaped unharmed.

Sitting on a low stool, she looked into her mirror, seeing behind her the reflected, reversed image of Mitzu and Nancy at their wedding, the dark black of Mitzu's suit and the pink of Nancy's dress. In a glass case next to the photograph two samurai warrior masks, dull gray metal festooned with strips of faded orange yarn, stared back at her. They were heirlooms of her husband's family. How meaningless they seem now, she thought. Who would take them after she and Yasuji were gone? Who would want them?

A museum, probably. Not Mitzu.

She rested her wig on the palm of her hand, so as not to disturb its shape, and set it carefully on the blotchy skin of her bald head. She had worn a wig every day for almost thirty-five years. Like all Japanese, she considered the parading of one's scars indecent and impolite, and not even her closest friends had ever seen her without a wig. She would have felt naked with her head uncovered. The wig she was putting on had just arrived; they wore out every few years, and you could hardly get a decent one for less than two hundred dollars, and so they received her close attention. She oiled and brushed them, and kept the wig blocks smooth and clean. Adjusting the gray strands around her ears, she could still imagine herself having hair, her rich flowing hair, when she was young, before the—

The thought broke off, as always, before it was completed.

She went to the kitchen to finish her dinner preparations. In the hall she passed the only painting she nad brought with her from Japan. It was four thousand years old, and even now the fragile square of rice-paper canvas meant more to her than any object she had ever owned.

It was priceless. Not in money, but in dreams. No one could trace where the painting had come from, or who the artist was, only that her family—her father's family and her father's father's family, and on back into the din of history—had owned this painting. An old man in gray brushstrokes looked down from the wall, his black robe in swaths of ink whirling around him. Four thousand years, Hiro thought to herself. What could people have been thinking then?

The buzzer in the kitchen sounded. The shrimp were cleaned, the rice was steaming, and now the soup was ready to be heated.

In the low-ceilinged living room Yasuji Nagata sat sipping sake. A weak, bastardized domestic variety, he mumbled to himself, but it would do. His hands, gnarled from arthritis like knotty wood, gripped an egg-shaped cloisonné cup, and he brought the mediocre brew to his lips. The cup had belonged to his mother's family. Her great-grandfather had been given a set of the cups when he joined the Imperial Navy in 1917. He had seen Japan invaded by the Russians and the Americans, had seen Commodore Perry's men march uninvited through the streets of Uraga, and had seen the samurai in their moment of greatness. The Japanese people had long before discovered a simple choice: allow your warriors to be true warriors, or be buried by an avalanche of foreign powers.

The Japanese chose the samurai. Then, but not now.

Yasuji Nagata sipped his sake in silence, and his wife remained in the kitchen, also in silence, and there, in their respective positions, a veil of tragedy in the air, they waited for their son.

The doorbell rang at precisely eight o'clock. Yasuji Nagata walked slowly to the door and greeted his son in Japanese.

"How are you, my son? How is your wife?"

Mitzu's mind shifted gears. First to Japanese, then back to English. He would not speak Japanese in his father's house, which was why he had so rarely been a guest there.

"She's recovering," Mitzu said. "She's resting."

Yasuji lowered his eyes and contemplated a demand. You will speak our language here, or you will speak not at all. But this was a sad day, and he laid his demand aside.

"Come in, your mother is waiting."

In the hallway Mitzu shrugged his coat off and donned a robe. Following custom, he stowed his shoes in the closet. In this concession to ritual he immediately made himself comfortable, and eased the tension always present when he entered his parents' home. He would not converse in Japanese, he would refuse to indulge his parents' predilection for living in the past. All this talk of long-dead relatives and family history seemed to him only an escape, a futile desire to inhabit a world that no longer existed.

Except, of course, that it did exist, as all memories exist, as palpable and real as the moonlight shimmering above the Bay and covering the spacious living room with a pale gold hue.

Only a single lamp burned in the room, a dim bulb in a high, narrow paper column. His mother and father talked about the hospital, but in a short time they exhausted their discussion of the previous twenty-four hours, each remarking in their own ways on the ineffable mystery of birth and the inexplicable horror that had entered their lives. They worried over Nancy's health, the trauma she might suffer, as they tiptoed through the minefields of each other's secret hurts and longings.

"Only through struggle do we grow," said Yasuji.

"Nancy's very strong," Mitzu said. "She's getting the best medical care in the city. I'm sure the doctors did all they could for the baby."

They were not truly speaking to each other, merely reciting monologues, like actors in a play.

Finally Hiro Nagata asked her question. Mitzu had been waiting for it.

"What was the cause?" she said. "Do they know any more now?"

"They don't know," Mitzu answered. "The doctors say it might have been that touch of the flu she had last month. But they'll never really know for sure."

Hiro Nagata stared into her son's eyes, beyond the surface of the flecked green, deep into the black center. She had been reading the feelings in those eyes for thirty-six years, and now she felt they were like a book to her, as open and telling as words on a page. She knew her son well. She knew the rhythms of his voice, the color of his feelings.

He was lying. She was certain he was lying.

"Then there will be other children," she said.

She knows, he thought. She knows.

They ate the simple meal—rice and rye, pickled vegetables, clear broth, and shrimp. It was the first time they had shared a meal together in more than a month, and the first time in a year that Nancy had not joined them. Photographs of the family hung on the walls around the table. The strong lines around Mitzu's eyes and the upward sweep of his forehead testified to the unmistakable resemblance he bore to his grandparents, whose images stared down at him from the sideboard. Against the opposite wall, facing Mitzu, a glass display case held two samurai swords, crossed. The swords had not been touched, as far as Mitzu could remember, since the day his parents had moved into the house. Six feet long, curved in the slightest arc, the *tsuba*, or sword guards, glowed in the half-light. Silver stripes, like bandages, wrapped the hilt of each sheath, snugly holding the handles of aquamarine inlaid with diamond-shaped pieces of gold. One of the swords had belonged to General Nogi, the victor of Port Arthur, who had committed suicide in 1912 so as not to survive the Emperor Meiji. Of the other's provenance no one was certain, although some in the family preferred to believe it had belonged to the Emperor himself.

Mitzu could not draw his eyes away from the swords. All during the meal he found his gaze straying to them, until finally, as his mother began clearing the dishes, he could see nothing else.

Why am I staring at them?

Of course, he thought to himself. Swords. I'll buy a set of swords to take to New York as a gift. How obvious! No one will think to question them. I'll ask Marie to clear them with the airlines. They'll be gifts.

"You seem far away," came his mother's voice, breaking through his obsession.

"No, not at all," Mitzu said, and to his own chagrin heard the words from his mouth spoken in Japanese. What have I been thinking?

His father's eyes widened, a smile creasing his cheeks. His mother' grip on the serving bowls faltered, and in the incalculable space of a single second she nearly dropped them.

Mitzu glanced at her. Quickly she averted her eyes. Mitzu noticed a fine film of makeup across her brow, and saw threads of netting drooping out from under her wig. He was used to the sight by now, but for some reason her injury pained him. The lengths she goes to every day to hide her scars, he thought.

The pain dug deep.

They moved into the living room, Mitzu and Yasuji, and stepped onto the narrow railed balcony overlooking the city. It was one of those rare nights when the sky had miraculously cleared, and the moon hung like a dazzling medallion on a field of velvet. Mitzu gripped the railing. In the marina below houseboats rolled on the water, their deck lights falling and rising as though seen through fog. A strong ocean breeze soared with the smell of salt. Mitzu was reminded of his walks along the dock as a child, when his father would mesmerize him with stories of ancient times, of warriors whose blood he shared. Sometimes they would drive south to the beaches, careful not to stray far from the main roads because of prejudice toward the Japanese. Then, Yasuji, taking his son by the hand, would describe the rich lushness of the Kanto plain, where Uncle Tadashi had lived. Uncle Tadashi's story was a recurring refrain in those days. He was the family's one genuine hero in living memory.

"He was a brave man," Mitzu's father had told him. "It was in January in 1945, only a few months before the—well, the Americans were approaching Luzon, the Philippines were encircled, and only a kamikaze corps could save us. Your Uncle Tadashi was a great pilot, willing to face certain death with honor and without hesitation."

On the balcony overlooking the city, Mitzu felt his father's presence beside him. He could almost hear the voice telling him the story. It was so uncanny he turned to see whether his father was speaking, so clear was the tale in his memory.

"There were no planes," the voice continued, "but at the last moment five planes, repaired and ready to fly, were available for an attack on the Philippines. Thirty pilots volunteered. Uncle Tadashi and I were among them, and he was selected. I went as his escort. I watched his plane vanish in flames as he hit the deck of an American carrier. He was a man of his country. He lived for the spirit of his country."

A warm hand touched Mitzu's shoulder. Mitzu turned to his father.

"What are you thinking, son?"

He was thinking of Tadashi, and the code of the samurai. He was thinking about the warrior code his family had lived by for forty centuries. Sacrifice, discipline, chivalry, service and faith to tradition. A tradition in which it is better not to live at all than to live disgraced. If I am to suffer this curse of history, Mitzu thought, this wound to my blood, then why should I live? My tradition, my family all ask me to revenge

71

this assault. Why, even my father, see him there staring at me, nodding his head, even he cries out in the silence for me to return to the truth of my past.

Mitzu brooded. Where did these crazy ideas come from? Am I hearing other voices? He permitted himself a moment to doubt his sanity.

His father's question had come in Japanese, and Mitzu, again to his surprise, answered in the language of his heritage.

"Of Uncle Tadashi," he said. "You used to tell me about him when I was little. Do you remember?"

"I remember," the old man said. "And now you remember your tongue. I am honored."

There was a soft clatter of cups against a tray behind them, and the sound of tea pouring. Hiro Nagata stood nearby, just inside the terrace door, listening.

"Do you have that old kendo robe?" Mitzu asked. "Uncle Tadashi's robe?"

"Why do you ask?" the old man said.

"I just wondered if you'd let me have it," Mitzu said, dipping his head slightly to look directly at his father. "I don't have anything like it, you know, something from the family."

Yasuji Nagata's eyebrows rose almost imperceptibly, wrinkling the rivers of flesh in his cheeks. He rocked on the balls of his feet, and the floorboards of the balcony let out a creak.

"This is an odd time," Yasuji said, "for you to ask for it. What prompts you?"

"I'm not sure," Mitzu said, recalling the words Tadashi had written before setting out on his mission. *Abandoning a fleeting life, my sovereign has risen to be among the gods. I follow him, my heart full of gratitude.* It was an old prayer before battle.

Mitzu went on. "I'm feeling . . . it's only that I need something to—"

"*Yamato damashii,*" the old man whispered. He disappeared into the house, his words still in the air. The spirit of old Japan.

It would do no one any good, Mitzu thought, to say why he wanted the robe. He was not entirely certain of the reason himself. He knew only that a soldier should be properly dressed for battle, and that he would be going into battle very soon.

His father appeared on the balcony, holding the long black robe in his arms.

6

THE RADIO announcer's voice droned on as Jill hung up the phone. "It's one of those Washington summers," the announcer said, "that drives politicians home and Virginia housewives to hounding their husbands once again for that retreat at the Maryland shore. Yep, it's hot. And that's the good news. The bad news is that it's going to get hotter."

Jill flicked the radio off and stared at the phone, a mute beige instrument. She reached for a cigarette. What am I thinking? I haven't smoked in four years.

Her apartment at 19th and M was ten blocks from the university and overlooked a small park—not a park, actually, more of a traffic island. But green grass was the first thing she saw when she awoke in the morning. The apartment building had six other professors in it, two lawyers, one lowly aid to somebody in the Cabinet, and a reporter for ABC News. Jill, still staring at the phone, was sitting in one of the Wassily chairs Burt had bought for her, with her feet propped on the eighteenth century green lacquered table she had brought back from Japan.

She could remember the day she bought it. She had not thought about that day in months, but now he had just called her. She had heard his voice, and she remembered five years ago as though it were only yesterday.

She had arrived in Tokyo for six months of hard work. There was, first of all, the language to learn. And there were classes and lectures and museums. She strolled through the center of the city, breathing in the bizarre glory of modern Japan. Row upon row of steel and glass towers competed for attention with the heri-

74

tage of centuries. Without quite thinking, Jill wandered into a side street—she could remember what it looked like, but not the name—and found herself in conversation with an antique dealer, a Japanese man who might have been fifty years old or eighty, and who was anxious to practice his English on a pretty young American girl. She, naturally, wanted to use her limited Japanese, and so they switched back and forth, he telling her how much he had loved his first visit to Washington, D.C., she explaining her research. All the while they talked she had been casting surreptitious glances at the green table, and when, in the end, she asked the price, he had simply given it to her as a present.

But what she recalled best about the day was that Mitzu Nagata had stood at her side the entire time, watching and listening with bemused detachment.

The night before she had met him at an American Embassy party. It was one of those provincial affairs with expensive liquor, inedible food, and false cheer. Every American in town seemed to have shown up, colonials in a far country on the Fourth of July. In the courtyard of the Embassy, Marines set off fireworks, and a band played the national anthem and the "Battle Hymn of the Republic." The ambassador's wife supplied sheet music for waltzes and polkas, and then danced with half the guests. A man from General Electric stood on the bar and juggled champagne glasses. A Sony executive from New Jersey organized charades in a corner of the grand ballroom. The *chargé d'affaires,* who looked like Gregory Peck but had a high, squeaky voice, spent the evening introducing people to each other, accomplishing his duty with such vigor that he frequently introduced the same people twice. A group of Jill's fellow graduate students smoked pot in the bathroom and giggled their way through the crowd.

Jill sat on a broad, brocaded couch and pretended to observe the scene, taking mental notes on the sociology of Embassy parties in Tokyo. A young diplomat, fresh from a post in Brazil and very lonely, tried to pick her up, but all he wanted to talk about was Richard Nixon and Jerry Ford and Jimmy Carter, and she had heard enough of that at home. A professor from Doshisha University quizzed her on why she had chosen to study at Tokyo University, and one of the Embassy *attachés,* a man from Dallas by way of London who had the most beautiful accent she had ever heard, insisted on recounting her own father's career to her. A subject which she already knew too well.

The party rolled on. She might have gone back to her hotel, still fatigued from her journey. But she was having a good time. At twenty-six, she liked thinking of herself as sophisticated. She was an Army brat, had grown up on bases where everyone wore uniforms and paid no attention to little girls who liked to read books, and the sight of so many blue-haired women in evening gowns and so many men decked out in comfortable old tuxedos attracted her.

It was even possible, she thought to herself five years later, that she was looking for the right man to go home with.

He introduced himself as Mitzu Nagata. She was still sitting on the brocaded couch, nursing the same drink she had been holding for two hours. He was towering over her, holding a gold lighter in front of her cigarette.

"All my friends call me Mitch," he said. "Even my Japanese friends."

He laughed. He had a warm, friendly laugh and a smile so glittering it seemed to take in all the glitter around him. She checked for a wedding ring and was pleased to see none.

Jill talked to him about her work, about exploring the Japanese character, about a trip to Kyoto she was hoping to make. And Mitzu listened. He listened for an hour, hardly interrupting except to ask a prodding question, until finally she wondered why he hadn't excused himself and walked away.

76

"Am I boring you?" she asked.

"Not at all," he said. "Would you like company on your trip to Kyoto? I know a little about the city, and maybe I could make your visit more worthwhile."

"How wonderful. Do you have time?"

"It would be rude of me not to make time," he said. "Americans in a strange country always help each other, don't they?"

His smile was so ingratiating, his manner so proper—almost courtly, she thought—that she found herself surprisingly charmed. And not disposed to probing his insistence on being American first, and Japanese second. It he wants to tell me he's a French land baron or a rodeo cowboy, she thought, that's all right, too. She had never so quickly fallen under a man's spell.

They toured Kyoto, once the capital of Imperial Japan, where in the twelfth and thirteenth centuries the Emperor reigned from many palaces, where nobles brought their ice down from Mount Hiei. They strolled along the Kamo River under a brooding gray sky, foggy but bright, as though transparent to the sunlight behind clouds. She thought there must be nowhere else on earth where so many cherry trees bloomed.

He took her to the houses of the shogun, to the ruins of the ancient granaries, and, at the end of their second day, before they returned to Tokyo, to a demonstration of *yabusame*. The demonstration took place in a modern arena. Ten men rode out on horseback, sheaves of arrows hanging on their backs. Each man wore a brightly colored robe and a wide-brimmed hat, a shallow cap like the Pope's. Jill knew that the Japanese had been archers for centuries. Each of the Japanese riders spurred his horse into action. They galloped around the arena, faster and faster, kicking up dirt, and just when Jill thought they could gallop no faster their riders began firing arrows as they rode, sending the missiles at incredible speed into targets at the center of the arena.

"It's an ancient sport," Mitzu told her, "except that *yabusame* was once a way of battle, not entertainment."

"Are they samurai?" she asked.

"There are no more samurai," he said flatly. "They're all gone now."

She wanted to ask other questions, but something in his tone warned her away.

They covered the city that night on foot, down a wide avenue a thousand years old. In the thirteenth century, when Indians still had the United States to themselves and Christopher Columbus had not yet been born, samurai warriors had proudly strolled the same avenue, their faces painted white, their hair tied under their black skullcaps. The samurai, the warrior class of a great Imperial nation, had fought with cleverness and determination and displays of unremitting violence such as mankind had rarely seen.

The night was unusually cold, and Mitzu draped his coat over her shoulders. As in Tokyo, modern buildings stood cheek by jowl with occasional wooden structures from centuries past—and, at the far end of the avenue, they could see what historians thought were the remains of the original gates to the city.

"Just think of plum trees and cherry trees," he said, "planted hundreds of years ago." Even as he spoke she could smell the blossoms.

"Just think," he went on, "and then remember the cruelty of the shogun, the corruption of his servants. You know all that, don't you?"

She did know, she was a good historian, and she told him so.

"But were the samurai any better?" she asked.

How could she let the question slip out? Once already she had felt his warning. Why try to discuss the samurai?

"There is a haiku," he told her, "a poem. 'May we die in springtime, the cherry tree flowers pure and lustrous.' That ought to tell you as much about the samurai as you need to answer your question."

She asked no more questions.

Above the avenue, and throughout the city, willows

hung high over the pavement, their glorious green limbs dipping to touch their heads and dangling in the moonlight as if burdened by their own sap. Tiered rock gardens, on a hillside, full of floral reds and yellows, shone in the darkness. Jill felt the presence of ghosts. Don't be a foolish romantic now, she told herself, not about this man. He's a nice young businessman who's maybe lonely and slightly confused about being in Japan because he's an American.

"The willows are beautiful," she said. "I've never seen a variety so lush."

"They weep well, don't they?" he said. "They live up to their name."

"I wonder why they weep," Jill said, trying to be clever and knowing she would elicit an interesting response.

Mitzu laughed softly. In a mere two days she had begun to fall in love with that soothing sound.

"They weep for history," he said matter-of-factly.

Jill turned, took his hand. With the cheerful arrogance of youth, she believed she understood more about him than he would ever tell, possibly even more than he knew about himself.

Somehow, that night, she found herself in his room at the Kyoto Hilton. They had come back to the hotel very late, and spent an hour over nightcaps in the bar. Although Jill was physically exhausted, she couldn't deny the sexual undercurrent between them. Nor could she miss the signs of his interest—the tilt of his head, the brush of his hand against hers. But it wasn't her style to go to bed with a man that quickly. She was still a bit old-fashioned. Still, the longer they lingered together, the more she wanted him. It wasn't only his charm, or the fact that he was physically beautiful—in fact, one of the most beautiful men she had ever known— no, there was something different about him. Underneath the sexual attraction was a deeper, nonsexual passion.

When they took the elevator up and rummaged for

79

their keys, she stood by the door of her room and watched him. It seemed silly to just say goodnight.

"I'll see you in the morning," she said shyly.

"I'd rather tap you on the shoulder," he said, "than knock on your door."

Their sex was more powerful than any she had experienced. It was delirious, and for the first time she knew what true sensuality meant. Her dreams were filled with his smooth hairless body, the curve of his muscled legs, and the smell of blossoms.

Mitzu was in Tokyo for two months as part of an American General team preparing to bid on Japanese nuclear plants, and Jill's office at the university was only six blocks from his. Three or four days a week, when he could get away, he would come by and take her to lunch. Most of the time they stopped at a stall on the street, a *yatai-mise*, or a *shidashiya*, Tokyo's equivalent of a fast-food restaurant. With paper containers of rice and raw fish, they toured and learned about the city together. Jill was surprised that the Japanese, who took such pride in the beauty of their art, didn't seem to care much about their streets, which were crowded and jumbled to the point of ugliness. Even the *shosen*, the subway, was not the spectacular artistic and architectural feat she had expected.

"The street is a public place," Mitzu explained as they walked down the crowded Ginza, the city's main artery. "The streets belong to nobody in particular, and so nobody worries if they're elegant. When people decide to put an effort into beauty, it goes into their houses and gardens."

"But the whole city is so disorganized," Jill said. "It's as if they didn't believe in city planning."

"I think they do it on purpose," Mitzu said. "Ugliness on the outside, and beauty within."

They dodged boys on bicycles carrying trays of food, street dancers advertising Coca-Cola, and Buddhist nuns with shaved heads. They bought sandals together, marched up the steps of the Imperial Palace to see the circular pattern of avenues radiating out from the center of the city, and drank sake in the taverns surrounding the university. He talked to her as no man had ever talked before. He took her seriously. Unlike David Peabody, her last boyfriend, who treated her as though she were an overaged nymphet who was doing something cute, like getting a Ph.D. Or her brother, who treated her as "kid sister," bright enough and nice enough, but still a kid. Or her father, who still thought of her as Daddy's little girl. Even her professors occasionally slipped, saying idiotic and offensive things like, "Inside your pretty little head is the brain of a potential scholar."

Mitzu never said anything like that. They talked about how post-industrial civilization had not entirely worn down the Japanese reserve, and how, in a chaotic society, the Japanese still found time to take a bath for sheer pleasure, not to get clean. They talked about social pathology in America, and the extraordinary organization of Japanese industry. And after a while it hardly mattered what they talked about, so in love was she with the sound of his voice. On some days they went to Mitzu's hotel suite and made love during their lunch hour, and then again at the end of the day, and once again before falling asleep. They did some of the things Jill had only fantasized about—tried new positions, used exotic lotions and creams, laughingly drank herbal aphrodisiacs that actually seemed to work.

During the first three weeks, Jill raised the subject of Mitzu's childhood only once. She asked if he had been back to the house where he was born.

"It's not there any more," he said with a note of weariness. "It burned down in the incendiary carpet bombings. Those B-29s were very efficient planes in their day."

"Don't you at least want to go look at the street?" she asked. "Some of the houses must have survived."

His face grew taut and the muscles on his neck stood

81

out. It wasn't an angry look, but something beyond that—an emotional chill that made Jill recoil.

"It's in the past," he said firmly, and then turned away from her.

But he would talk about almost anything else, and was in every way kind, warm, and loving. So this, she thought, is what love is all about. Twenty-three years old and I'm finally starting to understand. He took her to the theater, the Nikolai Cathedral, and the National Science Museum. During the Festival of the Three Protectors, a religious celebration dating back thousands of years, they met other members of his research team in a restaurant on the Ginza, and watched the revelries. Troupes of half-naked young men danced in the street, bringing traffic to a standstill. Jill, along with the other Americans, was shocked when a few store windows were smashed, but their waiter explained that the shopkeepers had not contributed to the festival, which was, after all, a celebration for the Deity. It had some of the antic feeling of New Year's Eve in Times Square, Jill thought, with thousands of people in brightly colored costumes partying as though Tokyo were a small town and this was the village square.

The following week they went to a party in Kawaguchi, a suburb on a hill overlooking the city. The Prime Minister's deputy in charge of energy projects was especially fond of Mitzu, and was giving the party for the American General team. When they arrived, Jill was amazed that only twenty minutes from the bustling city center, with its crowded streets and almost unbearable noise, there was an almost rural neighborhood. She had always thought of Tokyo sprawling on and on, and then suddenly ending in farms. But here, high in the hills, the noise of Tokyo could hardly be heard. The long, low house wrapped in a U shape around a central garden, with a small pond and rock path leading to the door. The door was made of paper, and pine trees towered over them, and *momiji* trees flowered orange in full bloom.

Although many government officials and diplomats were in attendance, Mitzu and Jill quickly became the favorites of the evening. Everyone wanted to know about the political situation in the United States—about the president and détente, Americans' attitude toward the Chinese. Some of the Japanese women came in Western dress, others in pink and blue formal kimonos belted with bands of yellow and white. One after the other came up to Jill to listen, almost as if she were holding court.

"They're all in love with you," Mitzu whispered with a smile. "You're really turning on the graciousness."

"Oh, Mitch, I'm not turning it on," Jill said, slightly miffed. "I'm just being me. Do you think I'm acting?"

He kissed her cheek. "No, of course not. I was only kidding. That's why I love you."

She tried not to think about Mitzu's going home. For a while she thought she might give up her fellowship and leave with him. But the moment she mentioned it, he told her not to be foolish. She was in Tokyo to study, she had spent years preparing herself for this, and it would be ridiculous to give it up for some crazy idea of romance.

"Mitch, I'm in love with you. This isn't an adolescent infatuation."

"I know, Jill, but let's see what happens when you get home. I'll come visit you in Washington, and if we still feel the way we do now, we'll go on from there."

He did visit her when she came home, making special trips to Washington whenever he could get away. At Christmas she flew to San Francisco to see him, and was more in love than ever. David Peabody continued to call her, and other men asked her out, but she put them off. A long-distance love affair had problems, but it was Mitch, and only Mitch, that she wanted. She was offered a post-doctoral grant at George Washington, but from a colleague at Georgetown she heard about an opening at Stanford. The George Washington job meant more money, a lighter teaching load, and a chance for tenure, but she applied to Stanford and planned on moving to San Francisco.

The head of the Stanford department telephoned her at the end of February, curious as to why she would want a position for which she was clearly overqualified. She explained her reasons the same way she explained them to everyone else: she needed a change of pace, a different climate, a new environment. It was slightly embarrassing to tell anyone, even Burt, that she was willing to disrupt her career and move across the country because she was in love. It looked too much like "man chasing."

In May, Stanford wrote that the job was hers. She was jubilant, and was getting ready to move when Mitch told her he had met someone else. He said he was sorry, but that it was serious, he thought he might even get married. He was so casual about it, as though what had happened between them amounted to no more than a fling. For a few days she moped around her apartment, unable to assimilate what had happened. Could this man she loved have been so cruel? Was she so out of touch with reality that she had misperceived everything about him?

She wrote Stanford that she had changed her mind. By pulling a few strings she managed to land a research spot at George Washington. And she put the memory of Mitzu Nagata behind her.

But he continued to call her when he was in Washington on business. She had never imagined she would find herself in the role of "the other woman," and she hated the idea of sleeping with Mitch when he was engaged to someone else. Yet she could not resist him. Even after Mitzu and Nancy were married, she continued to see him. She felt awful and cheap and dirty, but every time he called she accepted him into her arms.

It took more than a year after Mitch and Nancy were married for Jill to banish him from her life. But finally she had the strength to tell him it was over. They were finished. He shouldn't bother calling her again, she had her own life to lead, he should just go away. She drove him to Dulles a last time, wished him good luck, and said good-bye.

Now he had called again. He was coming to town on business and wanted to see her.

"I can't, Mitch, it's out of the question. It's no good for either of us."

"Look, Jill, Nancy's having a baby and we're very happy. I just want to see you for a drink, talk over old times, that's all. We're allowed to treasure our pasts, aren't we?"

She gave in. Against her better judgment she gave in. But as she hung up the telephone and stared at the green lacquer table, at the chips and scratches it had endured over the years, she thought about how odd and detached his voice had sounded. She went to the kitchen to fix a cup of camomile tea.

She walked idly around the living room touching familiar objects on the sideboard—a Steuben rabbit her father had given her, a vermeil tray from Alex. She settled down on the shag carpet in front of the bookcase and removed her favorite books one by one, held them, checked their bindings for decay, and replaced them in their proper slots. The books reassured her.

Treasure our pasts? The words were like the cracking of glass. Mitch had never used words like that before. In fact, Jill thought, she had never met anyone to whom the past seemed so specifically, so maniacally unimportant.

Maybe that was our problem, she thought ironically. I'm a historian, and he hates history. Especially his own.

She started gathering old newspapers for the incinerator. If anyone had pointed out her habitual response to anxiety—cleaning her apartment, examining her books, drinking camomile tea—she would have been surprised. But soon she was making pots of tea, dredging up dustcloths and bottles of Windex, and feverishly running the vacuum cleaner. Soon she had a foot-high pile of junk, which went, in a sucking whoosh, down the incinerator. By the end of the day she had blocked out the anxiety caused by Mitzu Nagata's call, and for all practical purposes was unaware that she had succumbed to anxiety at all.

THE GYMNASIUM was in a neighborhood Mitzu hardly knew. It was in one of those hidden corners of San Francisco that no lawyer or businessman from Montgomery Street would be likely to see, except from a highway or the top of an office building far away. Mitzu had found the address in the telephone book under "Schools-Martial Arts." There were jujitsu and judo and karate instructors, trained, according to the ads, "in the techniques for disabling your enemy without resort to dangerous weapons" and, more understated, "the ancient, classical forms of self-defense." Karate lessons Mitzu could do without, having studied as a child with neighborhood toughs. There was an ad for kung fu, which Mitzu thought was a grotesque fake, a pop-culture promoter's idea of Oriental behavior. He made several phone calls, asking each time for someone who knew anything about the samurai. Several of the gyms suggested he go to the library; others recommended history courses at the universities. Then Mitzu found an advertisement, buried in small type at the bottom of the page, that answered his need.

> Instruction in the samurai fighting arts. Training in precepts of the code of Bushido. The skills of kendo (fencing). Swords, ritual costumes supplied.

He dialed the telephone number in the ad, asking if night classes were available. At the other end of the line was a man who spoke only Japanese, or if he spoke English was unprepared to admit such treachery on the telephone.

Mitzu, following the man's precise instructions on how to reach the gym, discovered that he had driven in an almost perfect half circle around the edge of the city.

The gymnasium was housed in a cement block building covered, at one time in its history, by strips of redwood. But under the imprecations of time or vandalism the panels were now splintered and peeling, and pitted cement showed through. Two young Japanese boys lounged against the building, hanging out, nowhere to go, with a transistor radio blaring into the night. There was not a Caucasian face in sight.

"Hey, cap'n, spare some change," one of the boys called.

"Hey, cap'n, you lonely, you lookin' for company."

Mitzu had never suspected that so many poor Japanese lived together, as in a ghetto, in San Francisco. The Chinese did, of course, but he had thought Japanese ghettos a thing of the past. His eyes cautiously swept the street, and he looked back at his shining clean Audi, wondering if it were safe. He decided that although the neighborhood wasn't truly poor, neither was it rich. He gave two quarters to the boy with his hand out, and stepped to the gym's front door.

The inside of the gym, in contrast to its surroundings, was spotlessly clean. There was a hallway walled with mirrors and a carpeted floor. He reflected on the circumstances of his arrival. He had told Nancy he was going to a business meeting and could not be reached. She didn't mind; his mother was coming into the city to be with her, and would cook and keep her company. Nancy was still upset about the baby, and was taking Valium. He knew she would never think to check on his whereabouts because she trusted him without qualm. He had never lied to her before, but strangely he felt no guilt. He had come to learn what was necessary—to follow the way of the *bushi*, "to follow the right course in life."

It is better not to live, he said to himself, than to live disgraced.

Standing in the mirrored hallway and ringing the bell, all he could feel was rage. Instead of his own

88

image surrounding him, he saw the baby in the plastic box. And the faces in the photograph on the platform decked with flags.

His fist clenched. The muscles in his back snapped taut. Across his chest the fabric of his jacket wrinkled from the strain. He had always kept himself in shape, playing basketball on Sundays with the American General team, squash at the Racquet Club with Ed Stone, and jogging with the architect who lived next door. Now he reveled in his body's tension and the sense of power, of command, that his own physical strength gave him.

The mirrored doorway opened. A man dressed in a white shirt that crossed his chest in a deep V and black satin pants stepped through. He was short, much shorter than Mitzu, and Mitzu's height obviously surprised him. With a long, steady gaze, the man appraised Mitzu with what seemed to be unusual intensity. The expensive briefcase he singled out for a long glance, and the obviously expensive well-cut suit. Clearly most of his customers did not look like Mitzu Nagata.

"Mr. Nagata," the man said.

"Yes, I have an appointment for this evening."

The man extended a hand. "I'm Nakajima. You're here to enroll for the course in Bushido."

"That's right," Mitzu said, taking his hand. The man's grasp was so strong Mitzu felt a brief shot of pain. He noticed that Nakajima's chest, which at first had seemed broad and flabby, actually rippled with muscles.

Nakajima turned and beckoned Mitzu to follow. They passed through a mirrored room. On the swinging door was a poster of modern Japanese warriors in training. The soldiers wore helmets and jumpsuits. On the other side of the door was another poster, much older and yellowing, of soldiers with swords and bayoneted guns leaping through the air. Hanging at the other end of the room, on the mirrored wall, was a portrait of Yukio Mishima, the most famouse Japanese writer of the twentieth century, perhaps of all history. Mishima,

89

half naked, his well-muscled lithe body oiled and polished to a gleam, his hair trimmed short so that his skull shone through, cradled in his arms a samurai sword.

The instructor, Nakajima, saw Mitzu staring and stopped.

"You know Mishima's work."

"Uh, not really, no. I've heard of him, though. His suicide caused a big uproar in Japan, didn't it?"

"He had his own army," Nakajima said, a tone of reverence in his voice, "men he trained himself. Did you know that? They carried on the traditions of the samurai. But to the Army he was a nuisance. Oh, they invited his men to their maneuvers, but he was a threat to them. They were content to have a small force, and be unarmed. But Mishima believed in a rearmed Japan, and he protested in the only way he knew how. He took his own life." Nakajima turned and continued through the mirrored room. "November, just ten years ago. He chose a bright, beautiful day to die. It was in the morning, at the headquarters of the Japanese Army. They had tied General Mashita, the chief of the general staff, to a chair, so that he would have to watch and understand. I was privileged to be there as a witness. Mishima was standing on the balcony, calling to a crowd of young cadets. Do you know what he said?"

Mitzu stammered. "Uh, actually I don't, no, I—"

"He said, 'Awake, sons of Japan. Pacifism is a threat to the destiny of our country.' But they shouted at him. They *booed* him."

Nakajima's voice was so low as to be almost a whisper. The timbre had a touch of religious piety, as though harking not only in spirit but in fact to a lost civilization. Nakajima's eyes, set deep in his face, emitted a kind of glow, a martyr's eyes in the fire.

They had reached a small room behind the gym. There were six lockers against the wall. Nakajima waved Mitzu to a seat, then knelt at his feet.

"He was kneeling in front of us like this. He slashed his chest with his sword." Nakajima made the gesture.

"Then he plunged the blade into his stomach and disemboweled himself. *Seppuku*. Do you understand the term?"

Seppuku, Mitzu knew, was the ritual suicide of the samurai.

"He bled," Nakajima went on, "and his insides spilled out onto the floor. His stomach and his intestines, pouring out in front of us. Then one of his soldiers sliced off his head. The floor was a river of blood."

Nakajima closed his eyes and bowed his head, and a weird half smile came to his lips. Mitzu fought an almost irresistible urge to leave. What am I doing here?

Nakajima stood up, his face now normal again.

"The basic course," he said, his voice deeper and louder, "is three sessions of three hours each. We will penetrate and decipher the code of Bushido. We will explore the saintly and aristocratic road of the warrior. We will learn the maintenance and use of the swords."

He was almost benevolent, fatherly. Mitzu listened as though in a trance, receptive to hear truth. But his priest waited, as any priest will, for an invitation to bestow his prayer, and gazed at his supplicant.

I am Mitch, the supplicant thought. I am Mitzu.

Whoever he was, the priest did not care. He waited.

"Yes?" Mitzu said.

"There is a fee for our instruction," Nakajima said pleasantly.

"Oh yes, of course," Mitzu said, fumbling for his wallet. Nakajima wanted to be paid. And why not? To teach the right course to follow in life was worth more than mere money.

Mitzu counted out one hundred dollars in twenties. Nakajima took the money and the folded bills disappeared up his sleeve. From a drawer in the locker next to him Nakajima took a white shirt similar to his own. It bore a slight resemblance to Russian and Hungarian peasant clothing—no buttons, two long flaps that, when crossed and tucked in, made the body of the shirt. The

91

sleeves, belled and drooping, reached only down to the elbow.

"I've brought my own robe," Mitzu said, opening his briefcase. He unfolded Uncle Tadashi's black kendo robe and held it up for his instructor's inspection.

Nakajima pursed his lips. "You are a samurai," he said.

"My family was— Yes, I am a samurai."

"Please change," Nakajima said regally. "I'll wait in the gym."

Mitzu hung his jacket inside the locker, slipped out of his pants, and donned the ceremonial costume, tying the long strands of the shirt around his sleek body. His shoulder muscles rolled and rippled as he put his arms into the old kendo robe. A pair of sandals were lying at the foot of the full-length mirror.

He was shocked at the sight of himself.

No tie, no regimental button-down shirt, no tweed jacket. Bare flesh glittering murkily from the damp layer of sweat across his chest. And the rich foliage of whiteness from the shirt flowing into the blackness of the robe. He was lifted on a swell of pride.

I am a samurai ran the thought, wild and strange, in his head.

He opened the door to the gym and was instantly blinded by his own image surrounding him in the walls of mirrors, lit from above by a full panoply of klieg lights on ceiling tracks. In the unearthly brightness, he stared at his own body, silently squeezing his fist and bracing the muscles in his back.

Nakajima stood in one corner, holding two long wooden struts with carved handles. Both were five feet long.

"We will practice with these," he said.

Mitzu said, "I'd rather use swords, to get the feel of them. Do you have any? Your ad said swords were supplied."

Nakajima laid the two wooden struts on the floor mat and pushed one of the mirrored squares behind him. A panel in the wall opened, and he pulled out two swords. The handles were matched flawlessly, each with the hand-melded gold shield of Imperial Japan.

"These belonged to my grandfather," Nakajima said. "They are, as you can see, from the Taisho Era. But they are quite valuable to me. I would be willing to let you practice with them if you promise to treat them as your own. After you have learned."

Nakajima walked to the center of the room, and Mitzu, drawn to him as a moth to light, walked over and stood squarely opposite him, spreading his legs in imitation of Nakajima's pose.

"Follow me precisely," Nakajima said, "every motion and stroke, and you will learn the art of the sword."

Mitzu took one of the wooden poles. It was surprisingly heavy, and he swung it through the air to test its heft. Soft swirls of scratches showed signs of recent lathe work and polishing. Nakajima held his pole out in front of him at chest level, riveting Mitzu's attention on the shining wood.

Nakajima's pole flew up at an angle, close to Mitzu's face. Mitzu countered with the same gesture, pivoting on his heels in imitation. The poles met, lightly grazing each other.

Nakajima bowed. Mitzu bowed.

Nakajima's pole flashed from left to right, his body rigid and only his hand and arm in motion. Mitzu followed. Left, right, up, down, left, right, up, down . . .

The instruction had begun.

8

CHARLOTTE KIRKABY nervously buffed her nails, pacing her Los Angeles apartment. Charlotte could see, outside on Beverly Boulevard, the Hughes grocery store's rotating sign—"Open 24 Hours"—and rows of Rolls-Royces and Mercedes pulling into the parking lot of Chasen's Restaurant. The noise of street traffic blew through the windows. Her air conditioner had gone on the fritz that morning, and without open windows the air would be stifling and Janey would never get to sleep. Better the noise than the heat. Her landlord had promised to have an electrician there by six o'clock, but the man had never shown up. First it was the kitchen sink, and then a crack in the wall from earthquake tremors, and now the damned air conditioner. Six o'clock? It was already twenty to seven.

She considered calling Rory to say she would be late, and maybe he ought to get a sub. But Rory could find other dancers anytime he wanted, Los Angeles was literally crawling with out-of-work dancers, and this was a good solid job, too solid to risk losing by missing a performance. It was just what she needed until she went back to school in the fall. The club was sleazy, sure, but at least she didn't have to take off her clothes.

She dialed the baby-sitter's number and listened intently to the receiver's soft purr, as if by mind over matter she could force the result she desired. No one answered, which was a good sign. Betsy was on her way. Probably caught in traffic. Charlotte herself had been stuck often enough in rush-hour lunacy on the Hollywood Freeway.

In the fall, San Diego. Clean air, no freeways.

She crossed the cramped L-shaped living room and peeked in at Janey. Seeing Janey's head on the pillow was enough to lift Charlotte's dampened spirits. God love that child. Just look at that smile. She smiles when she's asleep, the little angel. Sweet and good and kind. If her father were alive . . .

Charlotte ducked out the front door and crossed Doheny to the Hughes market. A sudden craving for chocolate had struck. She chastised herself for leaving Janey alone, but her guilt passed quickly. Janey was ten years old, and Janey would be fine. She dodged a maroon Bentley insanely competing with a black Mercedes for a parking spot in the Hughes lot. Up above her the red rotating sign spelled out its message to the citizens of Beverly Hills and West Hollywood. "Fresh Fish. Open 24 Hours. Liquor." Next to the word "fish" was a small drawing of a fish with curving lines like the Pan Am symbol. She wondered if the same graphic artist had done both. Watch it, Charlotte. Crazy speculations again. Get your mind onto chocolate and stay away from speculations about grocery store signs.

The Hughes was crowded, but then again it was crowded round the clock. At two o'clock in the morning, when Charlotte came home from work, women in designer blue jeans and electric green blouses would be shopping for avocados and canned tuna and provolone. Charlotte headed straight for the center aisle, scooped up three hunks of Ghiradelli broken bars, and hurried to the "Express 8 Items or Less" lane. She managed to ignore the bustle around her, managed to avoid wondering what all these people did for a living. The same boy was at the register, Michael according to his name tag, the same boy who was there almost every other night of the year. She wondered about his future. Actor? Writer? Student? Would he always be in Hughes, even if she came back a decade from now? Would he never grow up, but remain a blond surfer until the end of time?

Stop it, Charlotte. Crazy speculations.

"Four dollars and thirty cents," he said.

She fished the coins and bills from her straw purse, thanked him, and walked fast, almost running, back to the apartment. She noticed that during her short excursion the mugginess actually seemed to have increased. From the bushes next door the sweet fragrance of jasmine wafted across the lawn, pure as perfume.

"Mommy, I want a piece."

Janey was nestled in Betsy's lap on the couch. The old cushions sagged under their weight.

"Charlotte, I'm sorry, but traffic was hell. I figured twenty minutes and it took forty."

"Thanks for coming, Betsy, that's okay."

"Mommy, you went for chocolate, didn't you? Can I have a piece?"

It's my own fault, Charlotte thought. I gave her the sweet tooth. She shouldn't really get chocolate before bedtime, but . . .

"All right, my love."

Charlotte ran her hands through the child's auburn hair and marveled at Janey's sensitivity. When I'm upset, Charlotte thought, I want chocolate, and Janey knows when I'm upset, like a seismograph. She knows my moods better than I do.

Charlotte broke off a piece of chocolate and held it while Janey snapped a bite.

"Mommy," the girl said, chewing, "where's Grandpa? Wasn't he supposed to sit with me tonight?"

"Yes, honey, but he's away and couldn't get back in time."

"When's he coming back?"

"Soon, honeybunch. Maybe tomorrow."

"I *miss* him," Janey said.

Yes, Charlotte thought, you do. So do I.

After Charlotte's husband had died, her father had become Janey's father, watching over her, escorting her on jaunts around the city, driving all of them to Disneyland and up to the Napa Valley and down to the desert, freeing Charlotte to grieve in private and meet new men and generally get her life in order. What would I do without him, and what would Janey do?

"If he comes home by Friday, honeybunch, we'll go out for Chinese food. How does that sound?"

96

"Outasight," Janey said, an expression she had picked up from television. "You better go, Mommy. You'll be late."

"God bless you, you little doll," Charlotte said. She kissed Janey's cheek and squeezed her palm. "Goodnight, pumpkin, sweet dreams."

The child hopped off to bed, and Charlotte tucked her in. In the living room she grabbed her costume bag and purse. With any luck in traffic at all, she figured she would make the eight o'clock show with plenty of time for makeup. Ever since Rory had allowed the dancers to park in the club's lot, life had become a great deal simpler.

Betsy came in from the kitchen, carrying a cup of steaming tea.

"Betsy, an electrician was supposed to show up by six to fix the air conditioner. He might still come, who knows? If Janey wakes up, she'll probably ask for orange juice. It's her latest fixation, and she can have as much as she wants."

"What time do you think you'll be home?"

"The usual. Two o'clock, two-thirty at the latest. Oh, and if her grandfather calls, wake her up and let her talk to him."

Betsy grinned. "You really spoil her."

"I know, but she's . . . she's all I've got. I can't help myself." She glanced at her watch. "I gotta run. I'll check in with you around eleven."

"Relax. Everything'll be okay."

Charlotte laughed at herself.

"I guess I worry too much. I *won't* check in at eleven."

She stepped once again into Janey's bedroom and saw her daughter's pink face against the white of the pillow. With that vision firmly etched in her mind, she allowed herself to leave, relieved to find that her bad mood, whatever its source, had dissipated, and that for the first time in weeks she was not only not dreading going to work, but feeling confident of better things to come.

9

ACROSS THE facade of the American General Building a few windows showed lights still burning, giving evidence of those who struggled on into the night, anxious to impress their bosses, or avoid their families, or simply to work because life offered no greater pleasures. It was the third night in a row that Mitzu had worked late. He would rather have been at the gym, tuning his body and perfecting his poise, but he had to prove to Ed Stone that he was functioning normally. He had to catch up on his late reports and get ready for the inspection tour. Otherwise Ed might decide he was too grief-stricken, or too far behind in his regular duties, to go.

He had gone home for dinner with Nancy, and now his gray Audi cruised down Montgomery Street and turned into the building's garage.

"Evening, Mr. Nagata," the guard on duty in the watch station said. "Putting in a hard week, aren't you?"

"I'm way behind, Al," Mitzu said. "Is Ed Stone still here?"

The guard scanned the rows of green tags on the board inside his cage.

"Yes, sir, he hasn't checked out yet."

Mitzu cruised down the ramp and rounded the same red column he had passed every day, twice and sometimes three times a day, for the past nine years. He could round this corner, seek his customary parking place, and slide his car between two yellow lines with the involuntary ease of breathing or blinking his eyes. He wondered what it would be like never to make these particular connections again—the turn, the guard, the ramp, the red column, and the painted yellow lines that seemed to be magically repainted whenever they began to fade. But he couldn't get beyond the last turn. Because it would carry him to an inevitable conclusion. To the act itself, to the final . . .

He turned the engine off. The garage was as still and noiseless as a ghost town.

On the next seat to him lay a paperback copy of Mishima's *The Sailor Who Fell from Grace with the Sea*. Nakajima had asked him to read it. He recalled that they had made a movie from the novel, setting the same story in England. Kris Kristofferson and Sarah Miles. Why had he not bothered to see it? What was it, then, that had stopped him from finding out more about Mishima? He stared at the words on the book's cover: "A Novel of the Homicidal Hysteria That Lies Latent in the Japanese Character."

He tossed the paperback into the glove compartment and stepped from the Audi. He was glad Ed Stone was still in the building. Despite his recent tragic loss, Mitzu wanted to assure Ed that he would be making his inspection tour anyway. Tragedy? Mitzu thought. It wasn't a tragedy. It was an omen. It was a deliverance.

He padded across the garage to the executive elevator that would carry him directly to the thirty-third floor, to Ed Stone's office. The elevator opened as soon as he inserted his key in the lock, and in barely a minute whooshed him upward to his destination. He watched the numbers pass, digital orange figures zipping quickly past on the door frame of the car. He felt the pressure of the rapid ascent, and the sudden rush of speed tugging on his body.

The light in Stone's office shot through the corridor, a beacon in the darkness as Mitzu stepped from the elevator. Stone was out of his chair before Mitzu reached the threshold.

"Mitch, what are you doing here so late again? You've been here almost every night this week."

"I've got to catch up, Ed. The regional sales charts are still on my desk, and I'm two weeks behind on approving changes for the operating manuals."

Stone let out a nervous, tired sigh. "Mitch, I want

you to realize that you don't have to be here. Benson's covering the Western accounts, and I'll send Cal Gifford on your tour and your—"

"Don't be ridiculous, Ed," Mitzu said. "I'll be all caught up in another week or so. And the tour next month is no problem. Next week I'll read the account histories and be ready to go."

Taken by surprise, Stone was speechless for a moment. "But I thought Nancy, I mean with her still upset, don't you want—"

"Nan's okay, Ed. She wants me to go on the tour. She knows how important this is to me, and she wants me right back in the swing of things."

Mitzu's voice was cold, cold as smoking dry ice. To Ed Stone it seemed to cut into his flesh, this hard tone coming from Mitch's haggard face. He had never seen Mitch look so tired. Why would he want to go on this tour? Why would he not want to stay near his wife at this shattering time in their lives?

The baby in the plastic box. Stone had only heard of it from the ward nurse when he went to see Nancy. And now the baby was dead.

"Mitch, maybe you should take it easy. You're under a strain now. Think about relaxing, taking some time off—"

"I'm *not* under any strain, Ed. Work is the best cure for all ills. Believe me, I'm in good shape, I won't blow it."

The voice Stone heard was undeniably Mitch's, but something—the harsh determination, the blithe indifference to pain—disturbed him, and he felt a chill. A literal chill. The hairs stood up on the back of his neck.

"Okay, Mitch, whatever you say. I'll tell Cal in the morning. But please do me a favor. Don't think you're missing anything if you don't go. I want you to just tell me if you're not up to it emotionally."

A surge of repulsion struck Mitzu at his core. This preposterous kindness! What did Ed Stone know? How could he grasp the torment, the rage, the fire of these days? What would he say about the newspaper photographs, the celebration, the sick and disgusting pride of those four men . . .

Move, Mitzu ordered himself. Move now.

"Thanks, Ed, I appreciate your concern, and so does Nancy. But we're strong. We'll get through this." Mitzu turned to leave, his hand sweeping his brow in a pretense of exhaustion.

"Okay, Mitch, go home and get some sleep."

"Yes, Ed, thanks, I'm very tired," he lied. He had never felt so energized. "It's finally getting to me, I guess. Good night, and thanks again."

Mitzu vaguely heard Ed's response as he reached the elevator door. Sleep, he thought. I don't need sleep. I could go for days now without sleep. I am as awake as I have ever been. I am electric. I don't need food or rest. I need to do my duty as a soldier.

The bronze elevator doors closed with a muffled thud, the car descending with a crisp whine.

Ed Stone watched the numbers change. He thought he knew Mitch Nagata as well as he knew anybody, but deep in his gut he was disturbed, and he didn't know why.

10

ST. BARTHOLOMEW'S was on a high patch of green near the train line in Elkins Park, outside Philadelphia. It was a long, low building of stone masonry, and its stained-glass windows depicting the Crucifixion and Resurrection squinted down onto a huge billboard of a yellow-helmeted workman, halfway into a manhole and holding up a newspaper. "In Philadelphia, everybody reads the *Inquirer.*"

Father Michael Farrell stood in the dressing room behind the altar looking toward the rectory. His view took in the billboard. He had overheard the monsignor just that morning asking someone at the archdiocese to see if a little leverage—a phone call or two—might influence the billboard's owners to remove it permanently as a gesture of friendship toward the Church. Maybe a call to the *Inquirer* would help. Let us all be brothers, and most of all let us all be good neighbors and not offend the parishioners with this eyesore as the first available sight to their eyes upon leaving the sanctuary on a Sunday morning.

Father Farrell picked up his two record albums, slipped out the side door, and jogged down the hill toward the rectory. A troupe of gardeners was still manicuring a Dutch elm that had once been in full bloom, giving shade to the downhill slope, but was now succumbing in stages to its indigenous blight. Although Father Farrell had never seen the tree in its summer ripeness, he was told that some of the older parishioners could recall its first buds.

"Good afternoon, gentlemen," Father Farrell called to the tree surgeons. "Think she can be saved?"

"Doesn't look that way, Father," one of the gardeners replied. "Too far gone."

A shame," the priest said.

"Yes, Father, it is. We'll do our best."

Father Farrell continued down the hill. In two weeks he would be celebrating his first Mass in the parish, and he had convinced Monsignor Raymond that some rock and roll music might entice the younger members of the church to attend. At the seminary all the younger priests said the Church was loosening up. And old Bill Raymond was no fool. If you wanted the "young people," as he called them, to appear in church, it wouldn't hurt to have a Saturday Mass that they could "relate to." So when Michael Farrell proposed a little bit of rock and roll—"My Sweet Lord," by George Harrison, and "Let It Be," by the Beatles, and "Precious Angel," by Bob Dylan—Monsignor Raymond had asked to hear the songs. The name Dylan he had heard of, but who, he asked, was George Harrison? A former Beatle, Father Farrell had said. Monsignor Raymond, a stodgy sort, was devoted less to his congregation than elevating himself in the Church hierarchy, and Father Farrell's suggestion had been met with consternation. What would the old people think, and wasn't it one of those Beatles who compared himself to Jesus Christ? Yes it was, Father Farrell explained, but not George Harrison.

Monsignor Raymond had graciously consented to listen to the songs, not least because Father Farrell would also be hearing his first confession in the parish following Saturday morning's Mass, and anything that would bring "young people" into the confessional might also swell their regular attendance.

Father Farrell stepped gingerly down the stone and slate steps to the front door of the rectory, ducking his head under the cupola above the door. At just over six feet, he was always having to watch out for his head in the unmodernized sections of the building. When the church was built at the turn of the century, people were generally much shorter. At the doorway Father Farrell had a sudden notion of being a monsignor himself one day, of having his own parish in five or six years, and of

103

ascending the Church hierarchy. The coming decade, he thought, would bring the flock back to the Church. The cult lunatics weren't going to disappear, but their very existence proved how hungry people were for faith in something larger than themselves, proved how desperately people yearned to define a purpose for their lives. Father Farrell was not himself altogether confident that the Catholic Church could provide answers. He had seen in the seminary more drunken priests than he had ever imagined could exist, and he could not but contemplate how faith seemed inexorably to lead to alcoholism.

Monsignor Raymond met him at the door and escorted him into the cottage's plush living room. Two Empire couches in brown leather faced each other across a hand-woven Iranian rug, a gift from two old biddies who gave more money to the parish than anyone else, as long as they could specify what it was spent for. And what they wanted it spent for was furniture for Monsignor Raymond's quarters. This had something to do, Father Farrell suspected, with Bill Raymond's extended teas with the women, and the prestige it lent them in parishioners' eyes.

"How are you feeling, Mike?" the monsignor asked.

"I'm pretty good, Bill. I've brought these records for you. I think you'll find them appropriate."

"I do want to listen to them, but I trust you, Mike. Do you feel ready to hear confession?"

Father Farrell took a deep breath.

"I guess so, Monsignor, but I have to say I'm having a lot of doubts these days."

"Doubts? About what?"

"Oh, you know, the same old stuff. My role in the Church. My right to grant absolution for anybody's sins."

The monsignor's red-veined face broke into a patronizing smile. He ran his fine-boned hands through his thick gray-white hair. Over the back of his desk chair his surplice and green chasuble hung, but he was still wearing his cassock.

"Mike, that's what a priest's business is all about," he said. "Faith and doubt, doubt and faith. You know that. Faith means doubt. Faith *requires* doubt. You're going to be a fine priest, Mike. Now let's listen to these songs you want to use."

The monsignor stepped to his stereo on the far side of the room. The figure of Jesus Christ guarded the cabinet. The stereo components, a gift from a parishioner who owned a hi-fi shop, were the best—two columns of Boze speakers, a Marantz amplifier—and could often be heard broadcasting the gloomy, overwhelming sounds of Bach chorales and boring Elgar symphonies. When Monsignor Raymond got a little tipsy he would blast the music at ear-splitting levels.

The monsignor slipped one of Father Farrell's discs from its sleeve, eased it onto the turntable, and lifted the tone arm.

"This Dylan fellow," the monsignor said. "He's Jewish, isn't he?"

"And also born again," Father Farrell said, smiling. "It'll be a very ecumenical service."

"Yes, well . . ."

"It's the second cut, side one."

Monsignor Raymond noticed Father Farrell's smile, returned it, and lowered the dampened tone arm. He sat near the speakers, sweeping the cassock under him as he lowered himself onto the couch. Bob Dylan's voice sang, ". . . to show me I was blinded, to show me I was gone . . .," to the accompaniment of sweet acoustic guitars. The volume was very high.

"Very nice," Monsignor Raymond said. "Mike, would you join me in a glass of sherry?"

"Love to," Father Farrell said, shouting above the music.

Monsignor Raymond poured the sherry and boosted the music's volume even louder. It occurred to Michael Farrell that not only was Bill Raymond a bit of a drunk. He was probably also damn near deaf.

11

MITZU ARRIVED for his second weekly lesson in high spirits. The Yukio Mishima novel assigned by Nakajima had given him a glimmer of insight into the rigid code of the samurai. The story told of a sailor who had deserted his calling, the life of the sea, for a woman. The woman's son and his friends could not accept the man's decision, and so they decided to kill him. The symbolism was obvious: a samurai who gives up the way of the warrior must die. Above all, Mitzu saw, the code of Bushido required loyalty and faithfulness to duty. From the story of Mishima's own life, and from a mimeographed short history of the samurai written by Nakajima, Mitzu understood that the aristocratic road of the warrior governed all actions. There was no complicated philosophy, no theoretical discussion. There was, simply, a right way to live.

Mitzu was already unknotting his tie when Nakajima opened the door into the mirrored gymnasium,.

"You have returned on schedule," the teacher said as Mitzu entered. "Please change into your robe."

After he had dressed, Mitzu came out of the locker room and found Nakajima sitting on a mat in the middle of the room. His legs were crossed in front of him, and his eyes were closed. Next to him was a small table, with a pot of steaming tea and two cups. Neither the swords nor the wooden kendo practice swords were visible. Mitzu gathered his robe around his knees and sat opposite Nakajima. At first the teacher did not acknowledge Mitzu, but Mitzu waited patiently. Patience was the way of the warrior. It occurred to Mitzu that in his office, waiting for a meeting to begin, he would have been making telephone calls or glancing through the agenda. Here he could only wait. His body was stiff from the tensions of the day—a morning sales conference, a hectic lunch with Cal Gifford and Steve Benson, dinner with his mother while Nancy rested. Now he felt himself relaxing. The twisted muscles in his shoulders loosened, his breathing slowed, and soon his eyes were closed. How remarkable, he thought. By following Nakajima's example, he had naturally settled into a meditative state.

He opened his eyes when Nakajima started to talk.

"The original name of Japan," Nakajima said, "was Wa. The word comes from the Chinese, meaning 'conjunction,' or 'harmony.' Harmony with all things, harmony between all things—this is the way of the warrior. You and I share our history, the history of the samurai. It began at the end of the eleventh century, at the time of the Minamoto clan. I gave you my impressions of this history. Tell me from your reading what you've learned. Why did the samurai arise?"

Mitzu stared into Nakajima's soft, unlined face. It had an entirely different character from when Nakajima held the wooden kendo swords. Now the instructor's eyes looked heavy-lidded and sleepy, without the heat and intensity of his fighting stance.

"The Minamoto clan," Mitzu said, "brought the country out of civil war. They took charge because the ruling classes were sinking into decadence."

"And what were their standards?" asked Nakajima.

"Loyalty to tradition," Mitzu said. "And an ideal of the warrior's pure dignity. Sadatsuna said it is the duty of the warrior to resemble a monk who lives in obedience to a rule."

"To what rule are you obedient?" Nakajima asked.

"To the rule of purity, of—"

"Ridiculous," Nakajima said. "You live in obedience to the rule of money. The true samurai were so unconcerned with money that they couldn't distinguish one coin from another."

"But you're charging me for these lessons," Mitzu said.

"I do not live in obedience to the rule of money, only to survival, and to bring honor to my family."

Nakajima poured tea, bowed his head toward Mitzu, and sipped from his cup. Mitzu followed suit.

"In the seventeenth century," Nakajima went on, "the samurai code, the way of *bushi*, was made formal. I think what is most interesting to me, after more than thirty years in the West, is how we, the samurai, make war, as opposed to the Westerner. There are two primary tenets to our code. Loyalty, as you understand, is one. *Chugi* is the Japanese word."

"*Chugi*," Mitzu said.

"The second tenet is equally important," Nakajima continued. "The Japanese word is *giri*."

"I know the meaning," Mitzu said. "Moral obligation."

"Yes," said Nakajima, "but to what?"

"Well, to . . . to . . ."

"To your Emperor," Nakajima said firmly. "And to your fellow man. To those above you and below you, to both your superior and inferior. This is why the code of *bushi* includes wisdom, kindness, and courage. Because your highest moral obligation is to the code itself, and to yourself as a samurai. The supreme sanctity of the samurai is the integrity of his word. *Bushi-no ichi gon*. The single word of the warrior."

"*Bushi-no ichi gon*," Mitzu repeated, testing the sound of the words. He liked the way they flowed from his tongue.

Nakajima smiled. "Your accent is very good."

Nakajima continued his stories of the samurai and their sacred values—a warrior's desire to bring honor to his family, to display courage in the use of the swords, to express gratitude to his country. As Mitzu listened, he felt light-headed. Looking at Nakajima sitting on the other side of the table was like looking into a mirror and glimpsing some hidden part of himself—a part that had been painted over, covered with a veneer built up, layer by layer, of education, career, and corporate status. But the truth of life could be found elsewhere: in the simple code of the warrior.

"Why did you come here?" Nakajima asked suddenly.

Mitzu was taken aback. Until now, Nakajima had

only given instruction, and had not asked a single personal question.

"To learn the way of *bushi*," Mitzu said.

"I know. But what prompted you to come?"

Mitzu considered his answer carefully. He was unsure how Nakajima would judge the worthiness of his goal. But if the way of the warrior stressed defending the honor of one's family and country, then how could the teacher object?

"There's something I have to set right," Mitzu said. "I have to correct an injustice to my country and family."

Nakajima took a deep breath and turned his gaze to the mirrored ceiling. The gym had grown warm while they talked, and beads of sweat dripped from Mitzu's forehead. Suddenly Nakajima's approval took on enormous importance. He is my true father, Mitzu thought. What if he probes for details? What if he demands to know what I'm planning?

But Nakajima stood and carried the tray into the locker room. When he returned he said, "Enough talk. We can go only so far with words. Now we will wrestle."

He knelt in front of Mitzu and raised his right arm. Mitzu assumed the same position. Nakajima reached out, grabbed Mitzu by the wrist, and tossed him sideways onto his back. Mitzu felt his head hit the mat with a clunk and for a second he was dizzy.

"Now," Nakajima said, "you try."

Again Mitzu put his arm up, and again Nakajima tossed him onto his back.

"You're trying too hard," Nakajima said. "You're struggling. The wisdom of the Zen archer says that if he aims too hard to strike the target, he will always miss. If he takes pleasure in the use of his bow, the arrow will find its own way. Now, again."

Mitzu raised his arm and mimicked Nakajima's twist of his wrist. To his surprise, he flipped his teacher onto his back.

"Very good," Nakajima said with a half smile.

They wrestled for half an hour. The purpose, Nakajima

explained, was not to learn how to fight, but how to be at one with the body. This was different from jujitsu. Wrestling promised its own reward separate from disabling an opponent. It was another facet in the perfection of the spirit.

"I sometimes think I was born in the wrong era," Nakajima said when they were done. "I would have been happy in the Edo Period, under the Shogun Tokugawa. I would have been happy to be a warrior."

As Mitzu was changing into his suit, it struck him in an instant of clarity that perhaps Nakajima was slightly mad. But Mitzu could appreciate the madness, and just as quickly as the thought had arisen it disappeared. There was nothing mad about the way of the warrior.

I am a warrior, he thought as the door to the gymnasium closed behind him.

12

THE MUSICAL was called *Alice and the Looking Glass,*
based, obviously, on *Alice in Wonderland.* If Charles
Dodgson, known to generations of children as Lewis
Carroll, had still been alive, he would have been sick at
the desecration of his masterpiece. But Broadway pro-
ducers are not noted for respecting the memory of the
dead. The book and lyrics to *Alice* were by Reuben
Morganstern, whose last two projects had collected a
shelf of Tony awards, a *Time* magazine cover, and
profits of roughly fourteen and a half million dollars.
The music was by Alan Hammerstein, no relation
whatever to the great Oscar, but whose previous foray
into the Broadway theater culminated in the enormously successful *Fleet Street,* winner of two Tonys,
rave reviews, and a *Newsweek* cover. And benefactor of
its limited partnership shareholders to the tune of
three million dollars.

You could get a nice long run, Stacy Berryman
thought, in a show with those credentials. You could
also become an overnight star.

The casting notice called for six women and five
men, Equity membership required. "Sopranos able to
belt," the notice said, "with a good mix of chest and
head voices, not necessarily pretty but with enough
power for a real ten-thirty number. Mezzos with light
coloratura possibilities. Rehearsals start September
19, out-of-town includes Balto, Chi, New Haven. Send
8x10, résumés."

Open calls horrified Stacy. You waited for five or six
hours and then they gave you five or six minutes to
sing and dance and do a monologue, and along with
several hundred other people, or several thousand, all
of whom were just as talented as you were, or more
talented, you competed for five roles. And in the end,

when you had suffered and worried and gotten your hopes up, they would give the part to an actress whose agent had power, or an actress whom they called at the last minute because they hated open calls as much as the actors and actresses and therefore stopped listening to the thousands of faces parading before their exhausted eyes.

It was hopeless. Thank you very much. That was lovely, dear. Don't call us.

Why did I ever want to be an actress? What made me think I had the talent or the stamina or the tolerance to be rejected by women in rhinestone glasses and tight black pants?

But she forced herself to go. All day long, starting at ten in the morning, she waited in the vestibule of a rehearsal hall six floors above Broadway at Fifty-fifth Street. The heat was stifling. There were no chairs. The floor, covered with candy wrappers and cigarette butts embedded in chewing gum, was too filthy to sit on. So she stood for a while, then used her *Times* as a cushion. Hundreds of others lounged on the steps, on the landing, in the lobby downstairs—listening for their names and bantering the kind of gossip heard in audition halls and theater bars around the world.

"She was in the chorus for six months, darling, and then bingo! Lucy gets sick and she's a star."

"I knew her when she couldn't dance, when she—"

"Of course he's gay, I mean that wife and two kids are great cover, but Sandy said he promised him the lead if he'd sleep with him, and Jack had to—"

"Great voice. Can't act her way out of a paper bag."

On and on it went. Good-natured nastiness, genuine unadulterated venom, and an ounce or two of admiration. The coffee machine in the lobby dispensed only hot water, and everyone refused to go out for coffee because what if someone made a mistake and they were called out of order? Stacy herself had arrived in full audition gear, fortified with sandwiches, doughnuts, a thermos, and an Anne Tyler novel. She was completely prepared. Her voice sounded wonderful.

She had lost ten pounds, as she had promised herself she would, and she was as confident as she had ever been. Of course they never hired an actress from an open call, and of course she didn't have a prayer, but . . .

"Stacy Berryman! Is there a Berryman here?"

The voice boomed down the stairwell.

Stacy jumped to her feet, squished her sandwiches, thermos, and paperback into her canvas bag, and dashed through the bodies on the steps to the doorway at the top.

"I'm Stacy Berryman," she said to the man at the open door. He was about thirty-five, cute in a gay sort of way, wore a blue turtleneck, and looked thoroughly bored with the proceedings at hand.

"I'm sorry you had to wait, sweetheart," he said. "I'm apologizing to everybody today. Go on in and do your stuff."

She walked into the rehearsal hall. About a dozen people slouched on folding chairs at the back of the room, and a thin, bearded man sat at the piano near the door. She recognized Reuben Morganstern right away because of his trademark white silk scarf, and Arthur Alpert, the producer, because he was the only one in the whole group past the age of forty.

"We're ready, dear," one of the women called out. Stacy recognized her, too. Libby Reinhart, the choreographer.

The accompanist took her music, propped it on the old spinet, and instantly started playing. From the moment Stacy heard the words soaring from her own mouth—*"Times have changed, and we've often rewound the clock"*—she knew she had never sounded better.

This was it. This was her lucky day.

Stacy took her time getting home. They had let her finish one song and then asked for another, and when she finished the second song they wanted a third, and they had asked her to dance. During the entire morning no other actress had survived more than ten minutes. She had been there almost twenty. "Thank you very much,

113

dear," was the way the session had ended, but they always ended that way. Thank-you-very-much-and-don't-call-us-we'll-call-you-thank-you-very-much-next-please.

She strolled crosstown on Fifty-seventh Street, blithely unaffected by the heat and sailing on the thought that she might get the part of Alice. The clothing in Bergdorf's window that she couldn't afford didn't bother her at all. *Things look swell,* she hummed to herself, *things look great.*

She saw Jason waiting for her when she turned the corner at Third Avenue at Seventy-third Street. She was two hours late, and he was sitting on the stoop. He had the most beautiful silver-yellow hair and dimpled chin she had ever seen, and she loved him with all her heart. He had probably forgotten his key again. She felt awful for Jason. He had more talent than she did and he hadn't worked in six months. Well, they would both make it someday. She just knew it, and they would do shows together, play opposite each other like Hume Cronyn and Jessica Tandy, husband and wife, the toast of Broadway.

"You forgot your key," she said as she leaned down to kiss him.

"No, my fair beauty, my Alice in Wonderland, I did *not* forget my key. Sit down next to me here. You ought to be sitting for this."

"For what?"

"Just sit down. I don't want you to faint in this heat."

"Jason, what *are* you talking about?"

He beckoned her to sit on the newspaper he had spread on the concrete stoop. She obliged him.

"You got a call," he said. "From Arthur Alpert's office."

"Jason, don't do this to me. You know I'm a sucker for—"

"I'm not kidding," he said. "Arthur Alpert's office called to say they were considering you for Alice and would you please come to a second call next Monday at exactly five o'clock."

She dramatically raised the back of her hand to her forehead.

"Omigod, I *am* going to faint."

He stood up, swept her into his arms, and started carrying her.

"Good," he said. "Faint. I'll carry you upstairs."

"Put me down, silly. You'll never make it up one flight."

He lowered her gently to her feet. "And your father called. He's staying out in New Mexico another week because the weather's good. And some guy called who said he knew you when you were five years old, said he was a friend of your father's, and was coming to town and wanted to see you. And Saturday we're going to celebrate with a picnic at the Cloisters."

"Jason, I don't have the part yet."

"I know, but let's celebrate anyway, and then if you get it, we'll celebrate again."

Impulsively she kissed him. He wasn't the least bit jealous of her. That's what she loved about him. He was so good and giving and caring, and he wasn't ever jealous.

She was humming again. Curtain up, light the lights . . .

13

WHO AND how? Alex Burgess dipped once again into his files, putting together a team. He had already called Toby Morrison, who had an instinct for terrorist behavior better than his own. Al Sanford would be perfect on the investigation end, if he was available. And Dr. Beckel, one of the Bureau's resident shrinks. Alex had already sent the letter down to Buck Weston for an analysis of sentence structure. Christ, Weston was a pain in the ass, with his gun collection and manic monologues all day, but stick him in a room with his computers and magnetic discs, full of notes from kidnappers and potential assassins and bank robbers, and he changed, like storm to sunshine, into the clearheaded professional he was.

The letter had also been sent for fingerprint dusting and paper analysis. Fingerprints were unlikely; the letter was a photocopy, probably a Xerox, and if whoever mailed it had taken that precaution, then he was probably careful enough to use gloves. Alex looked again at the photocopy on his desk.

> The past comes due. You have one week to shut down your nuclear power plants. All must be stopped. We know this takes time. If you do not start now, we will know. Honor and duty require it. Four children will die. And then thousands. Begin.

It was the strangest terrorist letter Alex had ever seen. And he had seen hundreds of them. The PLO variety, the Red Brigade Italian variety, the German Baader-Meinhof variety, and your run-of-the-mill American presidential assassin variety. All of Alex's training—as a lawyer, as an FBI agent, as a scholar of crime—had schooled him in rational thought, and when you were dealing with madmen you could sometimes forget that they, in fact, were not rational. Oh, they were rational on their own terms. In their own internal system of logic, they were often incredibly consistent. It was their system that was irrational. To me, Alex thought, red is red. To them, red is blue. One and one makes two for me. One and one makes six for them, or five, or eleven. All you had to do was figure out their mathematics, their logic, and you were a step ahead. Because they didn't understand yours.

The letter had arrived an hour before—at precisely three minutes past eleven—from the Nuclear Regulatory Commission. A secretary there had opened it in the course of the morning mail and simply laid it on a pile of public correspondence. Two hours later, in the normal sorting process, a clerk who routed letters to divisions of the public relations department had come across it, noticing first that this letter had no greeting, no signature, no heading. Just five typewritten lines in the middle of a page.

The Director's office dispatched the letter to Alex ten minutes after it came from the NRC. First question: is it real? Hundreds of screwballs sent letters every day. "I am going to shoot the President." "I am going to blow up the Washington Monument." "The People's Army is ready for combat. Beware." Most of the letters were harmless, but when somebody threatens to kill the President or bomb a city you at least have to pay attention. That was why the crazies sent a letter in the first place. They wanted you to pay attention. Even allowing for whatever political point they might be making, they wanted you to come after them, give them some gold-plated media exposure. Pay attention, they screamed. And you paid attention.

But not this one, Alex thought. Terrorists normally reached for grandeur in their threats. They decorated themselves with fancy names and symbols. Sloganeering, to the terrorist, is crucial. "Amerika must pay the price for its sins against humanity." That sort of stuff. They justified themselves with a Robin Hood state of mind. We are the saviors. We are the champions of the oppressed, or the victimized, or the innocent. Always champions of somebody.

But not this one. No slogans, no grandstand names. No championing of anybody. And most important of all, no implicit cry to be caught. There was very little here that would lead you to anybody.

At the sound of a tapping pencil Alex looked up to find Toby Morrison standing in his doorway. Toby was a big gentle ox with sandy hair and hangdog hazel eyes, a deceptively pretty man who seemed incapable of serious thought. But Toby had been a Rhodes Scholar at Oxford, a crack field agent, and frequent secret consultant, on loan to the State Department, to foreign governments. If Hoover were still alive, no agent would ever have been loaned to the Department of State, but with congressional oversight approval, exceptions had been made for Toby. In the space of two years the Israelis, the French, and with utmost caution the Saudis had called on his astringent mind. He was considered the Bureau's best-read man, outside of the shrink department, on terrorist psychology, and he kept a finger on every potentially serious case. Alex had requested his participation that morning, and he had a copy of the nuclear letter in his hand.

"Did you get a word-scan yet?" he asked.

"No, Buck's working on it."

"I thought you didn't like Buck," Toby said.

Alex chuckled. "Like him? He's my favorite gun collector. I'm recommending him for the National Rifle Association Nut-of-the-Year Award. What do you think he'll find?"

"I don't think he'll find anything," Toby said. "I also think you should tell the Director not to worry. This letter looks like a slow burn. Maybe even a crank."

Alex stood and planted himself against the window, looking up at the towering figure of Toby Morrison. This was not the opinion he'd been expecting.

"Really, Toby? Why do you think that?"

118

"Just a feeling. There's nothing here that fits the pattern. None of the usual attention-seeking bullshit. Some gumdrop thinks we'll shut down nuclear reactors on the basis of a crank letter. Although I have to admit this 'honor and duty' stuff worries me."

What disturbed Alex most was precisely what bothered Toby least. Maybe, Alex thought, that's Toby's blind spot. He understood political terrorism, the mind of the fanatic. But not the random madman. And despite whatever clues the letter might yield, Alex was operating on sixth-sense messages. He was responding to the same intuition that says, "Roll up your car windows, it's going to rain," and this time his intuition told him, "It's for real." Call it instinct, Alex told himself, call it superstition or intuition. Call it anything you want. But I'm not wrong too often, and this time I'm right. This letter was definitely for real, and out there, somewhere, a toys-in-the-attic looney-tune with squirrels for brains was getting ready to kill someone.

No, not squirrels for brains, Alex thought. In fact, probably intelligent. *Four children will die.* Okay, buster, which four kids did you have in mind? And when? And how can I stop you?

"Toby, I don't agree. I've got this feeling—"

"You and your feelings," Toby said. "The last time you had one of your feelings we ended up with a fifteen-year-old hot-rodder in Cleveland who hated his geometry teacher."

"Don't rub it in," Alex said, thinking that on that case, which was more than a year ago, he could just as easily have been right. Maybe the kid would have eventually shot his geometry teacher.

"I can tell, Alex. You want to run with this one, don't you? Full-scale, ten bells."

"Toby, let's look at this thing. What do we know? One, we have a postmark. San Francisco. Section Three says they might be able to come up with a mailbox radius of two square miles."

"Great," Toby said. "Seventy mailboxes in downtown San Francisco."

"And we have a paper sample. We ought to know the manufacturer of the bond and maybe who it was made for."

"Standard Xerox paper," Toby said. "Could be anybody's."

"Wrong! It looks like custom-cut paper. Maybe a big hunk of stock made for one company."

"But no watermark," Toby said.

"And what about the *words,* Toby? 'Honor and duty'?"

"I admitted that worries me. And the children will die business. But Buck is not going to turn those phrases up in his computer. And he isn't going to find 'the past comes due' either. There isn't a single sequence of words in this letter that he's going to find."

"Doesn't *that* worry you?"

"Alex, we've got to deal in *knowns.* What's the use of going full-scale with this until we have something more specific?"

Alex shrugged. "Well, we have a typewriter."

"IBM," Toby said. "A Selectric. Virtually impossible to trace. Oh, I'm all for running it through channels, but you're not going to turn anything up, believe me. And we don't have the people to spare for riot-gear response. Your basic terrorist doesn't write letters like this."

Alex leapt out of his seat, nearly tipping over his chair.

"But Toby, that's the point. This guy—"

"Or this woman—"

"Okay, or woman, isn't your basic terrorist. Look at this message. 'The past comes due.' Now what the hell does that mean? The guy has a grudge. 'We know this takes time.' He, or she, knows something about nuclear plants. And 'four children will die.' Now what the hell kind of threat is that? This guy's going to kill somebody, Toby. He doesn't tell us who, but he tells us why. Something about the past. And do you just ignore 'and then thousands'? How is he going to kill thousands of people? And why? Now, damnit, you can't tell me this letter means nothing."

"What I'm telling you," Toby said, "is that it doesn't fit any pattern. And we have *all* the patterns. We've seen every kind of nut case you can see. I think we can't do anything until we have some leads, any leads. What do the shrinks say?"

"No answer yet," Alex said. "Which means they're probably not even working on it."

"They're busy as hell," Toby said. He had not budged from his perch in the doorway. He folded the letter and casually slipped it inside his jacket.

"Let's assume," Toby continued, "for one minute anyway, that you're right. And you might be. You think whoever wrote this is likely to act fast, and so we ought to act fast. Who do you want? I mean, full time."

"You. Buck. Al Sanford from Special Investigations. Chuck Torrance in Research. And one of the shrinks. Beckel, if he's available."

"You can't have me," Toby said. "Not full time. I have seven open files."

"What about Buck? And Sanford and Torrance?"

Morrison smiled. "You're persistent, you muddle-headed dreamer. You and your intuition. Torrance you can have full time. I'll stop by Beckel's office and tell him to look at the letter. Sanford's on a case in Houston, I think. I'll check. Maybe we can get him back. Buck's got his hands full with new equipment and some trainees, but I'll try to spring him. Okay? You keep me posted."

Toby departed and Alex tossed his copy of the letter onto his desk. The paper, creased in the center, landed between the ashtray and the telephone, standing on edge. Alex lit a Lucky Strike—he was back into his heavy-smoking-and-coffee phase—and thought about what his mind was now labeling the nuclear letter. The longer he thought, the deeper the message bore into him, and the more upset he got. The fanaticism was so clear, and yet communicated in a low key. It was a studiously confident letter. He picked up a plastic ball Jill had given him—it fit snugly in the palm of his

121

hand—and juggled it back and forth as he circled his desk. I need to take a walk, he thought. But outside the heat was gruesome, and Alex could see tourists on Pennsylvania Avenue lugging cameras and sweating profusely.

The hell with it, he thought. I'll run. He carried his gym bag down the hall and changed into his jogging suit. He wasn't supposed to be seen in the hallways of the Bureau dressed like that, but Alex was in no mood to trek down to the gym and be cornered in small talk with handball players.

He trotted across the main court of the building and out onto the avenue. The sun was high in the sky and the white marble of the National Gallery's new wing, the intersecting triangles designed by I. M. Pei, sparkled in the midday light.

Halfway to the Capitol he started paying the cost for too many cigarettes. Thirty-five years old, he said to himself, and then laughed. He felt just like Jill, with the good old days of all-nighters and boundless energy behind him. One wife, one divorce, and three careers constituted more experience than even a healthy body should have to take.

He ran in place at a stoplight, then continued up Capitol Hill. Upstairs, he thought, they're going to complain if I tie up too many people on this letter. Run the standard checks, and if nothing comes up then stick it in a file and wait. Put the nuclear plants on alert and let the NRC worry. But Alex was certain, as certain as he was of anything these days, that anyone who wrote about "honor and duty" had serious intentions. Like murder, Alex thought. Or nuclear holocaust.

He crossed into the shade near the Rayburn Building and thanked the Government Services Agency for maintaining the trees and gardens. The light from the sun came in short vivid beams between the leaves, hypnotizing him into his rhythm as he ran.

Alex, he said to himself, they'll laugh at you. If you push this case they'll talk about those smartass jock lawyers, the ones who never climbed the Bureau ladder, running off half-cocked on backassward reasoning. I can hear them now, he thought, braying pompously because I was wrong. Because the damn letter's just a crank, doesn't mean anything, not worth the effort.

No, it's not a crank. This guy is trying to tell us something.

Alex pondered how he might explain this to the Director. Webster, as far as he could tell, was the best Director in the Bureau's history. Better than Hoover by a long shot. Not crazy. Downright sane. The older agents would just as soon shoot you for suggesting the idea that Hoover wasn't God's gift to law enforcement, even with all the stuff that had come out since he died. Hoover had been their king, and all they could do was shout, "Long live the king."

Webster will listen, Alex thought, huffing and heaving as he circled the Capitol and headed for the Hoover Building. My God, how could they name this building for Hoover? And how can they not change the name considering what we know about the old screwball now?

No question about it. Behind that letter lies a dedicated, sincere, thoroughly off-his-rocker madman.

Okay, madman, he thought as he steamed into the court of the building, nearly trampling a boy scout as he bounded down the steps. Okay, I know you're out there, I believe you. You're out there and I am going to find you.

He chugged to a halt in front of the identification security desk at the bottom of the plaza. His heart was pounding, his sweatsuit was soaked, and the tire-like treads of his Nike running shoes squeaked on the tiles. Although the desk agents undoubtedly recognized him, they nevertheless checked his card and logged his entry. Alex shoved his card into the turnstile reader and entered the building.

Toby Morrison met him in the hallway outside his office, grinning his wide dumb-ox grin.

123

"We just got a break, Alex. We have the original of the letter. The Seashell people got it. And to top it off, the NRC copy has prints. Not great prints, but prints."

"Probably doesn't mean a damn thing," Alex said, deadpan as he caught his breath. "You know about us muddleheaded dreamers and our intuition."

When the letter arrived at Seashell headquarters Lenny Horan had been finishing plans for a major demonstration in Florida. The nuclear plants on the south coast of the state had developed containment-vessel leaks, both for the second time in a month. Sentiment against nuclear power in the state was as ripe as ever. No one could have asked for a better time. Nothing like a disaster to get people riled up.

It had been a hard year for the Seashell Alliance. The head of the Boston office, a college classmate of Lenny's, had quit because he needed to earn more money—"I got two kids, Lenny, what am I gonna do?"—and taken a job with Common Cause. Common Cause had mountains of liberal-guilt money, and could afford reasonable salaries. An organizer at Common Cause could earn twenty-five thousand, while the highest-paid members of the Alliance staff were getting by on less than fifteen.

But with the Florida leaks money had come barreling in once again, and the presidential candidates could hardly ignore a potential nuclear catastrophe. The issues people for both the Republican and Democratic candidates had begun to yield on their candidates' adamant support for nuclear. Lenny Horan knew that the contenders believed in nuclear power, and just as surely he knew what he himself believed: nuclear power was the greatest threat to mankind since the plague. To make nuclear power safe might be possible, but the solutions were years away, a decade at least, and in the meantime every day of nuclear plant operation slapped the face of fate.

All these thoughts were on his mind as he coordinated the Florida demonstrations. The publicity and travel costs would run close to sixty thousand, and Seashell would be picking up the entire tab. Posters, print advertising, private security men, maybe a television ad or two. The locals had no money to speak of, but Lenny thought the expense well worth the effort. You couldn't always pick your times and places, and when the chance for mass media coverage presented itself, you had to be prepared.

The Seashell Alliance's Washington office was in a slightly seedy building just behind the Capitol, a few blocks into the Southeast quadrant of the city. In the third-floor warren of rooms, nine claustrophobic cubicles that had once been somebody's slave quarters, cardboard boxes of mailing labels, fund-raising lists, and bumper stickers cluttered all available floor space— Parkinson's Law, extended to collectibles, actively in evidence. Downstairs the Sierra Club was housed on an entire floor, and Lenny was on his way to meet one of their Florida representatives to ask for help over lunch when Ella Hufstedler, his unpaid volunteer officer manager, stopped him.

"Lenny, you better look at this before you go."

"What is it?"

"Just read it, Lenny. *Please.*"

The envelope was incorrectly addressed to Northwest instead of Southeast, but the post office had managed to get it there. It was not addressed to anyone in particular, just Seashell Alliance.

Lenny took the letter from the already opened envelope, wondering why Ella was so adamant. *The past comes due. You have one week to shut down . . .*

He skimmed the sentences without much concern. A nuclear nut. But the nuts were as dangerous as the opposition. The anti-nuclear movement was fragile enough without getting a name for breeding extremists. The first thought that crossed his mind was that one of the Alliance's members, somebody on their own mailing list, had sent the letter. Or why else send it to them?

125

"Lenny, you ought to call the NRC. And maybe the FBI."

"Call downstairs, will you, Ella, and see if they can wait twenty minutes for lunch. Don't mention the letter, okay? I want to talk to Gene."

The idea of calling either the Nuclear Regulatory Commission or the FBI didn't appeal to Lenny Horan. They'll think it's one of us, and use it to hurt us. Good God, it probably *is* one of us. He goose-stepped over a carton of coffee mugs, with "No Nukes" in blue Day-Glo, and walked into Gene Epstein's office. Epstein was their only staff lawyer in Washington. All the rest were volunteers. Epstein had walked away from a position at one of Washington's most prestigious corporate law firms to take the Alliance job, giving up not only his secure position in the legal fraternity but also half his salary. It was Epstein to whom Lenny Horan turned whenever he needed advice on strategy, or disputes with the Boston office, and it was Epstein who, in his cool, lawyerly way, worked out compromises.

He was on the phone when Lenny walked in.

"The civil liberties issue has to take precedence," he was saying in a soothing voice bent on persuasion. "The right to demonstrate is not an issue. Well, Jerry, I sympathize with the position you're in, but you have to make those hick cops understand. I don't want anybody hurt, but we're not stopping the demonstration. Get to the governor's office. Get . . . Okay, call me when you hear. Give my love to Candy."

He set the phone in its cradle. "The National Guard in Florida wants—"

Horan interrupted. "Gene, this came in the mail."

He handed the letter across the desk. Halfway through reading it, his eyes moving rapidly across the page, Gene Epstein dropped the letter.

"Who else has seen this?"

"Ella and me. What do you—"

"Anybody else touched it?"

"No, what are you talking about?"

126

"Fingerprints."

"Gene, why do you think it came here? If somebody in the movement . . . God, Gene, I hate to even think about it."

Gene Epstein leaned back purposefully in his chair. His lined, drawn face belied his youth, and as his fingertips massaged his temples he seemed a good deal older than his thirty-one years.

"Don't speculate, Lenny. You'll give yourself an ulcer. We could have gotten this for a hundred different reasons. I have a friend who works for Bill Webster. I think we ought to—"

"Oh no, Gene, not the FBI. They'd like nothing more than a chance to paint us as dangerous."

"You're a paranoid, Lenny. Not without reason, I'll admit. But we have to tell the FBI about this. I don't think it's a joke, and even if it is, it's not for us to decide. And if it's one of our own people, then we ought to find out who, and quick."

"But if this gets to the papers, Gene, the movement'll—"

"Lenny, the movement's in better shape than you think. But if some kook blows up a nuclear reactor, then you can kiss everything good-bye, all the public trust we've built up. Not to mention maybe killing a couple of hundred thousand people. Do you want to call Webster's office, or do you want me to do it?"

Lenny Horan thoroughly distrusted the FBI. They had kept files on him in the sixties, which he pried loose from them only after two Freedom of Information suits. When you came right down to it, he distrusted the entire federal government, from the President to the Director of the FBI to every single bureaucrat in the system.

"Gene, if they release this letter to the press, and say it came from our offices, you know what people will think."

"And what will they think," Epstein countered, "if we pretend we never got it and someone finds out we did?"

127

Horan mulled the possibility.

"Okay, call your friend. But see if they can keep us out of the story. And tell them they don't need *my* fingerprints. They already have them."

Horan rushed away to his lunch date. Gene Epstein picked up his telephone, praying that nobody besides the FBI had his lines tapped.

The simple five-line letter had been buried in the normal mass of Burt Britten's constituent mail. Angry citizens, venting their spleen on the upcoming defense appropriations hearings, had doubled the usual quantity. The increase was mostly the result of lobbyists from the defense industries themselves and the aerospace unions. All it took was a threatened cutback of missile development or reduction in airplane contracts to excite an avalanche of protest. Many of the supposed citizen comments would be identically written, copied from forms supplied by whichever special-interest group stood to lose the most. Still, everybody expected an answer, and everybody got one. Secretaries opened each letter, marked a code letter in the right-hand corner, and tapped a key on a computerized typewriter to generate a reply. "Thank you very much for your recent letter," all such replies began. "Your participation in the democratic process is what makes this country strong." At the end of the day the codes would be tabulated—telling Burt how many were for, how many were against, and how many were just generally angry at their government—and the letters would be signed by a machine that reproduced Burt's signature. Burt didn't approve of these thousands of impersonal letters being mailed out over his name, but there were lots of things congressmen had to do that he didn't approve of. You had to tolerate this rigamarole or else the machinery of government would grind to a halt.

Of all the mail-answering activity itself Burt was happily oblivious. A party caucus had consumed his entire afternoon. It was the sort of jockeying for power he liked, and a lesson, he thought, in one of the true functions of a legislature. The rise of one-issue political groups had fragmented the country's politics, but you didn't have to throw up your hands and succumb.

Burt returned to his office feeling pleasantly triumphant. His agenda for the hearings had been approved, he was firmly in control of at least six committee votes, and the Speaker had personally congratulated him, with an ironic glint in his eye, for being "a fine wheeler-dealer." John Connally's self-description had given the appellation an ugly sound, but the Speaker delivered the praise with a sparkling laugh—half as a joke, half as a tribute—and Burt was not the least bit surprised to find himself vulnerable to flattery. Especially when weeks of boning up on the facts, hours of phone calls, and vote-swapping to rival a backyard tag sale in Clovis, New Mexico, had paid off in so delectable and complete a success.

His administrative aide, a hometown boy named Tharp Williams, basked in as much glee as the congressman. Tharp was four years older than Burt, and had been working for one Massachusetts representative or another for the last six terms.

"You're gonna be a fine old pol some day," Tharp said as they rode upstairs in the Rayburn Building's members' elevator. "That's some of the handsomest playing with favors the halls of this venerable institution have ever seen. And who said you couldn't get powerful in Congress on brains alone?"

"It isn't brains," Burt said. "It's balls."

They enjoyed a laugh together and were still chuckling when they passed through the high mahogany-paneled door into the reception area of Burt's office. But both stopped short as they faced Burt's secretary, who stood waiting with a letter in her hand.

The past comes due. You have one week . . .

They read in silence, Tharp peering over Burt's shoulder.

"Tharp, find out if anybody else in the House has

received this letter. But *discreetly*. Just snoop around a little and see what turns up."

Burt walked into his office and reached for the phone. There was only one person he knew who understood these delirious outbursts of American madness, and that one person was Alex Burgess.

14

MITZU WAITED for the library to open. The morning air was briskly cool but turning warmer as office workers scurried across Larkin Street like lemmings. In the arched entryway near Mitzu a photographer with a Leica on a tripod seemed to be focusing on the fountains in the plaza below. A girl with a ponytail standing behind him said something about Beaux-Arts architecture, and then from inside there was a rattling of chains and the main door swung open.

Walking down the main hallway to the large reference room, Mitzu listened to the click of his heels on the marble floor. He had warned them, and now he had to carry out his plan. Patience and courage were the way of the warrior.

He turned the corner at the end of the hall into the main reading room. An old woman with blue-rinsed hair and the face of a sparrow sat on a stool behind the counter.

"Is this where you have the out-of-town directories?"

"Yes," she said with a bored sigh. "Which cities would you like?"

"Houston, Los Angeles, and Minneapolis," he said.

The woman slid a green card toward him. "I'll get them for you. Please fill this out."

Mitzu picked up a pencil and looked down at the green card—a snag he hadn't counted on. I can put down my own name, he thought. What does it matter? Then he saw a magazine cover with Warren Beatty's picture on the cover, and in the blank space on the card he wrote *M. Beatty*. Without thinking he filled in American General's address. The woman returned with the three directories, marked the card, and pushed the huge volumes across the counter.

"Just bring them back here when you're through, please."

Mitzu noticed her staring at his briefcase. The gold initials showed just above the handle. *M.N.* Quickly he grabbed the briefcase and the three directories, and made his way to a table underneath the high front windows. Taking the newspaper clipping from his pocket and a pad of yellow legal paper from his briefcase, he wrote the three names. The fourth, of course, he already knew, and needed no telephone number. With less effort he could have requested the information from the reference department at American General, but somewhere in his mind, in that region just below the level of consciousness but just as active as any willful decision, the possibility of detection had taken hold.

People might be watching. You never knew who was watching.

He measured his plans. He methodically considered risks and objectives, as though plotting a sales forecast. First, the names and numbers.

Dust motes floated into the sunlight like the glint of water on glass. With the pages crinkling in his hands, he thumbed through the Houston directory. He thought the old woman behind the counter was staring at him. He was tempted to glance over his shoulder. But he continued turning the pages. Here, the *B*'s. Banner to Beaton. Beaton, Berman, Berno. Next page, born with
what I can only call crippling deformities.

The doctor's voice, a soothing singsong, echoed through his mind. The grotesque, twisted form of his child, the huddled figures behind him in the ward, and the polished shimmering surfaces of metal and plastic and the box, the tubes.

It was his body, the twisted body. His own face merged before his eyes with the body of the baby boy. They were one body, one face, one injury. One spirit, the
spirit of old Japan, yamato-damashii . . . abandoning a fleeting life

for the spirit of old Japan.

Bernower. Bernstein.

There, Berryman. Oscar Berryman, Jr.

He copied the address and phone number, pushed the book aside, and opened the Los Angeles volume, scattering more dust.

He would abandon his life, he thought, for the spirit of old Japan. With that idea he returned to the telephone books, certain of his acts and of his fate.

The computer center occupied eleven thousand square feet two stories below ground level, resting on an independent foundation designed to withstand the shock of an earthquake no higher than 7.2 on the Richter scale. Of course any earthquake of that magnitude would destroy the building on Montgomery Street above, but the computers and their programs and their data would remain unharmed. Even if the street cracked and opened and swallowed cars and people, the sealed computer rooms, with their reinforced ceilings and poured foam foundation, were estimated to stand better than a fifty-fifty chance of escaping significant damage.

Mitzu had been in the computer center only twice in the past year, and as he stepped off the elevator he was struck immediately by the unearthly quiet. On the padded and carpeted floors no footsteps echoed. Not a soul stirred in the long, spotlit arcade. It had the feel of a medieval monastery—the dedication nearly religious, the sanctity imperturbable, and the mystery ineluctable.

He mentally rehearsed his answers to whatever questions the programmers might ask. Although he wore a clearance badge, entitling him to travel anywhere in the company's fortress at any time of day, someone was still likely to ask what he was doing there, particularly when he requested the safety procedures and security files for two of American General's installations. Bureaucrats behaved that way, sticklers on procedure. Just like me, Mitzu thought. Just like me. We are all

133

good company men. Faithful and loyal. I am the company. The company is me.

He felt in total control, having worked out what he thought was a logical explanation for his presence there, and knowing that underlings respond to authority with automatic deference.

He pushed through the pressure-dampened doors into the main terminal room and took a deep breath. He instructed his mind to plant an innocuous smile on his face, and unclipped his plastic-coated clearance shield.

"Department?" the desk clerk said.

"Domestic sales, nuclear," he answered crisply.

The clerk glanced halfheartedly at his picture on the card, punched four white buttons, and waited. On the television screen built into the desk Mitzu's clearance numbers appeared, one digit after another at three digits per second.

"Sign the book, please," the clerk said after completing the computerized transaction.

He signed with a flourish. All right, he said to himself, now you're in.

"Thanks," he said, offering his most gracious executive nod.

He crossed through the electric-eye monitors, two beams shooting from one stanchion to the other, knowing that he was being scanned for weapons. It occurred to him how idiotic these procedures were. The information in the computers gave him more power than doing damage to them. It might once have been true, as Mao had said, that power came from the barrel of a gun, but what was a gun compared to information? Knowledge was the greatest power.

The main terminal room stretched out before his eyes. Above him, rimming the cavernous space, hung a balcony veneered with panels of bleached white oak—the clean, spare look of modern design. All of this was Nancy's idea. She had selected the materials. Giant IBM and Control Data behemoths climbed straight up to the ceiling. Mitzu walked across the room to a bank

134

of IBM Series 7000's, where clusters of programmers were extracting perforated sheets as they tumbled, their gripper holes clicking in the ratchets, from the computer's printer. Mitzu casually walked by them and headed straight for the program key files.

In a matter of minutes he found what he wanted. Four separate entries were necessary to retrieve the information. He took the program key and began climbing the steps to the balcony.

No one had asked him any questions. No one had demanded to know why he was there.

He had once been awed by this room. The products of his company, of the men and women who created and sold them, had seemed to Mitzu, at another time, to promise untold rewards for mankind. And untold profits for American General. But now, as he reached the top of the steps, none of this mattered. Not American General or its products or its people. Not the untold rewards for mankind.

Honor and duty. The right course to follow in life. The spirit of old Japan.

These were what mattered now.

He gripped the railing, the light

in the sky, a canopy of white, blinding, the ground shaking and a spray of dust and a towering gray

filing cabinet next to him rotated toward the console operator. His palm was sweating, his heart thumping, and his mouth felt dry.

He let loose his grip on the railing and continued onto the balcony. White desks, like blocks in a child's Tinkertoy set, were lined up in a row. The main terminal was operated by a darkly tanned woman who, with her tawny blond hair layered in curls over her shoulders, and in the deft, assured sweep of her hands across the panel of buttons, bore a resemblance to Nancy, a similarity so startling that when she looked up he almost called her name.

"Department, please," the woman said.

"Domestic sales, nuclear," Mitzu said, handing her the program code.

She stared at the plastic chart.

"This is security material," she said.

"Yes, I know. I'm going out to meet the administrators on these jobs and I want to familiarize myself with the layouts. You know, to show the client we understand his problems."

She looked doubtful, but Mitzu maintained his fixed smile.

"Well-l-l . . ." She slapped the card against her hand. "I should really get clearance on this. I should call upstairs."

"That's all right, just dial Ed Stone's extension and I'll talk to him."

"We don't have to go *that* high."

"*I'll* be happy to call him," Mitzu said, "if you'll please hand me the phone." He put just a touch of frost in his voice, the brusque tone of an important man who believes in corporate democracy and who is willing to follow regulations, but who has taken as much interference from clerks as he's going to tolerate.

The woman got the message. "Oh no, that won't be necessary. I'm sure it's okay. This will take a few minutes to run, and there are four on line ahead of you. Where should I send the results?"

"I'll wait," Mitzu said, and without another word took a seat directly opposite her desk.

The woman held his glare for a fraction of a second, as though not quite accepting his determination. But Mitzu showed not the slightest interest, and she passed the plastic code card to the operator behind her.

Mitzu crossed his legs and smoothed the fabric of his suit, reminding himself of his competence.

They have trained me, he thought, to be efficient. They have trained me very well.

The meeting had gone on for three hours, and at Ed Stone's closing remarks, a ripple of applause broke around the conference table.

"We'll be looking forward to your reports," Stone said. "It's been an enormously successful period for all of us, and we are moving forward with great momentum. I want all of you to know how happy I am with your performance, and how much I appreciate your tremendous efforts. Let's get out there and show our clients what service really means. Let's show them we know as much about their business as they do. Let's show them we're the leader, and we intend to stay the leader."

Mitzu and the other nine men rose from their seats. Despite the camaraderie, Mitzu had not really been listening to the pep talk, to Stone's advice for their tours, or to the questions from his fellow executives. None of it penetrated the deep veil over his mind. The obsessed cannot be easily distracted. He was devoted to his private mission. Everyone, particularly Stone, had been aware of Mitzu's reticence. But they understood. Or thought they did. It was his personal tragedy. Who could blame him?

"Hey, Mitch," one of them said on the way out, "I heard about your kid. I'm real sorry."

Mitzu mumbled an appropriate reply, and then a few of the others approached him with equally solicitous words of comfort.

The buzzer on Stone's intercom sounded softly. Mitzu watched him take the call.

"Yes, Marie, who? The FBI? Threats? None that I know about . . . Well, call Stoddard and have him get back to me. Okay, I'll take it now. I'll be in there in a minute."

He wove his way through the crowd toward the door. Mitzu stopped him, laying a hand on his shoulder.

"What was that all about?"

"The FBI," Stone said, shaking his head in mystification. "They want to know if we've gotten any threats about our installations. They talked to the chairman this morning. It's probably some environmental group. Let me see what it's all about."

The FBI. Threats. They worked fast.

The time has come, Mitzu thought. Time to begin.

He dreamed that night, dreamed of swords. In his dream he stood in front of the mirrors in Nakajima's gym, his body oiled and glistening, like Mishima's body in the poster, and his hands pulling the arched curves of metal from their scabbards. His instructor stood next to him, but he saw directly through the man, as if he were a ghost, a projection of light. Nakajima's form shifted and changed in white puffs of smoke, taking on the shape of his father, his mother, beseeching him to come home. And then the kind and smiling face of his Uncle Tadashi in his airman's uniform, until finally the image became himself, but as a child, and he was staring into his own reflection. All the faces changed and flowed into one another. He was all of them.

But the voice was Nakajima's voice.

"The code of Bushido," his instructor said, "is the way of the warrior. The way of the warrior rests on two great pillars. *Giri,* the tie to your Emperor, your duty. *Chugi,* your loyalty, your course to follow in life. You are a *bushi,* a warrior. True courage is to live when it is right to live, and to die only when it is right to die. You are purity. You are simplicity. You were born a samurai . . . a samurai . . . a samurai . . ."

He awoke. Frond-like forms played on the ceiling in hues of gray and gold. Beside him Nancy stirred, her breath whistling through her lips.

He felt a deep inner calm, a great peace. He felt more peace than he had ever known.

15

BURT BRITTEN nervously tapped his cigarette, facing Alex Burgess across a table littered with coffee cups, sugar packets, and overflowing ashtrays. Two days had passed since the mysterious threatening letter had arrived at the Nuclear Regulatory Commission, at the Seashell Alliance, and at Burt's office. Now Alex's investigative team had been assembled.

"I don't understand," Burt said. "The NRC getting this letter makes sense. And I can see why the Alliance got it. But I don't work with them, I don't even *know* them. Why didn't anyone in the House besides me get it?"

Alex said, "I wish to God I knew."

"Alex, if the FBI doesn't have a clue, then what am I—"

"Calm down, Burt. You're starting to sound hysterical."

Burt snorted. "I could get hysterical very easily, Alex. I'm not handling any of this too well."

Alex rubbed his cheek. A sore was erupting inside from too much nicotine. "We've got some good sources on the Hill," he said, "and as far as I can tell nobody else received the letter. But who knows? It could be in a stack of mail on somebody's desk. What did Tharp Williams turn up?"

"He didn't want to panic anybody," Burt said. "I told him to be discreet. And he didn't find anything. Maybe in a couple of days . . ."

Alex picked up the phone. "Are Hollister and Alford ready yet? Send them in when they get here."

Burt chewed his lips. "What about the Seashell people?"

"Well, Gene Epstein's convinced it's somebody in the movement. He's terrified, as a matter of fact."

"And you don't think so."

"It's logical," Alex said, "up to a point. But it doesn't hit me right. No, there's something we just aren't seeing here. We're still going to run checks on the anti-nuke people who have histories of violence, but we're a little tight on manpower."

Burt sat straight up. "What do you mean? Tight on manpower?"

"I mean the Bureau's understaffed and ... and they're not taking this as a top-priority item."

Burt slammed his fist into his palm. "Great! I get letters saying people are going to be killed, and the FBI doesn't—"

The door opened and two men entered. Both were dressed in light gray suits, white shirts, and solid-colored ties. They were old Bureau men, of indefinite middle age. They had the nondescript faces so common to federal policemen—pale with narrow features, clean-shaven to the point of boyishness, and exuding unmistakable authority. The taller of the two reached out his hand toward Burt.

"Congressman, I'm Ken Hollister. This is Roger Alford."

Burt nodded to both. Hollister was the tall one, and his ill-fitting suit couldn't hide the fact of his well-proportioned body.

Hollister turned to Alex. "Has he agreed?"

"Agreed to what?" Burt asked.

"Burt, we're concerned about your safety," Alex said. "We'd like to keep an eye on you, everywhere you go. But we need your approval."

The idea stunned Burt.

"Do you think it's necessary?" he asked.

Hollister looked at Alford, and they both turned to Alex.

"Yes," Alex said, "we do. I know it doesn't make any sense, since you've never been a big booster of nuclear power, but everybody has enemies. Until we have some leads—" he took a breath, choosing his words carefully "—and until I can convince some other people around

140

here that this is serious, we ought to take the precaution."

Burt tried to imagine who would want to kill him. The thought that a stranger would single him out was hard to register. And then, unimaginably, he wondered how it would feel to be followed by FBI agents.

"I don't like it," he said, "but I'll do whatever you say."

Hollister sat down next to Alex. "Congressman, we don't want to be in your way. One of us, or both of us, will be with you all the time. We'll have another man outside your apartment twenty-four hours a day. You probably won't notice us too much, but try to let us know where you're going. On the Hill, we'll try to avoid being conspicuous, but you'll have to explain us to your staff."

Alford was already on his way out the door. "And don't run any red lights," he said with a smile. "We'll be with you when you leave the Bureau."

The two agents departed, and Alex closed the door behind them.

"So," he said.

Burt was suddenly weary. "You want to know the truth, Alex, I'm scared. How do other people react? You get this letter out of the blue and . . ." He licked his lips; they were dry. "Alex, I'm scared out of my goddamned wits."

"I wish I could tell you not to be," Alex said. "I wish I could say there's nothing to worry about. But Burt, I'm as frightened as you are, mainly because I don't know what any of this means. I have no explanation for why anybody would be after you."

"That," Burt said, "makes two of us."

I live in dreams, Jill thought. Reality is too much to bear. She had spent the afternoon in the library and was walking back to her apartment. Her ankle was still bothering her, and so she moved slowly, conscious of her slight limp. She could not, try as she might, put her finger on what was bothering her. All she knew

141

was that it had been going on for at least a week. While lecturing her attention would wander, and for the last several days she had felt not quite in touch with the simple daily tasks of life. She had accidentally paid her MasterCharge bill twice, had mailed the telephone company's check to the electric company, and only this morning had let the coffee heat so long that the pot boiled dry. Even stranger, she had unaccountably found herself daydreaming about her childhood, flashing on isolated moments that she hadn't thought about in years. She had thought about the brown mare she rode at her grandfather's farm in Chicopee, and remembered crying in the barn when the horse died of old age. She thought about her high school prom, and how being crowned prom queen seemed so important at the time. She recalled her senior year at Penn with unbelievable clarity, and driving to Harvard that June to Burt's law school graduation. With a visual image so strong that it made the hairs on the back of her neck stand up, she remembered feeling so proud for herself and for him, and wishing that her mother had been alive to see them both grow up and fulfill her hopes for them. She remembered landing in Tokyo and meeting Mitzu and . . .

Suddenly, as she crossed New Hampshire Avenue toward her apartment, Jill knew when her sense of distraction had begun. It had been Mitzu Nagata's telephone call.

At the doorway to the building she stopped in her tracks and dabbed perspiration from her forehead. "But it's all over," she said aloud. He's in the past. It was funny, she thought, how one telephone call could throw you off-balance. And it was ridiculous. I was younger then. I fell head over heels. I got hurt. That's life.

Riding up in the elevator she resolved not to think any more about Mitch. Alex would be coming from the Bureau soon, and she wanted to be in a good mood. Entering her apartment, she dropped her briefcase on the couch, flipped on the air conditioning, and glanced

142

around the living room, all its objects neatly in place. In the corner was an Isoli print she had forgotten to take to the frame shop. It had been sitting there for four days. Enough, she thought. Enough scatterbrained behavior. She shrugged off her dress, made a half-hearted and unsuccessful attempt to toss her bra onto the bedpost, and stepped into the shower. I was never good at horseshoes either, she thought.

As the water rushed over her, creating a kind of echo inside the shower cap, she found herself wondering who Alex Burgess really was. She was going to marry him, probably in January, spring at the latest, and it occurred to her that as much as she loved him, and even more important, truly liked him, she would never entirely understand him. She knew this was a commonplace thought: we never really understand anybody. We never really understand ourselves.

By the time she had dried herself off and squeezed into a pair of absurdly tight jeans, she heard Alex's key in the lock.

"Hi, hon."

"Hi, sweetheart."

He gave her his usual intense kiss. She loved that about him. He wasn't one of those fast-peck-on-the-lips types.

"How was your day?" he asked. "Making progress?"

"No," she said. "I couldn't concentrate for some reason. How's your case?"

Alex took his jacket off and tossed it onto the couch. As it landed he realized his cigarettes were in the pocket, and retrieved them.

"How many is that today?" she asked. She had promised not to nag him, but she couldn't help herself.

"Don't ask," he said.

"Just don't die in my arms of a heart attack when you're fifty," she said. "What about the case?"

"Nothing," he said. "No progress."

"I'm worried about Burt," she said, sitting down on the couch and straightening his jacket.

"You shouldn't be. Hollister and Alford are two of the best men in the Bureau."

"I know. But it's still a little scary. Have you turned up anything on the letter?"

"I hate to admit it," Alex said, "but we don't have much. There's nothing on the fingerprints yet. No luck tracing the copier paper. The original is on plain bond that could've been bought anywhere. We did narrow the mailbox down to one of thirty-seven in downtown San Francisco in the heart of the business district. Which means we are precisely nowhere."

He turned and went into the kitchen. A blue haze of cigarette smoke stayed in the air behind him. "Ice tea? Drink? Coffee?" he called out.

"No, thanks. What else can you do? I mean, without fingerprints?"

Alex returned with an iced glass of half milk and half coffee.

"I think the answer's in the letter," he said. "There's something odd about the language . . . Well, maybe Buck Weston will come up with something. Let's not talk about it, okay? It's bugging the hell out of me, and talking only makes it worse. Maybe it'll turn out to be a crank."

"You don't believe that for a second," Jill said.

Alex smiled. "No, you're right. I still don't. I might fool myself for a while, but not you. Do you have any idea how crazy I'd be without you in my life?"

Jill laughed. "*How* crazy?"

"Oh, I'd be even more compulsive than I am. I'd still be squeezing every drop out of toothpaste tubes and taking out the garbage twice a day and chewing out the dry cleaner for losing shirt buttons."

"You only stopped squeezing toothpaste like that because I won't let you," Jill said in a humorous taunt. "You still *want* to. So you're still crazy."

Alex drew himself up. "You're utterly correct, madame. The time has come for you to summon the men in the white coats and have me locked up for my own good. Shall I get you the phone?"

They leaned toward each other and kissed, this time longer. Jill had trouble admitting to her feminist friends that Alex's bear hugs turned her on, but there you were . . . he was a big, brawny man, a *physical* man, and she enjoyed that.

"Hungry?" she said.

"For you," he said.

"I mean for dinner."

"That too, but you first."

Jill laughed and walked toward the bedroom.

"On one condition," she said over her shoulder.

"Granted. I am your slave. What is it?"

"That you help me get back into these jeans. I practically sprained my wrist putting them on."

"I have a better idea," Alex said, following her. "You don't have to get back into them at all. I'll burn some sirloins for us, make mush of the zucchini, and we'll spend the night in bed."

Jill mock-swooned. "Oh, Alex honey," she said in a Southern drawl, "y'all treat me too well."

"Hush, Scarlett," he said, and closed the bedroom door.

16

THE STAGE door opened and a potbellied man with a cigarette dangling from his lips stood in the stairwell.

"Char, you ready?" he called over his shoulder. "You're on, baby."

"Comin', Wally, I'm comin'."

From inside could be heard a scratchy but well-rehearsed combo of trumpets and snare drums pounding out a syncopated disco version of "I Write the Songs." A platinum blond chorus girl strolled into view, propped one foot on a chair, and tugged at her black fishnet stockings. She stuffed a wad of cotton fluff and two sanitary napkins into her tight black lacy brassiere. Her body undulated with a dancer's confidence. Her back was straight and her legs sinuous, strong and full but not ugly. With her hands she cupped the underside of her breasts, studied them in the mirror and nodded approval to herself, and then, at the bong of a cymbal crash, strutted onto the stage.

"Ladies and gents," a cheerful voice shouted, "the star of our show, Miss Charlotte La Rue."

From outside Mitzu watched through the open stage door as she pranced out of his vision. The potbellied man in the stairwell clipped the cigarette between his thumb and forefinger, yanked it from his mouth, and spat onto the asphalt outside the door. He turned to see what dregs of humanity had been dredged up by the night to knock at his gateway to hell.

"Yeah, whaddaya want?" he growled.

"Is that Charlotte Kirkaby?"

"Char? Is that her name? Kirkaby? Yeah, that's Char. You know her? You wanna leave a message? You can't come in here."

"No, no, I was looking for her, that's all. Doesn't she have dark hair, though?"

"Char? Yeah, Char wears that for her act. Hey, look here, you some kinda peeper, or what? You wanna meet Char, you do it out front like everybody else, see? Don't hang around the door, see, or I'll take your head off, see?"

Mitzu stepped back before the door slammed shut in his face.

Mitzu's plane had landed in Los Angeles at five that afternoon. He had checked into the Beverly Hilton Hotel and confirmed his morning meetings. Everyone seemed to have heard about his baby. They were all sorry, they said. Why were they sorry? And from what did their sorrow spring?

They felt guilty. And they *were* guilty.

He had driven across Laurel Canyon into the Valley. The club had been easier to find than he could have hoped. "Duke's," the sign said in neon letters four feet high. "Stage Show. Girls." Now, seven hours later, he continued to stare at the doorway across the street. "Oh, you must mean Charlotte," the voice had said to him on the telephone. "Charlotte lives here in Los Angeles now. I can give you the address. No, she's still dancing. Do you remember? She always wanted to be a dancer. She married Hal Kirkaby, his dad owned the liquor store. That's right, you kids used to buy soda pop from him. Hal passed away, cancer, left Charlotte with a little girl. Well, yes, she's dancing at a club out in the Valley. I have the number right here, you'll never reach her at home, she works so late. Oh, she'll be thrilled to hear from you after all these years, what's your name again, I'll tell Mr. and Mrs. Bly you called. Mr. Beatty? You're not related to the actor, are you? No, I guess not. You'll recognize her, she's still wearing her beautiful brown hair in them curls. Yes, well, I'll sure tell 'em, they'll be home tomorrow, and you give Char my love if you see her."

Now he waited patiently, slouched low on the seat in his rented Datsun and trying not to breathe in the most polluted air Southern California had seen in

months. Literally seen, for smog had settled over the
Hollywood Hills, coloring the sky a ghostly orange and
painting the horizon a dreamy opalescent magenta.
Lines of cars chugged past, heading for home in the
vast reaches of the San Fernando Valley. Up Laurel
Canyon Drive stretched what seemed to be a never-
ending stream of headlights, white globes in the night
in counterpoint to the twinkling dots of houses precariously balanced on the hills above, and fading into
the smog far along the San Gabriel range.

There was a clanking on the car window, and Mitzu
turned to find a wide black face staring in at him.

"You can't park here, fella." It was a cop, aiming a
flashlight through the glass. Mitzu recoiled from the
glare. "There's no parking here, day or night."

"I'm waiting for a friend."

"I don't care if you're waiting for the comin' of the
Lord, my friend, this here ain't no parking zone. Didja
catch the sign? D'ya see any meters?"

"I'll move," Mitzu said, and started the engine.

He pulled away from the curb and the policeman
returned to his patrol car. Rounding a corner into the
first available side street, Mitzu drove slowly along,
searching for a parking spot. In his rearview mirror he
saw the prowl car, following him for no apparent reason.

I am a soldier, he said to himself. He reached out
with his right hand to the long black case on the seat
and flicked open the latch.

He checked the rearview mirror again. The prowl car
was turning. Mitzu closed the latch. It was not your
time to die, he silently told the policeman. You will die
only when it is right to die.

Suddenly he was lost. Why am I here? I should be at
the hotel resting for tomorrow's work. I'm tired. I'm so
tired. He could not remember why he had come to this
place. His foot hit the brake reflexively and the car
shuddered to a halt. A boy with a dog on a leash crossed
in front of him, and the boy stopped, caught in the
headlight's glare, his head craned toward the sky.

Mitzu was dazed. Where . . . who . . .

He closed his eyes. His head fell to his chest. I'm so tired. I'm

a soldier. You are following the code of Bushido, the way of

the warrior. Yes, the way of the warrior. He realized he could not be absent from his post across from the club's doorway for very long. She might appear at any second. It was already one-thirty, and he had to be waiting when she came out.

He circled the block, back to the main boulevard. Across from the club, on the tarmac of a deserted Mobil station, several cars were parked, and he pulled off the shiny main strip into the gloomy darkness. "No Parking for Duke's," a handwritten sign shouted uselessly. In Los Angeles such signs were as frequent as they were ignored. Mitzu turned off his engine.

Next to the gas station the neo-Gothic facade of a church jutted flush to the sidewalk. "Sinners in the Hands of an Angry God" in plastic letters called attention to Sunday's sermon. For a moment Mitzu wondered if this was a joke, and then the thought changed, as though a revelation, to *I am a soldier*.

He was transformed. The entire world revolved on its axis. He knew why he was there.

He reached into the back seat for his robe. It was Uncle Tadashi's robe, a black cloak festooned with orange squares of knotted yarn. A black padded breastplate with two gold shields lay under the cloak. Mitzu fitted the breastplate straps over his shoulders. He removed his jacket and tie and stepped from the car. In the darkness he wrapped the kendo robe around his body and tied the belt loosely at his waist. A couple scurried past the Mobil station and cast a short glance in his direction, barely concerned with the presence of a black-robed man—just one more bizarre, inexplicable sight in a city full of bizarre sights. A performer, they might have thought, or a tourist, or another cult member shilling flowers and record albums for money.

Mitzu opened the door on the other side of the car and leaned in. He snapped open the long leather-covered case. Strips of diamond-shaped filigree sought light from the night and shined like the surface of the sea. Loops of maroon velvet held two scabbards in place— one nearly four feet long, the other shorter and slightly wider. Nakajima, his teacher and guide to the way of *bushi,* had sent him to a withered old man with dim sockets for eyes and flesh the texture of parchment. These swords, the old man had proclaimed, sprang from the forge of the descendants of Goto, the great sword-making family. They were, it was true, of recent manufacture, but possessed the spirit of old Japan.

Mitzu unfastened the four purple loops, releasing the two sword guards. From one of them he slipped the long blade, running the tip of his index finger over its sharp burnished ridge. He began to sense the presence of Uncle Tadashi, hovering over him in the warm perfumed air, and observing him as he lifted a pouch from the corner of the case and extracted a slim opaque vial. Gently he pulled the cork from the glass tube and spilled a drop of oil onto the weapon's tip. With one continuous wipe of the pouch's chamois surface the oil softened and flowed, shining the weapon's sweeping curve.

Mitzu brought the blade to within an inch of his nose and smelled the rich odor, reminiscent of anise. He sighed at the beauty of the instrument, as pure as an Amati violin or the silver of Toledo. Touching the tip to his forefinger, he gazed at the golden curve jutting up from the sword's black lacquered grip, then suddenly swung the blade through the air. It sliced so cleanly there was hardly a sound, like a thrush gliding on the wind.

Yamato-damashii, he heard his father say, and he touched the ideogram for the family of Goto that decorated the weapon's hilt, carved into the surface in raised grooves.

The family of Goto, he thought, would be proud.

He coated the second blade with equal ceremony, returned the swords to their scabbards, and stood motionless in the dark night. His eyes were fixed on the doorway across the street. If a stranger had looked into his face, those eyes would have seemed to glow. But he was without emotion, steady in his course.

"Night, Char."

"Night, Wally."

"You want to send your costumes out to Doris, Char?"

"No thanks, Wally, I'll do it myself."

Charlotte Kirkaby gathered her skimpy costume together and stuffed it into her makeup case. The bodice needed new sequins as usual—with all the bumping and grinding in her closing number they popped off—but Rory didn't care who collected the costume repair allowance as long as you looked all right. Fifteen dollars was fifteen dollars, no matter how you figured, and Charlotte's old Singer, rickety as it was, could still tie and bind sequins. Why should Doris get the money?

"Char, there was some guy nosin' around for you tonight. A Jap, or a Chink maybe. Said he was gonna look for you out front."

Charlotte winced at Wally's racist slurs. To Wally you were either a Jap or Chink or a wop ginney or Afro-head, or any of a dozen other epithets he reserved for the varieties of the human animal.

Charlotte said, "I didn't see anybody, Wally. What did he look like?"

"Shit, Char, they all look alike to me. Big bucks, though. Strictly downtown."

Strictly downtown meant a suit and tie, as distinguished from leisure suits and white patent leather shoes, which were strictly Valley.

She stopped at a pay phone next to the callboard, checked the roster for Sunday's show, and dialed her home number. She liked to let Betsy know when she was leaving the club, just so she didn't worry.

"Hi, Betsy. I'm on my way home. How's Janey?"

"She's great, Charlotte, sound asleep."

"Terrific. See you in half an hour."

Slipping into her jacket, she pushed through the

steel stage door. For the second time that day she caught a fingernail on one of the rivets.

"Damnit!"

She ripped the nail off. At a dollar fifty-nine a pack she could afford new nails every week without bothering to grow them. Just six more weeks, she thought. Six more weeks of this and it's good-bye Rory Duke, good-bye drunks pinching your ass, and good-bye working until two o'clock in the morning. In six weeks she would be starting classes, living in a new apartment in San Diego, and could forget about nights at Duke's.

The club's lot had been full when she arrived, and she had parked across Ventura. Now where the hell was the car? She stopped on the sidewalk trying to remember. It was amazing how tired you could get. If my head wasn't screwed on I'd forget it. Then she saw the tail fins of her white Oldsmobile parked next to the church.

Even at two o'clock in the morning cars were zooming up and down Ventura, treating the street like a drag-racing strip. A noisy Corvette, belching smoke, careened past her, turning just as it reached her and skidding so close she could feel the heat of its exhaust on her legs. She tucked her makeup case under her arm and darted quickly, deer-like, through a brief letup in the hectic traffic.

The side streets were dark. She hurried to her car. A wave of purse snatching during the past week had put terror into the neighborhood, and one of the girls on the early shift, a waitress, had come close to being raped. All the merchants were screaming for more police, but the Proposition 13 cutbacks kept the force below full strength, or so the department said, and a minor crime wave might be exactly what the police needed to shake a little money loose from the county.

Charlotte studied the pavement with extra caution before continuing to her car. Not a soul in sight.

Mitzu moved noiselessly around the garage of the Mobil station, watching her ascent up the narrow incline. He wondered what she would do. Would she run away? Would she shout for help? He was not thinking about who she was, and found himself groping for the name he had known only seconds ago. The name, I need the name.

But try as he might, the name would not come.

It did not matter. The name would materialize, spring to his lips at the proper moment. He followed the way of the warrior. He was calm. He was strong.

He cradled the swords in his arms and stepped from his hiding place, listening to her short, fast steps on the sidewalk. She came into view, head ducked down and hands inside her purse. She had stopped by the white Oldsmobile and was searching for her keys.

"Mrs. Kirkaby?"

The name had come, as he knew it would. She spun around, dropping the keys, which clanked to the concrete. She leaned forward toward him, trying to make out his face in the darkness but seeing only two flashes of gold. Her open purse dangled from her arm.

"Yes, who's there?" Her voice quavered, shrill and tense.

He stepped closer. "My name is Beatty. I'm an old friend of your late husband's. I've been out of the country and didn't know about his passing away."

Standing there slightly confused, Charlotte Kirkaby failed to ask the sensible questions that might otherwise have occurred to her. She squinted into the light as the man approached. An Oriental, dressed in a black costume, flashes of gold. Wally had said "strictly downtown," nothing about a costume. Frantically she searched her memory of Hal's friends. Beatty? An Oriental named Beatty? Didn't Hal have a Filipino friend when he was stationed in Germany? Did I ever meet him?

She started to back away.

"Do I know you?" she said. "I don't think Hal ever mentioned you?"

"Actually, Hal and I hadn't spoken in years. When I talked to his mother . . ."

153

Her eyes suddenly opened wide. Mitzu could see he had said something wrong.

"Who are you? What do you want from me?"

"I was going to give these to Hal," Mitzu said, holding out the swords. "I owed him a favor, actually, and these—"

"Hal's mother is dead! She's been dead for ten years! You don't know Hal. Who are you?"

"As I said, these are presents for you."

He held up the long dark shapes. Charlotte began to back away from him faster now, frightened of the strange costume and the man who pretended to know Hal. What did he want? Was he going to rape her? Well, let him try, she thought. I won't give in. I'll fight.

"Please, don't be afraid. Look."

He removed one sword from its scabbard, then the other, and held them out to her.

"Swords," she said. "Oh my God. I'm going to scream. You better get away from me. I'm—"

"Yes, the swords of the samurai."

"I'm warning you, you better get away from me or—"

Panic froze her features. Her lips locked, like those of a wooden puppet, and her lungs sucked furiously inward, heaving in gasps. Instinctively her arms closed to cover and protect her chest. Not me, oh God no, this can't be happening to me. Oh Janey, sweet Janey, oh God no, please God no—

The sword in Mitzu's left hand swept up in an arc, and in one stroke slit her throat. She reached up and grabbed her neck, but the blood poured out. Mitzu stepped back to avoid the spray of blood as her body swerved in midair and thudded to the grass lining the sidewalk. He bent down and began dragging her across the pavement. A river of red ran into the cracks and crevices of the concrete, creating a map of veins amid puddles and pools.

When he had pulled the body behind the gas station he began his work in earnest. The sword in his right hand completed the stroke he had begun with his left.

Charlotte Kirkaby's head rolled away from her neck, severed as neatly and cleanly as a piece of cloth.

Mitzu picked up the bleeding head and placed it next to the body. The sword in his left hand cut a single diagonal line from her right hip to her shoulder, and with the other sword he drew the opposite diagonal with surgical accuracy. Crimson patches now seeped through her clothing, oozing from the wounds in an even flow and covering her body in a gaudy sacrament of death.

Mitzu felt no joy, no exhilaration, no ecstasy. He stood aside for a moment, transfixed by the sight of the swords in his hands. As though he were praying, the swords rose in front of him and their points met, and he was consumed not by gore or blood or death, but by redemption.

This was the right course to follow. This, he thought, is how Uncle Tadashi must have reconciled himself to his own death. The way of the samurai, the way of *kirisute gomen* in the seventeenth century. Retribution. To kill and to go away. This was the privilege of the samurai.

With the swords held high, rivulets of arterial blood streamed down the blades. Now it was time to execute the technique Nakajima had so strenuously taught him. With one strong swing of his arm he severed her right hand at the wrist, then the left. The body beneath him gave no more resistance than butter. Two puddles formed on either side.

He inspected the body that had once been Charlotte Kirkaby, and after a moment's hesitation, wiped the blades dry.

I have killed, he said to himself, as my own blood was killed. My resolution is fixed and unshakable.

Laying the robe on the rear seat of the car, Mitzu reached into the pocket of his suit jacket and found the newspaper photograph. Through one of the red circles he drew an X, neatly obliterating the face.

He returned the photograph to his pocket and looked

at his watch. His first business meeting in Los Angeles was six hours from now. Hurry. He must rest.

The lights on Ventura Boulevard blinded him as he steered from the Mobil station's lot. He blinked, turned left, and started the drive toward Laurel Canyon.

Betsy cradled the telephone in her lap. Charlotte should have been home by now. In ten months of sitting for Janey, she had not been kept waiting by Charlotte even once. When Charlotte called from the club and said half an hour, she meant half an hour.

It had been an hour and ten minutes since Charlotte's call.

Betsy turned the telephone dial one full circle.

"Operator, can you connect me to the police?"

17

IN THE fingerprint files of the FBI there are more than two hundred million sets of fingerprints. With a good impression, on metal, say, or glass, a print can be identified in less than an hour. With "latent fingerprints," those not from a police department or on record from a previous crime, using the print for identification is more difficult. A solution of ninhydrin, or a series of dusting powders, can bring the print into focus, depending, of course, on the quality of the print. The fingerprints found on the letter received by the NRC were less than ideal. The thumb had grasped the edge of the paper tightly and was relatively clear, but only three quarters of the impression was on the paper. The forefingers from both hands had lain directly on the page, but the prints were smudged.

The lab technicians were less than anxious to spend time on Alex Burgess's case. With seven major ongoing bank robbery investigations, a case of stolen negotiable federal securities worth in the neighborhood of three million dollars, and the murders of two teenaged girls in Oklahoma, the lab had its hands full. Not to mention that elsewhere in the Bureau Alex's case was being treated with all the concern that might be shown for a stickup at the corner grocery store.

There had been no further definite threats on nuclear plants. The NRC was in no mood to order shutdowns. The Oklahoma murder cases, everyone felt, had nothing to do with the letter from San Francisco. No additional letters had followed the first letter, as they often did.

No one believed Alex's intuition. You don't understand, Toby Morrison explained. They don't like you. You're on loan from Justice. To them you're not a real agent. They're processing twenty thousand fingerprints up there every day and they're overworked and you're an outsider with half a goddamn thumbprint.

On the second day after the letter arrived Alex awoke at four o'clock in the morning with a mounting sense of foreboding. *Children will die.* Children were going to die, he was certain of that, and whoever those "thousands" were, they were going to suffer at the hands of this lunatic, too. But who *was* he? And who were the children?

He sat up in bed. Jill tugged at her pillow, muttering in a dream. He was in her apartment, in her bed. What would Hoover have said? He knew, in fact, exactly what Hoover would have said. Hoover thought Ingrid Bergman's passport should be revoked because of her affair with Roberto Rossellini. Hoover transferred agents to Siberia if they were caught having an affair. Hoover hated Martin Luther King, Jr., and bugged his hotel rooms because he thought King was sleeping with white women.

Thank God for Bill Webster. Webster didn't give a damn where you slept as long as you did your job.

Alex slipped from under the sheets, boosted the air conditioning a notch, and trudged into the kitchen. The new coffeepot's glass basket rested on its stem, already filled. Alex held the pot under the running tap, lit a cigarette, and waited for the water to boil. Every morning he was tempted to make a quick cup of instant before the brewed coffee was ready, and every morning he resisted. Outside the sky was just beginning to turn light, but nothing moved on New Hampshire Avenue. Alex stared down at the empty silent street, and at the traffic island's lonely patch of grass.

For the next two hours he sipped coffee, five cups in all, and smoked cigarette after cigarette. He vowed to himself that he would raise some hell today. If he didn't get some fingerprint results he would charge upstairs to Webster's office and definitely raise hell!

At six o'clock, while Jill slept soundly, he wrote her a note, took a blazingly hot shower, and by six-thirty was on his way to the Bureau.

* * *

Toby Morrison was waiting in Alex's office, reading the morning *Post*. As usual, Toby's impeccable white shirt hung smoothly against his chest, as if it were starched, and his hair was styled and blown-dry to perfection. The front page of the newspaper was consumed with news of the presidential campaigns.

"Who's winning?" Alex asked.

"We are," Toby said.

"Who's we?"

"You and me."

Alex sat behind his desk and pried the lid from the Styrofoam cup of coffee he had bought downstairs. Steam wafted upward in a hazy column.

"What are we winning, Tobe? The war against inflation or the war against crime?"

"The war against bureaucracy," Toby said with a sly smile. "If you'll open that file on top of your in-basket, you'll find a little item I snatched for you this morning. It's called a fingerprint report."

Alex reached across his desk. "You little fucker, why didn't you tell me?"

"I just *told* you," Toby said gleefully. "You didn't want me to interrupt your morning coffee, did you?"

Alex opened the manila folder. "I've already ingested enough caffeinated water this morning to electrify every brain in Georgetown."

"Impossible," Toby said. "Most of the brains in Georgetown are dead."

The report had come from the Latent Fingerprint Section. The section had found nothing of use in the criminal files. But after building a portrait of the fingerprint—its ridges and dots as best they could be identified—the technician, on his own initiative, had begun searching the files on security clearances for government contractors in and around San Francisco. He had reasoned, his report said, that if a nuclear installation were involved, then anybody who could send the letter might have been fingerprinted. Employees in those kinds of companies often had access to classified documents.

"Recommend this guy for a promotion," Alex said. "So now we have this Anthony—" he looked down at the file "—Anthony Vosnecht, who works for American General in San Francisco. Who is he and why would he want to kill anybody and why haven't we picked him up yet?"

Toby expansively pressed his fingers together and cracked his knuckles. "We haven't picked him up because he probably doesn't want to kill anybody. He's sixty-one years old and he's been running a Xerox machine for American General for six years. Which means his fingerprints are on the top and bottom of every ream of paper loaded into the machine. Which explains why there weren't any prints on the original or on Burt's copy. Only one in every couple of hundred copies is going to be touched by anybody."

Alex spun a pencil between his fingers. "So we rule out Vosnecht. Let's have somebody talk to him anyway."

"Dick Werner's going to interview him this afternoon."

"Okay, let's assume that a guy who runs Xerox machines doesn't want to kill anybody," Alex said.

"Not to mention that he barely speaks English."

"I'm with you all the way, Toby. Vosnecht didn't write the letter. But American General builds nuclear plants. That puts us where we expected to be. First, maybe the NRC ought to increase security. Second, it could be anybody in that company. What's the payroll for the building?"

Toby consulted his notebook. "Three thousand, two hundred and twelve. Including janitors, lobby attendants, typists, and a couple of dozen vice-presidents."

Alex groaned. "A mere three thousand. Let's see, full background checks on three thousand would only take—what, Toby, a couple of months? Do you think Mr. Honor and Duty will wait?"

"We should take out an ad," Toby said. "In the *Chronicle*. To the attention of Mr. Honor and Duty. Give us two months and we'll stop you."

"Right," Alex said. "If he wanted to be stopped. But he doesn't." He stared intently at Toby, who was examining the cork soundproof panels on the ceiling. "You'd better find out if Burt's introduced any legislation or made any public statements about American General. Maybe it's an angry employee or . . ." He broke off. "No, that's bullshit."

"We should check just in case," Toby said.

"Sure, but five'll get you ten it's a waste of time. No, let's work with what we've got. Who uses the Xerox machines? Is the print shop open to anybody who walks in or do you have to fill out an order? If you wanted to use the machine when no one was there, would you need a key to the room?"

Toby looked doubtful. "That's not going to get us very far."

Alex lit a cigarette from the tip of the butt burning in the ashtray. "You're right, but what else do you suggest? We can check every typewriter in the building and compare impressions. What else?"

"Alex, you smoke too much."

"I know," Alex said, inhaling deeply. "I'm quitting next week."

"That's what you said last month," Toby said, smiling good-naturedly.

"Well, this month for sure. As soon as we break this case. Has Buck Weston come up with anything new? What about the shrinks?"

"The shrinks aren't talking. Buck's still feeding word combinations into the computer. He thinks maybe sentence rhythms will give him something. Number of words, implied accents, that kind of thing. But I gather he thinks it's hopeless."

"Very encouraging," Alex said.

"How's Shorty holding out? Is he getting along with Alford and Hollister?"

Alex laughed. "Poor Burt. He calls them Lenin and Bakunin. It's bugging the hell out of him. And it's eating at Jill, too. I don't know, maybe she's upset about her book, too, but there's this faraway look in her eyes I've never seen before."

Toby had picked up the paper-clip caddy from Alex's desk and idly begun hooking them into a chain.

"It's love," Toby said, "the strain of loving you."

"Would you do me a favor, Tobe?"

"I know, would I please go fuck myself?"

"No, Tobe, just get us a list of everybody who had access to that Xerox machine and start with the guys on top and work your way down. We'll turn up something."

"Okay," Toby said, standing.

"Do I get the idea you're taking this seriously now?"

"Sure," Toby said. "I'm convinced. And if you want some action out of Buck Weston, why don't you give him a call? He likes you. He's the only one down there who does. He thinks you're his friend."

"God save us," Alex said, "from our friends."

18

A STIFF unseasonably cool breeze rattled the row of arched stained-glass windows on the west side of the church. In the center window's intricate panels, the Lord on His cross appeared to be weeping as the muted orange glass refracted the setting sun, and his apostles, on the next window, cast a sad appraising eye over the rectory. The walls of the church, built of layered stone slabs, spanned the bluff above the road like a sixteenth-century Tudor manor. As Father Michael Farrell circled the building, he marveled at the craftsmanship. You couldn't buy masonry work like that nowadays, even if you could afford it. There wasn't a man within a thousand miles who could assemble a wall of stone slabs and have it stand for sixty years.

There had been a funeral Mass the day before—old Miss McPartland, who'd been faithfully attending Mass every morning for well on forty years. Today the handyman was working in the rectory, and so a few bright white and purple blooms of lilies and anemones littered the path between the pews. Father Farrell entered the sanctuary, crossed himself, and bent down to pick up one of the flowers. He smelled its pungent bouquet, then started gathering, one by one, the broken blooms.

The parish was beginning to feel like home now. His experimental rock and roll Mass had gone well indeed, and there was talk of his leading a youth group. Monsignor Raymond had received several calls from parents who were pleased at the Church's attempt to make their children feel more welcome, and someone had written a note to the archbishop and asked why more young priests weren't in tune with the times. Faith was a hard commodity to come by these days, and the Church needed all the help it could get. The letter had pleased Michael Farrell enormously, not least because Monsignor Raymond had been doubtful about the whole enterprise. Poor old Bill Raymond.

Now to the matter of the devil. Father Farrell, in preparation for his Sunday sermon, had been reading Luther in the morning. "The best way to drive out the devil, if he will not yield to texts or scripture, is to jeer and flout him, for he cannot bear scorn." I don't suppose I can quote Luther, Father Farrell thought, but I can use the same idea. I can talk about Satan not being the opposite of God, and give a little advice on temptation, materialism, and those sorts of things. But what I really ought to say is that the devil is all around us in the most common places: in the grocery store where the owner overcharges us, in the policeman who solicits a bribe, in the government where politicians play fast and loose with the taxpayers' money.

If I say that, Father Farrell thought, they'll probably skin me alive. Oh well, it's the only way I'll get the idea through to them. They won't throw me out on my ear for one provocative sermon. Or will they?

When he reached the front row of pews, Father Farrell glanced quite automatically at his watch. Ten minutes to seven. He had no idea whether anyone would come for confession. Lots of people were away on vacation. In any event, Monsignor Raymond had been hearing most of them. At the end of the aisle the young priest paused to scoop the last of the flower petals from the floor—four cylindrical red blooms with puffy balls at the stem, *Aloe variegata,* and grayish-white speckled cones with stamens tipped yellow, *Azalea lutea rubicunda.* Damn, I'd have made a good botanist. He curled the flowers' downy flesh around his fingers, and thought that when God went to work on the subtleties of nature He left no doubt as to his powers of invention.

Stepping into the triangular office carved from the corner of the sanctuary, he dropped his handful of petals into the wastebasket and set to work transferring the calendar of parish events onto his report for the diocese. Fleetingly he regretted relinquishing botany for the Church. Well, the parish would have its own greenhouse one day, and he could do both.

He heard a car pulling up outside. It might be Cornelia Wade, he thought. She had said she might come to talk about fund-raising. But no, that wasn't her car. Standing at the window, Father Farrell saw a man wearing a black robe standing beside one of those new small Chevys. A cassock? No, it was crossed and tied at the waist, and underneath was some kind of padded shirt with gold emblems. An Oriental Catholic? Certainly not a member of this parish, he thought. I've met most of the regular congregants.

The priest closed his calendar and turned toward the sanctuary.

Mitzu read the board near the church's front door. Two pastors were listed. Raymond and Farrell. One of them would be the senior man. He held his case under his arm and stood for a moment staring at the brass panels on the door.

I am a warrior. The privilege of *kirisute gomen* is mine. To kill and go away.

He was about to knock when the church door creaked open.

"Can I help you?"

A young man with ash-blond hair faced him. Yes, this was the one. Even from the grainy photograph Mitzu recognized the similarity of the features on the man's face.

"Father Farrell?"

"Yes, I'm Father Farrell. Have we met before?"

"May I come in?"

The priest, flustered, backed away. "Yes, of course, I'm sorry."

Mitzu eased past him into the sanctuary. "I'm an old friend of your father's, and he told me if I was in Philadelphia I should look you up."

The priest seemed doubtful. "What was your name again?"

"Nagata," Mitzu said. "Mitzu Nagata."

The priest tugged at his chin. "Gee, I don't think he ever mentioned you. Where do you know him from?"

"We met at a conference last year."

"Really? He's retired now, you know. I thought he had stopped going to those things. He—"

Mitzu ignored him. "I brought you a present." He set the case down on a pew in the last row and snapped open the clasp.

"What on earth—? Look, Mr. Matz . . . Magatzta. I think you have the wrong Farrell. Are you sure you're—"

Mitzu had taken the two swords from their scabbards and pointed them up. Shafts of sunlight shone through the stained-glass windows, reflecting in blue and green from the oiled blades.

"These are for you," Mitzu said, now grasping the swords by their hilts and holding them outstretched. "They are beautiful specimens from the forge of Goto."

"Oh, I see, that's why you're wearing—"

Mitzu swung the longer sword toward the priest, but the young man was agile and backed away. The blade had only grazed his chest.

"Who are you?" Father Farrell gasped, slowly stepping backward. "What do you—"

Mitzu stepped quickly and once again swung the sword. This time it reached its target, drawing a slash across the priest's black robe. The gold cross around his neck turned red.

"Why . . . who . . ."

The priest gagged and staggered toward the organ behind him, grabbing frantically for a hold. The bells in the church tower clanged the hour. It was seven o'clock.

Mitzu assumed the proper stance—legs spread, rolling on the balls of his feet—and drove the longer blade into the priest's abdomen, opening his chest cavity. His arms flailed to push the blade away, but by then it had pierced straight through him. He heaved forward onto the blade, coughing, spitting red foaming blood onto the floor. The wound in his chest opened as the blade tore more deeply into his body. Spots of red spattered his arms and shoes.

"Te . . . absolvo . . . nomine patri . . ." came the stifled cry from his throat.

Mitzu vaguely understood the words. Absolution. But I am already absolved. I am a warrior.

Outside on the road, past the church, the car lights flickered like clusters of candles. The quiet summer evening would be disrupted by dinner, talk of tuition payments, and secret infidelities among the bedroom commuters from Philadelphia. None of this impinged on Mitzu Nagata as he pulled the ragged newspaper photograph from his pocket. The newsprint was damp from the heat of his body, and in only a few days the cheap pulp paper had turned yellow, fraying at the edges. The four individual faces, circled in red, had begun losing definition.

Mitzu took a red marker from the glove compartment of his rented car, drew a neat symmetrical *X* through the second face, and watched as the rough surface of the paper unevenly absorbed the ink. A shudder passed through him, a wave of heat, as he stared down at the black robe on the seat and the breastplate's gleaming gold medallions.

He bowed his head.

I am a soldier.

At a quarter past nine, when Father Farrell failed to return to the rectory on his way home, Monsignor Raymond trudged up the path to the church. The old elm tree was down now, its stump sealed with black pitch. The forsythia bushes had deposited a downy bed of yellow on the lawn.

Probably Mike's practicing the organ, the monsignor thought. Maybe he's using the earphones, or maybe I'm not hearing so well any more.

But as he approached the door, he heard no sound, and no lights shone from the sanctuary. The door was

167

unlocked, so Mike must still be in there somewhere, but why no lights?

Monsignor Raymond entered the church through the back door. He knelt at the altar and crossed himself.

"Mike? Are you here?"

He started down the steps.

"Mike? Where are—?"

He smelled the grisly scent of death before he saw the pools of blood, a trail leading from the last pew to the organ, and then he saw the prone body, entwined in the purple cloth from the organ bench, and then the severed head and hands.

Monsignor Raymond was instantly sick. He retched.

The police from Elkins Park arrived in a blaze of flashing lights and sirens, followed by reporters and rapidly joined by St. Bartholomew's curious neighbors.

By midnight half the town knew that a killer was loose. They locked their doors tight, activated their burglar alarms, and slept fitfully, oblivious that the threat had passed on, and that it had no interest in their aborted affairs, their sorrows, or their triumphs and defeats.

19

THERE IS nothing like a single clue to galvanize doubters, and Alex Burgess was discovering how quickly the Bureau could shift into action. Fourteen men had been assigned to run security checks on American General employees. Two agents had grilled Anthony Vosnecht for six hours. They were incontrovertibly convinced that he was innocent of any connection to the threatening letter, and further convinced of his inability to help in isolating who might have used the print shop's copying machine. On the other hand, he was able to pinpoint the particular machine used, among the shop's four, by noting the spots on the glass and the padded print belt. This fact also proved useless. Anyone on the thirty-second, thirty-third, or thirty-fourth floors of the building could have used the machine, which left Alex Burgess and Toby Morrison with a list of more than eleven hundred suspects.

Less than three thousand. But still impossible.

Alex and Toby began sifting field reports on the eleven hundred as they arrived, learning more about the private lives of those people than they had any desire to know. Interviews with American General executives helped hardly at all. Half of them were out of town, and the rest were fairly mystified by vague questions about their colleagues.

In the FBI's basement computer center, Buck Weston pursued his bloodless quarry like one of his own hunting dogs. A dog requires only that the object of his desire pass through a field long enough to leave a trace of his smell, and the same was true for Buck. He had not spent two and a half years of his life cataloguing and cross-referencing bank robbery notes, ransom demands, and terrorist manifestos from all over the world only to be defeated by one oddball assemblage of phrases.

Later he would remember the actual moment when his memory saved him. The trigger was a song, performed by one of those faceless, nameless orchestras that fill elevators and department stores with lush renditions of old standards and current hits, all sounding alike. Buck heard the song on his way to work, and not until the last few bars did the title register. The song, which he hadn't heard in years, and doubted twenty minutes later that he would have been likely to identify, was "New York State of Mind."

"This isn't telling us anything," Toby said, sitting across from Alex and hunched over the desk. He delved into the three-hundredth file of the eleven hundred.

"Let's keep looking," Alex said.

"Do you want to read all of them? Ferguson's been through this half, and Morefield the other half. They didn't find anything either."

"Just keep reading," Alex said.

"Only if you promise to limit yourself to one cigarette every half hour. The smoke's gonna make me batty."

Alex's response was to reach around his chair and crank the ventilating system in his office to "high."

Purvis. Warner, Atlas. Goldstein, Stuberovski. Manley.

Alex had worked through six more files when the telephone rang. It was Buck Weston.

"Alex, can you come down here for a minute? There's something I want you to look at."

"What is it, Buck?"

At the sound of Weston's name Toby rolled his eyes. He had long since given up hope that Buck's computers would be of any help.

"I'm not sure, but come on down, will you?"

"On our way."

He hung up the phone and closed the Manley file. Ashes dribbled down his jacket as he stood.

"What is it?" Toby asked.

"I don't know. Let's find out."

"Crazy Buck. You don't suppose he's really on to something?"

Alex stubbed out his cigarette. "Buck may be crazy, but I'll take anything now."

They waited at the elevator. Alex tapped his shoe on the polished tiled floor while Toby repeatedly pushed the already lit button. Both were at the edge of their respective tolerances. They wanted a break. Any break. Somewhere nearby water rushed through the building's plumbing, more audible than one would have expected in a multi-million-dollar monolith, and the flourescent lights emitted a continual hum.

"Ruins your eyes," Toby said.

"What?"

"These lights. The goddamn flickering ruins your eyes. I just saw an OSHA report. They're going to replace every light in the building this year. Turns out they not only ruin your eyes, they give children cavities in their molars."

The elevator opened and a messenger with a cart pushed past them. Alex and Toby rode down in silence, each praying that Buck Weston had stumbled onto something meaningful, and that whatever pedantic lecture he delivered would be mercifully short.

Buck was waiting for them as the elevator doors opened.

Stepping out, Alex asked, "What have you got for us, Buck?"

"Maybe a winner, maybe not. Do you remember that gang of kids who took over the armory in New York about ten years ago?"

"Chinese," Alex said. "A protest about Formosa, wasn't it?"

"Nope. Japanese."

"Japanese," Toby said. "What about it?"

Buck now sped ahead of them, practically jogging to his office. Toby and Alex followed suit. From the rear Buck's cowlick looked remotely comical, like a circus clown's wig.

They swung as a group into Buck's cubicle, where

computer printouts covered every available surface. Three video terminals glowed in the corner.

"Take a look at the screen," Buck said.

"Also bad for your eyes," Toby said. "Causes cataracts."

"Not this kind," Buck said. "The green cathode-ray tube screens cause cataracts. This is conventional television."

Alex sat in front of the terminal. On the screen was a summary of newspaper clippings about the armory incident. Alex now remembered it more clearly, recalling that he hadn't paid much attention at the time.

"It was when that crazy writer killed himself," Buck said. "You know, the one who split his stomach open."

"Mishima," Alex said. "Muscleman, wasn't he?"

"And a national hero," Toby said.

"These Japanese kids," Buck continued, "took over the armory to protest Japan's treatment of their warrior class. The kids kept sending out statements to the press, but they were really aiming for the Japanese papers. They got their coverage and then said they had made their point. Then they invited the cops in. The cops booked 'em for trespassing, for illegal possession, and let 'em loose. Hell, there were so many demonstrations then, I don't think the Bureau had anything to do with this one. It was all over in a couple of days."

Alex was reading the summary. There was nothing on the screen to connect the armory takeover to the threatening letter.

"Okay, Buck, what's the connection?"

Buck punched two buttons, the screen cleared, and a new file spit onto the tube.

"Here it is," Buck said. "Listen to this. 'The text of the following newspaper statement was reprinted in full in two Tokyo newspapers.' Let's see now, it's here somewhere. 'Name of our great . . . sons of eternal Japan . . . our destiny . . .' Here it is. 'Honor and duty require an end to our silence,' and wait a minute, there's one more, it's here somewhere, 'and the past comes to the present and future.'"

Buck stepped back from the screen, his arms folded proudly across his chest.

"Remarkable," Toby said dryly.

Buck's arms dropped. "You might think it's only a coincidence," he said, "but when you add up the number of word pairs I tried and—"

"Okay," Alex said, interrupting. He wanted to think.

"—and the number of phrases I—"

"Okay," Alex said again.

"—put through the tapes, and that they all clicked through without a single—"

"Please be quiet," Toby said. "Alex is trying to think."

Alex, in fact, had already completed his thought, which was that Buck had providentially provided the only solid detail in a haphazard mosaic of speculation, circumstance, and accident. From here they had a direction to go in, other than in the circles Alex had dizzily been marking out in his mind for two days.

"Who were they?"

"What?" Buck asked.

"Who?" Toby asked.

"Those kids," Alex said. "Who were they?"

"Just a gang of—"

"No, Buck, not just a gang of crazy kids. They had a reason. I mean, what was their name? What did they call themselves?"

"I remember," Toby said matter-of-factly.

"Toby's famous memory," Alex said, nodding to Buck. "Okay, Tobe, what did they call themselves?"

"The Sons of the Samurai," Toby said, more than a little pleased with himself. "Yep, I can picture the headline. They signed all their dispatches the same way. The Sons of the Samurai. I was at Columbia and we went down to the police lines one day to watch."

"Print that article," Alex said to Buck. "Toby, let's run through those American General files and see if there are any Japanese names. There were a couple, I think. And we'll have to look at the women, see if they might be Japanese but married to Americans. And I want to check every one of those kids in the armory takeover. Are any of them living in San Francisco? Do any of them work for American General? Do any of them *know* somebody who works there? It could be anybody from a messenger to a secretary to an executive."

Toby said, "We probably have Open Survey on those kids. Code 40, I think."

Alex frowned. "I thought the Bureau stopped that stuff during Watergate. We don't keep open files on dissidents now, do we?"

"Look, Alex," Toby said, chewing his lip, "theoretically the Bureau keeps its nose clean with domestic politics. We don't tail anybody, we don't tap their phones. Theoretically, that is. So you just leave it to me. Give me a couple of hours and I'll get you whatever we have on every dissident of Japanese descent in the country."

Alex said nothing for a moment. Every time he found himself in one of these situations he felt the same kind of internal conflict. You couldn't keep tabs on everybody who protested government policy, because then you were as bad as the worst totalitarian regimes. Watching American citizens just because of their opinions put you right at the top of a slippery slope into a police state. On the other hand, the United States was still supporting murderous dictators around the world, and sometimes we had to choose between one murderous dictator and another only slightly less evil. Alex had always known that sections of the Bureau operated in secret corners protected from congressional scrutiny, protected even from the senior Bureau managers themselves. Maybe even the Director couldn't keep an eye on everything the Bureau did. Hell, what was right any more? What was wrong?

Toby interrupted his reverie.

"Alex, don't think about it. You ought to talk to the NRC again about calling a security alert. Put the pressure on 'em. I'll get you through to the Director and he'll back you up. In the meantime, you let me handle this. Okay?"

"Okay," Alex said, a bit uneasily.

He turned to leave and Toby stood to follow him. Halfway through the door he turned back. The video screen's printer was spewing out the newsclip file.

"Buck, I'd appreciate it if you'd send a copy up to the shrinks, attention Beckel. And send one to DomIntel. You'd better cross-check whatever you have on the nuclear dissident list, too."

"Immediately," Buck said, "if not sooner."

"Thank you, Buck."

"Thank me when it breaks," Buck called out a moment later, but Alex and Toby were already down the hall, around the corner, and out of sight.

20

FOR HANK Robbins the week had started badly, and it was about to get worse.

At Toms River, New Jersey, thirty miles southwest of New York City and equidistant to Paterson and Newark, the Crescent Park nuclear power station was operating at full power, feeding 660 megawatts from Unit 1 and 550 megawatts from Unit 2 to the northeast power grid. A million and a half gallons of water flowed through its cooling towers. This was five hundred million dollars' worth of electricity-generating machinery, and it was virtually brand-new.

Hank Robbins had problems, because it was brand-new to him, too. He had been general systems manager at Crescent Park only since early March. The plant was, as he said, "my baby." But for the first time since the summer blackout of 1977, the inhabitants of the great urban corridor stretching from New York to Washington were consuming electricity at all-time highs. Air conditioners from Oyster Bay to Chevy Chase were running full blast. A heat wave still building after two weeks showed no signs of abating. The National Weather Bureau predicted higher temperatures yet to come. And the capacity of the entire grid was being sapped. To make matters worse, two plants belonging to Consolidated Edison of New York had gone off-line for unscheduled repairs, provoking system-wide strain. Hank Robbins was smart enough, and suspicious enough, to know that no matter how well built, no matter how thoroughly tested, a nuclear plant at seventy percent of its power was far less likely to cause him difficulties than a plant operating at its peak.

During his first three weeks on the job that spring, Hank had thought continually of summer, and about readying the staff and the plant itself for operation under stressful conditions. He knew that during its first summer Crescent Park had been forced to cut out of the grid because of sloppy staff work, and he was determined that no "downtime" would besmirch his record. But on Monday two of his best and most experienced control room supervisors had called in sick. On Wednesday a poorly maintained transmission circuit had overheated and come perilously close to tripping the plant into "scram," or shutdown. That would have meant at least thirty-six hours off the grid. And now a routine check of the plant's security apparatus had revealed not one, not two, but five nonfunctioning solenoid relays at the control room checkpoints.

By the time Mitzu Nagata showed up at his office, Hank Robbins was seething mad.

"You picked a fine time, Mr. Nagata. I don't want you to get the wrong idea or anything, I'm glad you're here and all, but American General just isn't my favorite corporation this week. I had a transmission circuit go bad on me, and half the solenoids in our control room bypass circuit are dead. And that's your equipment, sir. Equipment that's not supposed to break down on me. Right?"

Mitzu had been driven directly from La Guardia to reach Crescent Park. He knew that if his letter to the Nuclear Regulatory Commission was taken seriously, the plant might be on alert now. He had to find out. There was a risk that showing up before his appointment could cause suspicion, but this part of his plan could not be executed without a preliminary visit. He had come too far, and invested too much, to veer from his course. All he needed was a good view of the control room; once the personnel there had seen him, and knew he could be trusted, he would have no trouble immobilizing the security procedures. Then they would understand his resolve. Then he would redeem the violence to the blood of Nagata with the same violence directed at others. And his duty would be done.

Hank Robbins, he noticed, had given no sign that the

177

plant was on alert. Despite regulations, Mitzu doubted whether he would be able to hide the fact. No, to judge by his demeanor, Robbins was genuinely upset by the solenoid problems, and happy to vent his frustration on an American General executive. If he's acting, Mitzu thought, then he's a very good actor indeed.

"I'll be glad to give you a hand," Mitzu said to him as they sipped coffee in an office outside the plant's main building. "Why don't we tour the plant? You tell me where your problems are, and I'll make sure we have some of our people here this week to work things through with you. How does that sound?"

Robbins blushed and ducked his head. "Gee, I guess I shouldn't be taking this out on you. I'm just letting off steam. Sorry about that."

Mitzu smiled his tolerant smile, a kindly parent accepting the excesses of an infant. "How long have you been systems manager, Mr. Robbins?"

"Hank, call me Hank. I used to be assistant manager out at Hummock Point. Then Herb Conti, he used to be here—"

"I know," Mitzu said. "They kicked Herb upstairs."

"Yeah, he got himself a desk job. And took his number-two man with him. Hummock's got a World-Horvath installation, and it isn't even a close cousin to yours. I tell you, they're not making things easy on any of us."

"Hank, American General wants all of its installations to run smoothly. I'm here to listen to your complaints, and do everything I can to help you do your job."

"That's what I need to hear, Mr. Nagata, that's what—"

"Mitch, call me Mitch."

"That's what I need to hear, Mitch."

"Why don't we take a look at your control room situation?"

"Sure," Robbins said, swigging the last drops of his coffee. "That's a good place to start."

* * *

Robbins returned to his office two hours later, a good deal more relaxed than he had been earlier in the morning. That Nagata fellow had promised to send him an engineer for a week to run through all of the system's fail-safe mechanisms, and to stick around until everything was tested. The World-Horvath people had never so much as telephoned him to check out problems at Hummock Point. If it hadn't been for the NRC, Robbins figured that World-Horvath would have forgotten they even built the plant. They only came around when they wanted to show the place off to potential new customers.

Robbins settled down to work, scheduling overtime for control room supervisors. With two men out sick, his regular force of seven would have to divide the extra hours and fill in the holes. He had hardly made a dent in the schedules when his telephone rang.

"Robbins," he answered in a clipped voice.

"Mr. Robbins, this is Harvey Clark at the NRC. How are you this morning?"

Whoops! What would the NRC be calling about? What the hell have I done wrong now?

"Pretty good, Mr. Clark. What can I do for you?"

"You're general systems manager there, is that right?"

"That's right," Robbins said. "Look, if it's about those compliance papers, I put 'em in the mail last—"

"No, Mr. Robbins. I'm not in that department. We're calling a security test alert for three days, starting today. It's just a *test,* mind you, standard operating procedure. You'll be getting a confirmation of this by wire, but that'll take a couple of hours and we want you to put the alert into effect right now."

"Just a sec," Hank said. Holy smolly, a security alert. He put the telephone call on hold, reached into his back pocket, and pulled out his keys. Behind his desk was a forged steel safe, which required both a key and a combination to unlock. As he was reaching for his keys, Robbins buzzed Travis Webb, his chief security officer.

"Webb here."

"Travis, it's Hank. Can you come over here and dial the combination of this NRC safe? They're calling a test alert on security. Have you ever been through one of these?"

"We had one right after we went operational. Did you get a wire on it?"

"No," Robbins said, "they're on the phone."

There was silence at the other end for a moment. "On the phone, huh? That's not normal, Hank. That's not normal procedure."

"Hell, Travis, they're on the phone. I don't care if it's normal. Would you come on over?"

"Be right there," Webb said, and the line clicked off.

Robbins punched the button on his phone. "Mr. Clark, I'm getting out the code numbers now. But look here, my security officer says these things normally come by wire."

"You'll have a confirmation," the voice at the other end said. "But we want to see how fast we can move in an emergency. That's the purpose of this test."

Robbins thought for a moment. What if this were someone trying to penetrate the plant's security system? What if this wasn't the NRC calling at all, but instead somebody who wanted to set off an alert to see what happened?

"Mr. Clark, why don't I hang up and call you right back?"

"Very good, Robbins. I'm at extension 451. You have the toll-direct line, is that right?"

"Yeah, right here in front of me."

"Fine, call me back then."

Robbins dialed three numbers on the toll line to the NRC. He gave the extension number to the operator.

"Clark."

"Okay, Mr. Clark, hold on. I gotta get the safe open."

Travis Webb came through the door of Robbins' office. He was a burly man with a beer-belly gut and a flat, squashed nose that gave him the look of a prizefighter.

"Hi, Hank. Now what kind of alert is this?"

"The NRC says it's a test to see how fast we can respond in an emergency."

Travis Webb rubbed his jaw. "Well, it sounds funny to me. I never heard of test without a wire order."

"Travis, I called back to make sure it was the NRC. Would you open the safe for me?"

"You're the boss," Webb said. He walked over to the safe and dialed the combination. "Your turn."

Robbins inserted his key, flipped both handles up, and opened the door. The security codes were in a manila envelope.

"Okay, Mr. Clark," Robbins said. "I have the codes."

"I'll give you a six-digit number," Clark said, "and then a four-digit number. Do you know where to look on the code chart?"

"Yes sir, it's pretty well marked. Shoot."

Clark read the codes slowly while Hank Robbins followed the security index instructions for the two series of digits, moving his forefinger across the page. Both codes were accurate.

"Okay, Mr. Clark, that checks out. We're going on total security alert."

"Thanks, Robbins. I want you to call me if anything unusual happens. You have my number."

"I thought this was a test," Robbins said. "Are you expecting something unusual?"

"Nothing, uh, nothing at all. Well, we'll be talking to you during the next couple of days. Thanks very much."

The call ended with a click and Robbins found himself staring into the receiver, as though, perhaps, a face might materialize in front of him.

"He hung up," Robbins said to Travis Webb.

Webb positioned himself on the edge of Robbins' desk and started putting the code index back into its envelope.

"What did he say?" Webb asked.

"He said to call him if anything unusual happened, and I said I thought this was a test. What do you make of it, Travis? What the hell's going on?"

Webb stroked his jaw again and, performing his

181

favorite tic, hit the tip of his nose with his closed fist. "Damned if I know," he said. "But it's kinda funny. And we can't stage a total alert for the next couple of hours anyway. Those solenoids won't be hooked up again until tonight. We should announce it though. You wanna do it?"

"Yeah, I guess I should," Robbins said. He picked up the microphone from the metal cabinet next to the safe, and turned the indicator to *All Stations.*

"Can I have your attention please?" he began. "Crescent Park is now under a test security alert by instructions of the Nuclear Regulatory Commission. The test will last three days. Any employees unfamiliar with alert procedures should see their supervisors. Supervisors should call Travis Webb. We are now beginning a three-day test security alert."

Robbins clicked the public address system off.

"Damned funny," Travis Webb said. "Damned funny procedures if it's only a test."

21

BY THAT afternoon Toby Morrison had located all but one of the fourteen Japanese students who had taken over the armory in New York ten years earlier. The only one he couldn't find had, as far as he could tell, moved to London in 1974 and had never returned to the United States. But Alex had asked Toby to make sure. As long as they had decided to use the Bureau's clandestine information services, they might as well slide down the slippery slope a little further and find that missing student. Neither of them had the authority to request an overseas report. Less important, but still to be dealt with, it would have to go on somebody's budget card.

Alex was leery of going to the Director again. Getting the NRC to call an alert had been hard enough. So Toby somehow did an end run around Operations and queried Scotland Yard via Interpol shortly after three o'clock. Alex didn't bother to ask how this was accomplished; he didn't want to know. In fact, the less he knew, the better. And Toby didn't volunteer a hint of who had actually wired the request, or who was paying for it.

Half an hour later, at eight-thirty London time, the report came back. Toby buzzed from downstairs and told Alex to meet him on the second floor. The missing student, it turned out, was actually in London, had been there for six years, and worked in marketing at Harrods.

"The rebels of yesteryear," Alex said, standing outside the wire room. "Times change. So much for the Sons of the Samurai."

Toby laughed. "Where have all the protesters gone?"

Alex suddenly snapped his fingers, spun on his heels, and crossed the hall to the Day Book wires. Here all the reports of crimes from around the country were logged; cases in which local police asked for FBI help were catalogued in a separate volume.

Alex started thumbing through the uncatalogued logs. Each occupied its own plastic sleeve.

"What is it?" Toby asked.

"I'm looking for a report from Philly on that priest who was killed. Why the hell didn't I think of it? Did you see it? The guy was sliced up in a church by swords. We got a forensic follow-up. Two curved blades, different lengths. Samurai swords, the follow-up said."

"Shit," Toby said.

Alex flinched. Toby rarely swore. He considered profanity the refuge of illiterates and children.

"Shit," Toby said again. "There was one just like that last week in Los Angeles. A girl sliced up in a Mobil station. No, outside a Mobil station. Two o'clock in the morning."

Alex stopped turning pages and pulled one of the plastic envelopes from the binder.

"Here it is." He flipped a few pages forward. "And here's the L.A.P.D. file. Nothing about Samurai swords here, but they look the same."

"You call Philly," Toby said, already moving down the hall at a trot. "I'll call Hardison in L.A. He always comes through for me in a hurry."

Both of them ran to their offices.

"They weren't children," Alex was saying three hours later. He was in Toby's office on the other side of the building. Outside, night was descending. "The priest was twenty-eight and the dancer was thirty-three. The dancer had a daughter."

"And the priest?" Toby said with the wry smile of a talk-show host.

"A dozen out-of-wedlock orphans," Alex said sourly, "which he fathered in Malaysia and left in an orphanage."

"Okay, he didn't have any children," Toby said. "I was only trying to lighten things up a little. But what if *they* are the children?"

184

"Who considers a woman of thirty-three a child?" Alex asked.

"Wait a minute," Toby said. "There's no apparent relationship between the dancer and the priest, right? But the letter said *children* would die. And we're all somebody's children. So now the question is, whose children are *they?*"

"Of course," Alex said, slamming his fist onto the desk. "That's it. That's exactly it."

The files on Charlotte Kirkaby and Michael Farrell were, on such short notice, far from complete. They were bare police statistics. Neither indicated who the victims' parents were.

Toby looked at his watch. "It's three-thirty in Los Angeles. We'll have the names of the dancer's parents in half an hour. I don't know about the priest."

He picked up the phone and pressed a five-digit number.

"Where the hell are they?" he asked Alex. Then, into the receiver, "Fergie, do me a favor and get that cop in Philadelphia to find out who the priest's parents are. That's right, *parents*. Hall of records, I don't know, maybe the church's files. Somebody'll know. Fergie, go down to Philly yourself if you have to. Get Ben Hill on it, I don't care. But find out." He put the receiver down. "Ferguson wanted to know if he would get paid overtime."

Alex stared thoughtfully into the middle distance, the pictures in his head shifting from position to position like pieces of a jigsaw puzzle.

Toby said, "Let's go back to motive. Who wrote the letter and why?"

"Tobe, what do we know that we're not using?"

"Clairvoyance," Toby muttered.

"Toby, *please.*"

Toby pursed his lips and fiddled with his wristwatch. Alex lit a cigarette. For a few seconds they both sat staring at each other.

"How far have we gotten with the American General

list?" Alex asked. "How many Japanese names did we come up with?"

Toby felt idiotic. "You're right, what's wrong with me?" He bounded out of his chair to the credenza across the room, picked up the summary of the American General files prepared by Torrance in Research, and riffled the stack of pages. "We've got three surnames. Ikeda. She's a marketing analyst hired last spring. Nagata. He's a sales and marketing vice-president, been with the company for eight years. Uyehara, a systems engineer. Four years. Then we have two married women, Klein and Mastropieri. Both Japanese descent, both hired in the last six months, both secretaries. We've got positive location in San Francisco on Ikeda and Klein and we're working on the other three."

"When'll we hear?"

Toby looked at his watch. "Another couple of hours. Midnight at the very latest."

Alex lit a new cigarette from the butt of the one in his hand. "We've got a dead priest and a dead dancer," he said. "Something had better break quick. Our samurai sword killer is moving fairly methodically. And he isn't wasting much time."

At six o'clock rush-hour traffic on Third Avenue had come to a standstill. Bumper-to-bumper taxis seemed permanently fixed in a sea of yellow like eggs in aspic. At Seventieth Street Mitzu sat sweltering in a cab without air conditioning. The cab had moved only three blocks in ten minutes.

"I'll get out and walk," Mitzu said to the driver. He looked at the meter, calculated a fifteen percent tip, and pushed four dollar bills into the cup in the partition separating him from the driver.

"Watch my door!" the cab driver shouted as Mitzu stepped out into the middle of a lane of traffic. There wasn't much need to watch the door, he thought, considering that nobody was moving fast enough to do any damage.

He darted to the west side of the street and stopped

to orient himself. Walking uptown, he checked the numbers on apartment buildings. He was amazed by the number of people walking in the unbearable heat, carrying paper bags and briefcases. At the corner of Seventy-third Street he stopped and bought an Italian ice from a street vendor standing at a rolling metal wagon. The number the maid had given him was 223. Drinking the ice's sugared syrup, he turned west toward Lexington Avenue. 217, 215. The wrong direction. He turned around and began crossing the street, not waiting for the light to change. Three buildings down, on his right, was a soot-covered brownstone with blue-and-white tiled numbers above the door. 223. The boy on the phone had said they would not be home the next day, that they would be leaving early in the morning. Mitzu had called as her father's old friend Mr. Beatty, and the boy said she would be home that evening.

He would have to find her tonight.

He climbed the steps. Under the bell for apartment 4B were two names embossed on plastic tape: "Hammer-Berryman." So she did not live alone. She must live with the boy he talked to on the telephone.

Mitzu rang the bell.

"Who is it?" the boy's voice said.

Mitzu said nothing.

"Who's there?"

Still Mitzu did not answer.

He waited half a minute with his ear pressed to the glass door, watching and listening. Then he rang the bell again.

"Who's there, damnit?"

He did not answer, instead rubbing his hand across the grating over the microphone, creating a scratching, static-like noise.

"This isn't working," the boy's voice said. "I'm coming down."

Mitzu turned and walked out of the building. He crossed the street and waited behind a green industrial dumpster, which overflowed with garbage, pieces of lumber, and hunks of plaster. The building behind him was being renovated. He fixed his eyes on the doorway to the building across the street.

The boy came down. Through the glass exterior door it was difficult to make out his face very clearly, but Mitzu could see that the boy was tall. As though obliging his secret observer, the boy stepped out onto the stoop and looked in both directions, up and down the street, for whoever had rung his bell. He shook his head and went back inside.

He was tall, fair-haired, and lean. Mitzu decided he would recognize him again, and decided to wait until morning.

22

BY ELEVEN o'clock Alex's eyes were bloodshot. Staring at the field reports, he could feel a vein throbbing behind his right eyeball, and he could no longer focus on anything so small and fuzzy as a teletype dispatch. He wanted to quit and go have a drink with Burt. But two reports were yet to come from San Francisco, and in them he might find an answer.

He had spent the evening assembling files on the two victims of what newspaper readers in Los Angeles and Philadelphia were learning to call "the sword murderer." Headline writers in both cities had succumbed to the same sensationalism, and the afternoon papers had somehow discovered the Bureau's involvement. You had to hand it to the reporters. They cultivated sources inside police headquarters, and the sources paid off. Now they had a new angle to play with and could run their stories all over again: the FBI is on the case. Murder was good copy, Alex thought, the kinkier the better. It was sort of sickening, but the republic could probably withstand an onslaught of bad taste.

These files, he said to himself, are telling me zilch. He turned out his desk lamp and walked around to Toby's office. Toby was on the phone.

"Uh huh," Toby was saying. "You talked to this guy Stone yourself? And what about Uyehara and Mastropieri?" Toby waved Alex to sit down. "Right, okay. You run with it. You know where to get hold of me."

Toby hung up. "We've got our man," he said.

"Which one?"

"Nagata, first name Mitzu. Vice-president of marketing. Mastropieri, the secretary, has been at work every day for the last two weeks. Uyehara's been locked up in his office with a dozen other engineers. But Nagata was supposed to be in New York at the

Waldorf, and he isn't there. Then he's supposed to be at the Mayflower here in D.C. Nobody's heard from him in a week. Now catch this. The guy's wife had a baby a few weeks ago with terrible birth defects, and the baby died. But the man went right on working, didn't give an inch."

"Did they talk to the wife?"

"Can't find her," Toby said. "They're looking."

"Let's get Beckel in on this," Alex said, picking up the phone. "Is Gary there? No? Get him at home, will you, and ask him to call me. Thanks." He hung up, and rubbed his eyes in fatigue. "All right, what's the connection between the dancer and the priest?"

"Search me," Toby said. "You've read the files."

"There's nothing," Alex said, "except that both of their fathers were stationed in New Mexico during the war. What's that worth?"

"Ought to be worth something," Toby said. "Let's get their military records."

"I already sent for them. But they're in Rockville. It'll take a while."

Toby exhaled a deep sigh. "How soon?"

"Hour, maybe two. Operation put a pad through half an hour ago. But it's a forty-five-minute drive."

"At least we know who we're looking for," Toby said.

"You've got the hotels covered."

"Yeah, but he's not going to walk right into our arms. We have to find out who those two other children are. And fast."

Alex slipped into his jacket. "I'm going over to Burt's. As long as I'm doing nothing, I might as well do it over there. If Beckel calls, see if you can get him in here to whip up a personality profile."

"Take a nap," Toby said. "I'll call you."

On his way to the elevator Alex stopped at the duty station and told the nighthawk he would be at Burt's if anybody wanted him. When a case was this hot Alex never stayed out of the Bureau's reach, and his home phone was equipped with call-forwarding so that when he slept at Jill's his calls were automatically routed there.

Alex flagged a cab on Pennsylvania Avenue. "Fifth, Southeast, just off Independence," he said. He leaned back in the cab, feeling as if he had been on a drinking binge and pre-hangover stupor had set in. The truth, of course, was that he had imbibed nothing stronger than eighteen or nineteen cups of coffee, the effect of which, on his particular constitution, could approximate the same kind of wired-for-sound euphoria as too much liquor. He lit what he guessed to be his fiftieth Lucky Strike of the day. *Now let's see, I started with a pack half-finished this morning, two packs during the day, and half a pack here . . . nope, this was closer to the sixtieth cigarette. You're out of your gourd, Burgess. You're going to die of lung cancer and all your friends will sit around moaning that they told you so. I'll quit, I'll quit after this case. You said that the last time. And I quit the last time. For two months.*

The internal dialogue ended. Razzing himself, he knew, only wasted his declining mental energy, in precious short supply by now.

Hollister and Alford were parked outside the townhouse in an unmarked, lipstick-pink Firebird. A genius in procurement had finally realized that plain blue or green stakeout sedans were a waste of money. Any crook worth his prison record could smell them a block away. The two agents watched Alex coming toward them from the taxi.

"Evening, gents," Alex said as he leaned in through the window. "Nice wheels."

"Hi," Hollister said. "Toby tells us we're looking for a Jap."

"Right. How's the congressman?"

"Nervous," Alford said, leaning toward Alex. "Bites his nails a lot."

"He always bites his nails," Alex said. "Any unusual calls? Breathers? Hang-ups?"

"*Nada*," Alford said. "His secretary, his wife, Senator Eagleton, Congressman Brokaw, Congressman

191

Gasner. His dry cleaner dropped his shirts off. Granger opened them."

"Granger's upstairs?" Alex asked.

"In the hallway."

"I might take the congressman out for a walk," Alex said. "Stick with us."

Hollister yawned. "We'll be there."

Alex rang the bell on the building's intercom.

"That you, Alex?" came Burt's voice from the small speaker.

"Don't *do* that," Alex replied. "All I had to do was say yes and you'd have let me in. Wait for people to identify themselves."

The lock on the door buzzed and Alex pushed through. As he came onto the landing on the third floor he saw Granger's profile through the translucent glass panel in the doorway at the end of the hall. He walked right past Burt's apartment and Granger stuck his head around the corner.

"Hi, Burgess. All clear. He's in for the night, snug as a baby."

"We might go out. Are you on all night?"

"I'll be here when you get back," Granger said. "Hollister tells me you and Morrison came up with a lead."

"Looks that way. We'll let you know."

When Alex turned back into the hallway Burt was waiting for him.

"Hi, Shorty. How're you holding out?"

"Don't call me Shorty, Alex."

Alex followed him into the apartment. The old townhouse had been broken up into two spacious apartments on each floor, and Burt's wife had taken advantage of the thirteen-foot ceilings to build shelves to display her collection of Belgian crystal. There was not a bare wall in the place.

"What does Marge say?" Alex asked.

"How did you know she called?"

"You know they've been listening to your calls, Burt. I told you they would."

Burt exhaled in angry frustration. "That's right, I forgot. Alex, this is driving me bananas. Brokaw spotted Lenin and Bakunin outside the hearing room today. He knew who they were, and he wanted to know why. They have FBI written all over their faces."

"Do they? I told them to stop doing that. Where was it? On their cheeks?"

Alex's attempt to dispel Burt's irritability with humor wasn't entirely successful.

"I'm spooked, Alex. I'm jumping at shadows. I see those two following me and I get so nervous I want to tell 'em to go home. Marge is scared out of her wits. She begged me to let her come back."

"You told her to stay where she is, I hope."

"Naturally," Burt said, heading for his study. "You want a drink?"

Alex followed him in. "A shot of gin would do me up just fine," he said. "Marge couldn't get back here anyway."

"What do you mean? Why not?" Burt asked, his voice cracking.

"Because we have a tail on her, too. If she tries to come into town, he'll stop her. We have enough trouble watching you."

There were two Chesterfield couches in the study, surrounded by bookcases. Burt poured Alex a shot of Tanqueray and a healthy dose of Dewar's for himself.

Burt asked, "Are you any closer to finding out who sent the letter?"

"Actually, I think I know who he is," Alex said.

Burt passed Alex his glass of gin. Then, with sudden gravity, he said, "Play straight with me, Alex. Do you honestly have something?"

"Yep, we do." Alex loosened his tie, took off his jacket, and rolled up his sleeves. "Do you remember when a group of Japanese kids took over a building in New York ten years ago? Spring of 1970."

Burt rested his drink on the arm of the couch and stretched his head back to loosen his neck muscles.

"Japanese kids," he said. "It was the armory, wasn't

it? On Park Avenue? You and me and that gorgeous brunette down the hall were getting ready for the bar review course. I remember. What's that got to do with me?"

"The slogans those kids used in their manifesto are the same words used in the letter you got. Did you ever meet a man named Mitzu Nagata? He's a vice-president of American General."

"Never heard of him," Burt said. "Why?"

"Take a second and think about it," Alex said. "Does the name mean anything to you? Did he ever testify in front of you?"

Burt sipped his Scotch and flexed his neck again.

"No, I'm sure," he said. "Don't know the guy from Adam. Why?"

"Because in the past ninety-six hours two people were stabbed to death and mutilated by samurai swords. A priest in Philadelphia and a dancer in—"

"Los Angeles," Burt interjected. "I saw it in the *Star*. What's the connection?"

"I don't know. Not yet. Except that this Nagata character has disappeared. He's on a company trip and he didn't check in to any of the hotels he's supposed to be staying in. We're waiting for a full briefing on him and interviews with his family."

Burt held his glass to the light of his captain's lamp and swirled the Scotch. He paced around the couch, padding quietly in his bare feet. At the bay window he stopped and parted the gauzy curtain.

"Do those two listen to my calls?"

"No, we have a man on the line in a house down the street."

"I know it's my life you're protecting, but isn't that illegal?"

"You gave us your permission," Alex said. "You helped draft the law. If one party knows the call is being listened to, then the tap is legal. Moreover, I have a court order, which was easy enough to get as soon as I told the judge you approved."

Burt put his glass on the window ledge and slouched onto the couch.

"Now let me get this straight," Burt said. "An executive with American General, who happens to be Japanese, is missing. The Xerox machine was at American General. Two people were stabbed to death with samurai swords, and you think this guy . . . what's his name?"

"Nagata."

"You think this Nagata wants to kill me."

"All we know is that the words used in the letter you got are the same words used by those Japanese kids ten years ago, and that Nagata had access to the Xerox machine used to copy the letter. I'm just adding two and two and getting six, Burt. The fact that he's disappeared and apparently isn't making the stops he's scheduled for—well, it makes me think that at least we're on the right track."

"But what's the motive, Alex? What's the connection?"

Alex frowned. Concentration creased his forehead. "We don't know. There's nothing in either victim's files to connect them to each other. If I could find out that they met once, or had something in common . . ."

"But they don't," Burt said.

"Well, actually they do. Both the priest's father and the dancer's father were stationed in New Mexico during World War II. Toby figures that's what 'children' means in the letter. But their fathers were at two different bases. It's probably a coincidence. Other than that, we—"

Burt gagged on his drink. Sputtering, he asked, "Where were they stationed?"

"What is it, Burt? What's the matter?"

Burt recovered from his coughing fit, asking louder and more urgently, "Where were they stationed, Alex?"

Alex called up the pictures of the two files in his mind. "The dancer's name is Kirkaby," he said. "Her father was . . . let me think . . . an Army corporal in Santa Fe. The priest's name was Michael Farrell, and his father was at an air force base in—"

Burt ran from the room toward the kitchen. "My father was stationed in New Mexico!"

"Where are you going?" Alex yelled after him.

"The picture," Burt shouted over his shoulder. "The picture in the *Post* from Los Alamos."

In the kitchen Burt stood over a pile of newspapers stacked on the dishwasher, discarding them one by one onto the floor as he searched the dates on each front page.

"Oh God, look at this, Alex. Look at the caption."

He handed the newspaper to Alex. On the front page was a photograph of the ceremony at Los Alamos. There were four men in the photo, with General Britten third from the left. An American flag was prominent behind them.

"Look at the names," Burt said, reading over Alex's shoulder. "Bly, Farrell, my father, and Berryman."

"The dancer's maiden name was Bly," Alex said, with mounting horror as the meaning of the photograph dawned. "There's your four children, all right. That's why you got the letter."

They stood staring at the picture, mesmerized by the idea that was simultaneously taking shape in both of their imaginations.

"But did *they* get the letters, too?" Burt asked. "And why didn't they call the police? And if he's working his way across this picture, then that means I'm next."

"Unless somebody named Berryman is next," Alex said, and ran out into the hall.

23

MITZU AWOKE in his bed at the Abbey Victoria Hotel shortly before six o'clock the next morning. He needed no alarm clock, no call from the desk. His own interior clock was comfortably and efficiently at work, rousing him from a sleep as sound as death to a state of sharp wakefulness in the time it took to swing from under the blanket and sit up.

He showered and shaved meticulously, then quickly folded his clothes into his suitcase. As he knotted his tie he stared through the grimy window at Seventh Avenue below. A bum in tattered clothes was urinating onto the curb. Mitzu picked up his suitcase and the long narrow case that held his two swords.

With the two cases he took the elevator down to the checkout desk in the lobby. A lone clerk manned the cashier's window. Mitzu had paid for his room in cash the night before, so he simply turned in his keys.

"Thank you, Mr. Beatty, please stay with us again," the clerk said without much conviction.

Outside on Seventh Avenue Mitzu hailed a cab. Today he would need a car. On the block adjacent to the hotel's entrance he saw more bums, these sleeping in the gutter, and farther downtown the lights of Broadway's porn parlors were still pulsing in the last shadows of the disappearing dawn. Even without the heat of the city's life, the air was already filled with mugginess.

The cab crossed over Fifty-first Street to Eighth Avenue, passing souvenir shops and a theater advertising live sex shows. A delicatessen owner struggled to push aside the accordion-like grating that protected his windows. The cab rounded the corner and sped through synchronized stoplights straight to Columbus Circle. Mitzu tried to make out the message on the

Paramount Theater, circling the marquee in flashing white bulbs. But the driver was moving too fast. Now, Mitzu thought, my journey will soon be at an end. Now I have met my responsibility to my family, to my country. To *yamato-damashii*. Now I am a worthy soldier, loyal to the tradition I once spurned.

The cab dropped him at Seventy-sixth Street. At the enclosed newsstand he bought a copy of the *Times*—he would need it later—from a blind, crippled man whose eyes rolled listlessly in his head.

"That ain't the late edition," the blind man said. "It ain't come in yet."

"Thanks," Mitzu said.

He turned toward the red-and-white facade of the Avis office. No one else was on the sidewalk.

Behind the Lucite-walled cage inside, a black woman was folding car rental contracts and labeling them. All the banks, Mitzu noticed, had plastic cages now, too, so you couldn't look anybody straight in the face. So many robberies, he idly thought. So much violence.

"Nagata," he said to her. "I have a car reserved."

She looked up at him, then turned wearily to the rack on the wall and pulled the contract with his name in heavy black letters. He would have preferred using the name Beatty, but none of the car rental agencies would give you a car without a credit card.

"A sedan," the black woman said. "Can I please have your Wizard Card, credit card, and driver's license?"

Mitzu passed her the three cards through the opening at the bottom of the cage. She zipped the contract through the credit card press and imprinted an American Express form.

"Will you be returning the car here?" she asked, reciting her litany.

I won't be returning it at all, he thought.

"Yes," he said, signing the forms and returning them.

She picked up a phone and her voice echoed from speakers in the garage behind her. "Sedan, two-door, up front. Customer waiting." She turned to Mitzu, tearing the top copy of the contract and pushing it back at him. "The tank is full. You can fill it before you bring it back, or we'll fill it and charge you for the gas."

He stepped outside with his two cases. The sun, only minutes ago shrouded in haze, was so instantly bright he stopped in his tracks. Across the street a huge van was disgorging cases of canned goods into the storage well of a grocery store, and on the van's crenellated exterior was an enameled red sun rimmed in white. "Red Sun Label. Fine Food." A flag. An omen. A reminder.

At the entrance to the garage the car was waiting, a new Chevrolet. He wondered, looking at the car, if the one he had rented from Hertz had been traced yet. He opened the trunk, deposited the smaller of the two cases, and threw the other one into the back seat. Climbing in, he was overwhelmed by the smell of cleaning fluid, and opened the windows.

Now. They can't stop me now. What does an individual mean? The individual is nothing unless he is connected. Otherwise he is invisible.

They had been Nakajima's words. Now they were his.

He drove through the dazzling forest of Central Park toward the East Side. How early, he wondered, could they leave their apartment? Not at seven in the morning. Not this early. Anticipation gnawed at him, and he stepped harder on the gas. When he reached Fifth Avenue the light was green, and he did not hesitate. He imagined what his last moments would be like, how all the world would hear his message. His mother would know, and feel redeemed. The flame of the samurai code would burn again for her, and for his father. How happy his father would be with the spirit of old Japan revived. He would offer his father the ultimate sacrifice in what Nakajima had described as the etiquette of death. It was wonderful what the tradition had bred, he thought, in its ideals and its language.

The green industrial dumpster was still sitting at

the curb, and Mitzu parked next to it. He slouched down behind the steering wheel, propped the *Times* in front of him, and settled down to wait. The tremors of anticipation were gone now. The impatience he had felt driving through the park had evaporated. Now there was only waiting—calm, purposeful waiting.

A soldier, he said to himself, is serene in his valor.

Stacy Berryman, still half-asleep, stroked Jason's neck. Her hand drifted down his spine and he purred.

"Up, up, sleepyhead," she whispered. "Let's get there before the crowds."

He rolled over and they kissed. "Sex or food," he said. "Feed me."

"Food," she said. "I want to see the Unicorn tapestries in the morning light."

Stacy raised the shades and their one-room apartment was flooded with light. After a quick breakfast of toast, orange juice, and Haitian coffee which she had traveled great lengths on the subway to acquire, Stacy took the picnic lunch from the bottom shelf of the refrigerator and started packing the wicker basket Jason's mother had given them after cleaning out her house in Quogue.

"Do you think your mother would buy us an air conditioner?" she asked him as she filled the thermos. "I don't know how much longer I can take this heat."

"She might," Jason said, calling from the bathroom. "Can we afford the electricity?"

"No, you're right. Unless I get the part in *Alice*."

"Then we ought to ask Mom for an air conditioner," he said. "Because you're going to get the part."

"I *am*, am I? How do you know?"

"Mom's astrologer said so. And I had a dream this morning. You were accepting a Tony award from Angela Lansbury. It was wonderful. You looked so happy."

Stacy laughed. "How did *you* feel in the dream?"

"Me? I was happy because I was starring in a revival of *Most Happy Fella* and got great reviews."

"You don't look like Robert Weede," she said.

"But I could play the part," Jason said. "I have the voice for it. I'd be terrific in it."

"You would," she said.

She heard the water beating on the shower curtain and finished packing the lunch—fried chicken, cucumber salad, half a pound of Fontina. Jason came out of the shower dripping water all over the floor.

Stacy said, "I'm amazed Buzzy's lending us the car."

"He loves us," Jason said. "He wants to sleep with both of us."

"He wants to sleep with *you*, Jason, not me. Does it have gas, or do we have to stop?"

"It has gas. Whether the engine'll hold up is another question altogether."

Jason threw aside his towel and stepped into his underwear.

"I love your body," she said. "Especially when it's wet."

"I love your body wet *or* dry," he said.

When he was finished dressing, she handed him the picnic basket, picked up a bottle of California Cabernet her uncle had given them, and they headed out the door. Just as Jason turned the key and heard the police lock fall into place, the phone started ringing.

"Oh hell," he said. "It's probably my mother."

"Skip it," Stacy said. "We'll call her later."

The phone continued to ring. Stacy was humming, *Something's coming, something good,* as they raced down the steps and pushed through the downstairs door onto the street.

Mitzu almost missed them. They skipped down the stoop so rapidly that if he had not looked up from the *Times* at the last moment they would have been down the block and out of sight. They were coming directly toward him, and he slouched down farther behind the newspaper. Yes, that was the same boy who had answered the bell. Hammer. She was Berryman. The boy was carrying a large wicker box with handles, probably a picnic basket. Mitzu wondered if he should wait

201

until they came home, and then he decided to follow them. Assuming they would get on the subway, he was ready to open the car door when he saw the boy stop at an old black Porsche roadster.

When they had gotten in, driven to the end of the block, and stopped at a red light, he turned the key. The light turned green and he pulled out of his space, watching the Porsche turn right onto Third Avenue. Then, when they had made the turn, he zoomed up the street and sped around the corner. They were in the far left lane. He stayed well behind them.

The traffic was just light enough to keep pace and not lose sight of them, and just heavy enough to avoid being spotted. Heavy trucks thundered past, bouncing in and out of potholes, shaking the pavement. Taxis weaved from lane to lane, swerving like drunks. A meter maid crossed in mid-block, oblivious to stoplights, traffic, and her own safety.

Where were the boy and girl going? Where would you go to have a picnic in New York? Mitzu glanced reflexively at the gas gauge—it's full. I can follow them anywhere.

The Porsche turned at Ninety-sixth Street, wound around Madison Avenue, and entered Central Park. It continued straight across town to the West Side Highway. This was more than Mitzu had bargained for. He thought about turning back, parking in front of their building, and waiting till nightfall.

But time was running out. He knew that eventually he himself would be pursued, and eventually, too, that they would find him. He was unafraid of being caught, and in the end he wanted them there, all of them, because the end was foreordained.

But not now, not before he was ready.

True courage is to live when it is right to live, and to die when it is right to die.

On the highway up the West Side of the city the Porsche stayed in the right lane, allowing traffic to pass. On the left the Hudson River gleamed, mirroring the hot morning sun, and on the opposite New Jersey shore tall white buildings hovered over the narrow channel. Mitzu recalled the view, which he had seen on television during Op Sail. But he had never seen the entire city from this angle, and did not know where the highway led. As the George Washington Bridge leapt into view on the horizon he was reminded of the Golden Gate, of home. The thought that he would never see Nancy again unexpectedly saddened him. She would never understand, as his parents would. She would never comprehend the way of the warrior, the code of *bushi*.

The black Porsche continued past the bridge on the winding Henry Hudson Parkway. The road was narrower now, and most of the traffic had taken the exit for the bridge or the New England Thruway. Mitzu remained several lengths behind the Porsche as it dipped from view and rose again in the highway's rolling bends. He drove across a narrow bridge—grandeur, a touch of paradise. This stretch, on a plateau above the river, was called the Spuyten Duyvil, or Spitting Devil, by the original settlers of Manhattan island. On the right, jagged cliffs. On the left, down a sheer face of rock, the glittering river. The rocks' glare radiated sparkling fingers of light down onto the highway and the water, washing through the trees in kaleidoscopic patterns and colors.

The car! Where was the Porsche?

Mitzu looked to his right. "Fort Tryon Park—the Cloisters" said the green highway sign. The Porsche was climbing the exit ramp. Mitzu had missed it. He took the next exit, feverishly doubling back. He felt a rising panic and beads of sweat popped out on his forehead.

A soldier is serene.

He crossed through a stretch of parkland, and then, on a hill in the middle of a forest, saw the outlines of a medieval castle. What was this? As the road crested he looked down, and there was the Porsche pulling into a parking lot crowded with cars and buses, one of them a red English double-decker Leyland.

He cruised slowly down the hill, stopping near the entrance to the lot as the boy and girl got out of their car. He waited while they locked the car's door and started across the broad expanse of lawn to the castle. They had not taken the picnic basket with them. They would return.

He pulled into the lot, parked in a spot near the entrance, and sat staring as they climbed the knoll and entered the castle.

Gregorian chants echoed in the background, awesomely real and comforting, and transporting Stacy and Jason to the Middle Ages. In the vast main hall of a Romanesque chapel from the Notre Dame of Langon, they stared at the lancet stained-glass windows of Mary Magdalene wearing a red halo and Isaiah unfurling a scroll. The chapel seemed so real. The fourteenth-century sculptors from Évron who had made this church, who had carved these windows, could have been nearby practicing their craft. All around Stacy and Jason five centuries of art celebrated the passion and the resurrection of Christ.

"Every time I come here," Jason said, "it makes me want to start going to church again."

"You're the worst kind of Catholic," Stacy said.

"Why?"

"What did the Church do to us? First it sold us sin. And then it sold us the antidote, salvation. The problem with you is that you still believe in sin, but you don't believe in the salvation."

"So what do I do?"

"Give up the idea of sin," she said. "Besides, you're so decent that St. Peter will welcome you into heaven with open arms. It's the *real* sinners, like me, who have to worry."

"You're a hopeless cynic," he said, "but you're not a sinner."

"I have all the terrible sins," she said. "Envy being the worst. If I don't get that part, I'll kill whoever does."

"What about lust?" Jason asked. "I have plenty of lust. Isn't that the worst sin?" He kissed her neck.

"Let's go look at the tapestries," she said.

She wanted most of all to see the Unicorn tapestries and the Chalice of Antioch. The tapestries had been given to the museum by John D. Rockefeller, Jr., and as far as Stacy was concerned made up for a lot of terrible things he had done in the pursuit of money. Rockefeller had also paid for the Cloisters, which were composed of the remains of five French monasteries and a Spanish chapel that had been artfully assembled and reconstructed in this magnificent park overlooking the river. Rockefeller had also purchased twelve miles of the Palisades across the Hudson as a backdrop for his creation. Here, in the heart of the old Dutch section of the city, where the last English governor of New York held sway before the American Revolution, and where farmers organized underground resistance to British troops, was a setting practically rural, a stately retreat from the clamorous streets of Manhattan.

"The unicorn is a mythical animal, right?" Jason asked.

"I don't think anybody's sure," Stacy said.

The white, deer-like creature seemed to dance in the myriad woven flowers.

"Jason," she whispered, "that man's been following us."

"Who?"

"Don't look! He's over there by the Magi. He's staring right at us."

Jason crossed the granite floor into the small garden courtyard and looked at the man while pretending to study the ornamental trees. Nonchalantly he walked right past the man to Stacy.

"You mean the Chinese guy in the robe?" he whispered.

"Yeah, he's been following us since we got here. He hasn't taken his eyes off us."

"You're imagining things."

"The hell I am," she said. "I'm going to the gift shop.

I want to buy some postcards. You'll see. I'll bet he follows me."

Jason watched her go. The Chinese man in the black robe had moved on to the next room, where he was gazing up at the risen Christ.

"This wine is unbelievable," Jason said. They were sprawled on a blanket at the edge of Fort Tryon Park, in the shade of the forest.

"If it weren't for your mother and my Uncle Joe, we'd never get a taste of the good life."

"Where did he get this stuff?" Jason asked.

"He shipped it back from California," she said. "He bought three cases of it last year when it was seven dollars a bottle. Now you can buy it in New York. For twenty-two dollars a bottle."

Jason yawned. "It's worth it," he said. "I mean, it's worth it if you can afford it."

"I learned everything I know from him," Stacy said. "Did I ever tell you how when I first got to the city he took me around to all the furniture stores? He taught me how to find the most beautiful things. And then he took me to the wholesale stores and showed me how to find the same things cheaper."

She cut the brick of Fontina into chunks and passed one to Jason.

"I'm sleepy," he said.

"Why don't you take a nap? I'm going to pick some flowers."

He sprawled out on the blanket. His eyes were closed. He's a prince, she thought. He's such a prince. She had visions of their long life together. A bigger apartment facing the park filled with the sounds of children, with crayon drawings and Tinkertoys and a big fat sheep dog and slinky Siamese cat.

She watched flies beating their wings around the edge of the empty wine bottle, and she saw them sink in, land on the bottom, and drown.

* * *

Through the trees Mitzu watched them eat. The boy was putting his head down on the corner of the blanket and the girl was coming into the forest. A crook in the tree, latticed with leaves, shielded him. She bent down and plucked a bunch of white flowers sprouting in clumps around a dying tree stump. Leaning against a vast oak, dwarfed by its girth, she hummed a song and sniffed the flowers.

Her footsteps crunched on the forest floor as she came closer to him, branches snapping loudly. He peered around the tree, and suddenly she was only a few feet away. He slithered along the trunk, careful not to disturb the branches. She walked past, bending to pick more flowers. Her auburn hair bounced as she swayed among the trees, humming aloud.

He moved parallel to her, staying a few yards away, the metal shafts along his legs shining mutely. He stopped as she bent down once again, and he slid the swords from their sheaths, the *hemons* decorated also with the ideogram of the family of Goto. Mosquitoes buzzed around his head, alighting on his cheeks, and bugs of all kinds nipped at his arms, attracted by the oil on the blades. Stealthily he began crossing the forest toward her.

She turned and saw him.

"Stacy," he called out, in the hope she wouldn't scream.

"Who are you? Why are you following us?"

"I'm an old friend," he said. "I wanted to be sure it was you. I have a message for you."

She moved closer to him, and when she was barely two feet away he swung the sword at her, instantly slashing her throat. A strangled scream was shuttered in her lungs. Blood dripped from the half-moon gash as she threw her hands up, too late, to protect herself. She stumbled forward onto the forest floor, her white peasant blouse now spattered red. Mitzu finished his stroke, slicing her head off.

"Stacy," a voice called from the edge of the forest. It was the boy.

Quickly Mitzu pulled the swords away. Hurrying through the trees, stripping off his robe, he heard the boy's anguished cry.

He pulled from the highway into a cul-de-sac. Another car was there, and a woman and boy looked out over the Hudson. The river seemed to be painted against the sky, an endless mural, a mirage. Mitzu reached into his pocket for the photograph. By now the yellowed newsprint was in shreds, but the middle section remained, and with his red marker he drew an X through the third face. He touched the slender blade on the seat. He brought it to his lap and caressed it lovingly. He was almost finished. Redemption was at hand.

24

"WE WERE too late," Alex said. "He got to her before we did."

He had returned to Burt's apartment after a night of no sleep at the Bureau. Now only caffeine and Dexedrine kept him awake. He leaned on the kitchen counter, listening to the slap of a whisk against the side of a metal bowl as Burt scrambled eggs.

"What happened?"

"We couldn't find Oscar Berryman," Alex said. "He and his wife are driving cross-country in their trailer. Then we found the housekeeper. But by the time we figured out where the girl lived she was gone. The New York field office didn't call her until this morning. She'd already left. He got her at the Cloisters." Alex shook his head. "A picnic. She's an actress. Pardon me, was an actress."

Burt was speechless for a moment. He stopped beating the eggs. "Who found her?"

"Her boyfriend," Alex said, his voice hollow. "He's in Bellevue. Catatonic."

Burt poured the eggs into the sizzling butter, and the yellow liquid foamed and turned brown. The smell made Alex a little dizzy. He knew he had to eat, you could only survive so long on candy bars and coffee and dex, but the thought of food turned his stomach. He saw Burt's hand shaking.

"Did you get any sleep?"

"An hour here, an hour there. Not really."

"You're going to spill that all over yourself. Let Hollister do it." Alex leaned into the hall. "Ken, come in here, will you?"

Hollister bounded into the kitchen.

"Ken, can you finish this for us?"

"Sure," Hollister said, and took the spatula from Burt's hand.

They went into the living room. Sections of the morning *Post* littered the Chesterfield couches. Through the closed shutters sunlight fell in lines across the highly polished floor. The world goes on, Alex thought. People are brushing their teeth and going to work and cursing the heat, and a sad, sick man, to all appearances perfectly normal, is getting ready to kill again.

Alex peeked out through the shutters, spotting the two teams of men now in their cars at either end of the block. He looked up; on the roof of the house across the street shadows moved. Two gunsights poked over the parapet.

"He's coming after me," Burt said softly.

"If he sticks to his pattern," Alex said. "And he will. He's been methodical up till now, and there's no reason to think he'll change. We may be able to stop him on the way. But you can't check every license plate coming into the city, and there are lots of blue Chevrolet Monte Carlos. We're watching the trains and planes, but he won't come that way. He's still got the car."

"What do you want me to do?" Burt asked.

"Go to your office. He might show up on the Hill. Although, by now, if he's as smart as I think he is, he's going to wait for you to go out. Which is exactly what you'll do."

"You mean I'm bait."

Alex smiled. "I guess so. But we'll be on your tail every minute of the way. You have nothing to worry about. The one thing I'm sure of is that he won't give up. He'll hang around until he gets you. Betty Ammonds is upstairs. She's going to bustle around in here, stand by the windows, go shopping. When you come home, you'll both walk past the windows, and then you'll go down to the corner to buy some cigarettes and a quart of milk. And you'll do that tomorrow night and the next night and the next night, until we see him."

Burt rested his chin in his hands and drummed his fingers against his cheek. "Okay," he said with forced brightness and a nervous laugh. "I'll go attend to the business of my constituents."

"And I'm going to get some sleep. I'll call you later."

Alex stopped in the hallway outside. The building was remarkably quiet. Behind the translucent-windowed door he could see Granger's silhouette.

Alex walked over and tapped on the glass. The door opened. Sweat dripped from Granger's forehead.

"Frank, I'm going to sack out. He's going up to the Hill. Keep your eyes on the street and stay on your toes. You might get a visitor." Alex turned to leave, then said over his shoulder, "And Frank, if anything happens to him . . ."

Granger just nodded, and Alex headed down the stairs.

"The Japanese never speak of freedom," Jill read to her class, "but their warriors were always free men. They fought, strove, out of loyalty, and they expected to act under discipline, under an obligation to nation, clan, family, and their personal honor. The forms have changed but the force is still there."

In the airy seminar room her students had ceased taking notes. Her "Patterns of Culture" course was, she thought, her best, and her seven students sensed her passion and were intrigued as much by the subject matter of her lecture as by the urgency of her voice, intuitively hearing a commitment to knowledge they rarely found in a classroom. Their rapt faces, young and full of the search for understanding, were all turned toward her.

"Now what did Morton mean?" she asked. "What does it mean to say that the forms have changed but the force is still there? That's the question I want you to answer in seven hundred and fifty words by Wednesday. What does national character mean? Is it only an idea, a historian's shorthand? Or are the Japanese truly different from the Germans, and the Germans from the Chinese, and the Chinese from the American Indian? Do you believe in a national pysche?"

A preternaturally serious young man whose honor

thesis concerned the peasants of Western Samoa raised his hand.

"Miss Britten, are you asking for our opinions? Or do you want us to justify what Morton wrote?"

Jill couldn't help smiling. Even the best of undergraduates these days were afraid of expressing opinions.

"Mr. Kenworthy, I'm asking you to formulate a response to the idea of national character. That doesn't mean I want *only* your opinions. I want your opinion combined with your scholarship, with your total understanding of what we've read in this course. Friedrich in *Modern Japan* says the Japanese are warlike. Dussault, in *The Fatherland,* says the Germans have a love affair with authority, any authority. Tomlinson and Shack write that Americans are anarchists at heart, and that's what makes democracy possible. Does any of this resonate in you?"

The student stared at his hands, studying a rubber band stretched between his palms. Suddenly he looked up, as though struck by a revelation.

"Then you *do* want our opinions."

"Yes," Jill said, "I do. If for no other reason than it'll help you get them written."

The class grinned. Jill glanced at her watch.

"I'll see you next week," she said. "Remember, have your papers in my departmental mailbox by Wednesday."

The class quickly disappeared into the twilight, leaving nothing behind but their cigarette butts and scraps of notepaper. Jill followed them onto H Street, watched them disperse in five different directions, and began walking to her apartment. Down Pennsylvania Avenue she could see network television crews parked in front of the Old Executive Office Building and, on the horizon, the dome of the Capitol bright against a robin's-egg-blue sky. She had never posed her questions to a class with such vehemence, and she knew the class had understood. The problem was, she did not quite understand herself. What was it that she wanted to know?

Mitzu's call that morning had set her off, set her

thinking again about all the things she wanted to forget and had buried away.

She stopped at a phone booth and tried to call Alex at home, but the Bureau answered his phone. Toby told her Alex had worked through the night. But what was happening? Was there a break in the case? Toby wouldn't say. She hung up and remembered when Alex had disappeared for four days during the Pittsburgh Bomber case. She knew she had to accept that Alex wouldn't always be there when she needed him, but today she could use some support, a brief phone call. She picked up the phone again and dialed Burt's office. After she talked with Tharp Williams she felt better. Burt was in a committee meeting, so everything must be all right.

She took a mirror from her purse and examined her face. Half-moons of gray hung under her eyes, visible through her makeup. She wished there had been some way to tell Mitzu that she no longer had any desire to see him. I stopped transferring your name from one address book to another two years ago, she could have said. I haven't thought about you at all, she could have said. I'm too worried about my brother to think about you, she could have said.

But the simple fact was that she had said, "Dinner sounds fine. It'll be fun to catch up after all this time."

Although the sun had been setting for half an hour, the heat remained, so stifling it seemed to impede all motion. The buildings on Twenty-first Street were still emptying lawyers and insurance salesmen and secretaries into the evening like a giant factory producing facsimiles of human beings, and they appeared to move with exaggerated slowness, as though conserving energy to fight the heat. A man at the corner of N and Twenty-first carried his suit jacket over his shoulder while blotches of perspiration broke out on his shirt as he waited for the light to change. His briefcase hung from his hand like a steel weight. He probably looked quite distinguished this morning, Jill thought, and now he looks as if he might keel over any second.

I could tell Mitch I don't feel well, she thought. I could tell him I'm too tired to be good company. He would stay for a drink or two and then leave. Maybe she could disappear into the library, where she told Alex she would be, and not be home when Mitch arrived. Maybe . . .

But none of this was possible. Try as she might, she couldn't run from her true feelings. She wanted to see him. She even wanted to make love to him. Even though she knew it was wrong, and would lead her to an unwelcome betrayal, and to guilt.

The traffic along the old canal road leading into Washington was stalled almost to a dead stop. Despite his tiredness, despite the fact that he had driven four hours straight to Washington, Mitzu was alert. Tonight he would have to repeat the drive, but he would be strong.

I am strength, he thought. Hardness, purity, beauty.

In the half-light of dusk he could see the couple in the Volkswagen next to him. The man, who had the face of a well-fed hog, was perspiring profusely and honking his horn. The woman was shouting at him.

Weakness, Mitzu thought with scorn. Softness, impurity, ugliness.

The traffic began to move, and Mitzu's headlights picked out joggers running along the water's edge. As the parkway changed into Foxhall Road, he saw a group of teenagers spraying "Artie loves Rosemary" on a bridge abutment, merrily defacing an otherwise clean cement wall.

It had been a long time since his last trip to Washington, but this route was as familiar as if he had driven it yesterday. The bright green foliage, the languid pace of traffic, the bleak stretch of empty buildings breaking into the fringes of Georgetown, where suddenly the world was comprised of cute shops, banks designed in ersatz eighteenth-century architecture, and fake small-town ice-cream parlors.

He could imagine Jill's creamy skin, her blissfully alabaster flesh, and the suppleness of her body which remained in his memory like a favorite painting or a golden past romanticized as paradise. She had been sweet to him, touched him deeply, yet he felt no tenderness as he touched the clasp of the case next to him on the seat.

He passed the Nigerian Embassy on Twenty-second Street and began looking for a parking place.

"At hearings before the House Appropriations Committee," the radio announcer was saying, "General George Britten called for renewed emphasis on development of the country's nuclear arsenal. In testimony delivered this morning, the former high aide to the Joint Chiefs of Staff told the congressmen that America was falling behind the Soviet Union in nuclear capability." The announcer paused and the general's taped voice came on. "We must arm our armed forces with the best in nuclear weaponry, not with outmoded armaments that will be useless in the event of war. The nuclear trump will someday have to be played. It is our duty as citizens to support the guardians of our security. Nothing less than our national honor is at stake."

Duty. Honor.

Mitzu laughed softly. His throat caught and he chortled, a deep-throated gurgling laugh. He pulled to the side of the street and threw his hands up in hysterical cackling, rolling sideways on the seat, yelping with glee in a crescendo of laughter until he could no longer control himself. Louder and louder he laughed, the sound caroming off the glass. His head jerked back and forth as demented cries issued from his throat, and he was grasping his cheeks in his hands when he fell in a paroxysm onto the steering wheel, weeping and laughing, laughing and weeping, weeping, laughing . . .

Jill spent an unpleasant hour in her apartment. She arranged and rearranged the Wassily chairs, adjusted the tiered reading lamp into all of its possible positions, straightened the jade figurines on the lacquered table. She pulled books from the shelf, examined them, and replaced them. The air conditioning's thermostat clicked on and off twice during the hour, and both times she was startled. It's ridiculous, she thought. It's ridiculous that I should be so goofy about this. We'll have a nice dinner, we'll talk, we'll wish each other good luck in the future, and that will be that. Old friends. Just old friends, lovers no more.

The security horn in the kitchen squealed like a siren. Someone was at the downstairs door.

"Yes," she said, pushing the *talk* button.

"Jill, it's Mitzu," came the metallic voice.

She buzzed him in.

She raced into the bedroom, ran her hands through her hair, and smoothed the bedspread. Very good, she said to herself. The bedspread. Now why do you suppose you did that if he's only here to take you to dinner?

In the living room she took two fluted glasses from the cabinet and set them on the breakfront.

The doorbell rang. She tried to form a smile on her lips, and went to the door.

"Jill, oh, Jill, how are you, you look wonderful." He kissed her on the cheek.

"Mitch, it's been so long, it's good to see you. How was your flight?"

He was as beautiful as she remembered. His fine, high cheekbones gleamed like polished china. The deep wells of his eyes were like bottomless jewels of aquamarine. From the merest touch she could feel the stiff strength of his body. She tingled, warmth rippling through her chest. He was magical.

"Pretty good flight," he said. "The stewardess spilled a cup of coffee but missed me, and two babies cried the whole way."

They were standing in the doorway. He had a suitcase in one hand, and a long, narrow carrying case in the other.

"I brought these up, I hope you don't mind. I didn't want to leave them in the car. And there's something I want to show you."

"What?"

"Not right now. Are you going to invite me in?"

"I'm sorry, I'm a little dazed, come in, sit down, what can I get you to drink? Sherry?"

She poured Bristol Cream into the fluted glasses, observing him from the corner of her eye as he strolled around the apartment. When she turned with the glasses in her hands he was sitting on the couch, running his hand along the edge of the lacquered table.

"I remember when you got this," he said.

"I remember, too," she said. She was anxious to change the subject. "How's Nancy? Did she deliver yet?"

"A baby boy," he said. "Six pounds, five ounces."

"Oh, Mitch, that's marvelous. What's his name?"

"Tad," he said. "For my Uncle Tadashi. He's a big healthy kid. Looks just like his mother."

She thought it strange that he would name his child after one of his relatives. He had never liked talking about them. Idly she wondered what her children would look like if he were the father.

"Mitch, how could you take a business trip after you'd just had a baby?"

For an instant his face changed, sharpened. And then the expression softened as quickly as it had arisen.

"Well, you know, I'll only be gone a few days. And this is an important trip. There's a good chance I'll end up heading the division when my boss retires. Nancy understands. How's your brother?"

"Burt? He's all right. But this terrible thing's been going on. He got a crazy letter in the mail and we can't figure out what it means, and now he has the FBI on his tail. They think someone might want to kill him."

"The FBI? What's it all about?"

"I don't know, but it's scaring me to death. Look, let's not talk about it. As a matter of fact, I was hoping

217

you'd take my mind off it. I made a reservation around the corner. Let's get something to eat."

"Let's, I'm hungry," he said, standing. He reached across the table and took her hand. "I've missed seeing you, Jill. I can't tell you how good it is to see you."

She wanted to pull her hand from his, but it seemed childish. It's only a simple dinner with an old friend.

"It's good to see you, too, Mitch."

A simple dinner. He's happily married, he's just had a baby boy, and we're just old friends.

25

ALEX HAD slept until seven o'clock that evening, when his alarm clock shook him out of his stupor. He was still groggy twenty minutes later when he started his third cup of coffee. Eight hours just wasn't enough. After checking in with Toby he called Jill at home, but her machine wasn't on. He assumed she was in the library working on her book. But she was so meticulous about the answering machine. And if she had gone from her afternoon class to the library, why had her machine been on this morning?

Toby was waiting at the Bureau with no news, which was bad news.

"No sign of the car," Toby said. "Maybe he ditched it. We didn't spot him on the Jersey Pike, but it's possible he got out of Jersey before the state police started looking. If he's on his way here, they should have seen him south of Philly."

"He could've gone around the Penn Pike," Alex said, "if he thought anyone was watching."

Toby nodded. "Maybe. And the Penn troopers could miss him. But coming into the capital he has to pass us three times. If he gets through, it's only because he knows every back road in town."

"I want every cop on the streets looking for him," Alex said. "If he makes it into the city, he's liable to park and take the subway. Christ, he could get on in Rockville or somewhere out there and then we'd lose him for sure."

"Yeah, but the minute he tries for Burt, he's ours. A worm couldn't get within six blocks of Burt's. We'll find him."

"Sure," Alex said doubtfully. He ran his hands over his stubbly beard, wishing he had taken the time to shave. His skin was starting to itch. Coffee, dex, not enough sleep—his body begged for relief.

Toby said, "I'll bet he hasn't even left New York. They'll pick him up in the city, or tonight on the Penn Pike."

Yes, Alex thought, that was possible. Nagata had seemed to move without particular caution until now. He had managed to kill Charlotte Kirkaby in San Francisco, then go to a business meeting in the afternoon. He had inspected a nuclear plant in Philadelphia on a morning four days later, and then slaughtered Michael Farrell on the same day. Then he had decided to lie low, missing an appointment in New York and not checking into the Waldorf. He had given them just enough time to get onto his scent, and then he had disappeared. Less than fifteen hours after a positive identification, he had killed Stacy Berryman. How had he managed to follow her to the Cloisters? How had he even been able to position himself to follow her?

"Let's talk to Beckel," Alex said.

"He's waiting for us."

The Bureau's Psychological Analysis Unit was tucked into a small, cramped corner in the basement, the result of its inability to compete successfully for space with Chemistry & Toxicology, Mineralogy, and Serology. The older hands joked that if the shrinks were really any good, they ought to be able to manipulate the Director into allocating half the third floor to their work. But it was only in the past two years that psychological profiles of various criminal types had been given passing credence. Before Hoover's death, money for psychiatrists was scarce unless they were weeding misfits out of the Bureau itself.

Gary Beckel's office—nothing more than two partitions and a desk—was at the front of the section. Alex had originally requested Beckel partly because he was young and ambitious, but mostly because the psychiatrist had studied criminals in prison for his post-doctoral research, and wholeheartedly believed there actually was such a thing as the criminal mind. Alex had heard him lecture on the kinds of character disorders that led to crime, and had found himself unusually impressed.

"Hiya, sleuths," Beckel said, standing to greet Alex and Toby. "You have a real strange one on your hands."

"I'm sorry to keep you here so late," Alex said, "but I was out cold all day."

"That's all right. Sit down and take a load off your feet."

Beckel's eager good looks combined with his white Brooks Brothers shirt, rep tie loosely knotted, and dirty buck shoes gave him the air of a model preppie. Alex, sitting down opposite his desk, was sure this accounted for his liking Beckel so much. I have bad tendencies, Alex thought, toward elitist snobbery. But he dismissed the idea from his mind and concentrated on the young shrink.

"What do you think, Doc?" Toby asked.

Beckel propped a file in his lap. "Nagata's an interesting set of contradictions. Ideal citizen, good employee, your basic, solid middle-class American. Or is he?" Beckel gave them a grave look. "He spent the last eight years of his life at the same job. Young managers don't do that. They move around from company to company. Why didn't he? Well, his parents live in San Francisco, and his boss, Edward Stone, says he's very loyal to them."

Alex asked, "Did you get that from the file? I didn't see that."

"No, I called him. So why is Nagata loyal? Well, it turns out the parents are old-style Japanese. Never really assimilated. Stone says they even live in a Japanese-style house, and the father speaks Japanese to his son. And they brought him to San Francisco just after the war. Now that gets us to this baby boy who died. I talked to the doctor, name of Bellows. Bellows says—"

Alex interrupted. "How'd you get hold of him?"

"From the file. Bellows says when he told Nagata about the boy, Nagata displayed no emotion. Didn't cry, shout, or scream—nothing. Cut off from his feelings, cold as hell. Okay, so his wife goes home from the hospital and Nagata throws himself right back into his work. Now what do you make of that? I mean, anybody else would take a couple of days off to recover, or at least stay home with his wife. Not this character. Now it turns out that Nagata was near Hiroshima at the time of the blast, and Bellows says that's probably what caused the deformities. An alteration of the genes."

Alex whistled. "Is that possible? Or common?"

"Oh, sure. Mutagenic response to radiation, absolutely. Teratogenicity of radiation? Unquestionable."

"Terato— What?" Toby asked.

"From the Greek," said the psychiatrist. "Meaning, literally, monster-forming. Bellows wanted to get a tissue sample for some very expensive gene analysis on Nagata. But Nagata never came for the appointment. Well, I'll tell you what I think. Understand that this is guesswork. But I think Nagata snapped. I think you have a situation here with somebody already on the edge, ready to fall. A personality already balanced precariously, so when the kid is born, whammo! The kid dies, Nagata knows there won't be any more kids, and then he sees the picture in the paper, and he says to the picture—"

"You mean," Alex interrupted, "that he said to himself."

"No, to the picture," Beckel continued. "The picture becomes alive for him, he anthropomorphizes the image, the people in it are real, and he says to the picture, if I can't have kids, neither can you. You set off the bomb, but you have your children. An eye for an eye. Now, I don't know anything about Nagata's parents, but I'll bet you there's a samurai background there. Nagata suppressed it, became utterly American, and not just any American, but a quintessential American, even married an American girl, a Protestant beauty from a solid old family. It's like the guy was living out some fantasy of not being Japanese, but every time he looked in a mirror he had to face the contradiction. Well, you walk around with that long enough, and the personality, already rigid, is in deep trouble. It's as though you or I looked in the mirror every day and saw ourselves as Cary Grant, only with Nagata it was much worse. We could get away with pretending we were Cary Grant. But Nagata was headed for disaster."

Beckel sat back and closed his file. "It's all speculation, of course, but that's what I think."

Toby asked, "Did they get anything from the wife?"

"They just turned her up an hour ago at his parents'. I'm waiting for word that I can talk to her, and I'd like to hear from the parents, too. But I think I'm on the mark. Now what you want to know is what he'll do next. The note says thousands will die, and he works for a company that builds nuclear plants and we're talking radiation here, so—"

"I'm ahead of you, Doc," Alex said. "The NRC already has the whole Northeast on alert."

Beckel smiled. "He's going to blow one of them up if he gets the chance. He's going to spread enough radiation to kill all the children he can, and to stop anybody else from having children. We took his kid away, and now he's going to metaphorically take ours."

Toby said, "I would hardly call blowing up a nuclear plant a metaphor."

Beckel nodded. "The metaphor is in his mind. The reality doesn't matter. I suggest you be ready for him. He's a samurai now. He's got those swords and he's living in a seventeenth-century dream. He's on a holy mission, and he's not going to be easy to stop."

"We'll get him when he goes for Burt," Alex said.

Beckel sat up hard in his chair. "Burt?"

"He got the letter," Alex said.

Beckel's face screwed up in concentration. "Well, sure, but what about the general's daughter?"

Alex looked from Toby's shocked face to Beckel's.

"Oh my God," he said, and was up out of his chair.

26

DINNER HAD been a slow luxurious affair. The restaurant had pretensions to French elegance, with slow service, too many waiters filling water glasses too often, and a captain who after each course insisted on inquiring as to the quality of the food. By dessert Mitzu and Jill had consumed two bottles of Pouilly-Fuisse, and Jill, feeling light-headed, was entranced. Not that Mitzu had uttered a romantic word, or even an innuendo. If anything, he had been very proper, practically diffident. She had rambled on about her teaching and her book, and he had joked about the perils of corporate-ladder climbing. If Jill had not been affected by the wine, she might have noticed that his conversation was mechanical, that he steered her from one topic to another, never allowing any train of thought to sustain itself for very long, as though he were following a script.

But Jill was wrestling with too many wild emotions. She felt guilty for even having dinner with him. Guilty for betraying Alex. She was confused about her feelings toward Mitch, having a wish for him to disappear, and a simultaneous wish to make love to him. Had she been less confused, or more sober, his casual touching of her hand or the brush of his leg against hers might have seemed purposeful, but as it was she did not realize he was actively seducing her.

Walking back to her apartment up Connecticut Avenue they passed a couple, young lovers, holding hands and kissing, and staring in the windows of the American Express office at the corner of M Street. The words "honeymoon," "wedding," and "money" rose above their murmurs.

"Cognac?" Jill said when they entered her apartment.

"Just what the doctor ordered," Mitzu said. The doctor . . .

the doctor said what I can only call crippling deformities.

Jill sat next to him, holding out the glass and thinking the evening was turning out to be easier than she had expected.

Mitzu drank cautiously, but each sip added to the heaviness in his chest. Moderation in all things. A samurai denied weakness and attractions to temporal excess. The figure who sat with him on the couch had harmed his family, had harmed the seed of his life.

She was the destroyer of his child.

No, she was Jill.

She was the enemy of his family.

In the way of the warrior, there is wisdom and valor.

She refilled her glass twice while he continued to sip on the first drink she had poured him. His spirit would be dulled by further consumption. You are a soldier. Be strong. Be benevolent. Be victorious.

"You know, you really seem different," she said.

"How?"

"I don't know, maybe more serious. More . . . I guess just older."

His eyes strayed to the two suitcases lying in the hallway between the living room and the bedroom.

"We're all a little older," he said. "I'm getting to be middle-aged. I don't move as fast as I used to, the muscles creak."

She laughed. "You sound like me. My . . . my brother says I sound ancient. Any minute now we'll need canes and walkers."

Alex. It was Alex who had said that. Why don't I tell him about Alex?

He laid his hand on hers, but she resisted his touch, sliding away from him.

"I love the way you're wearing your hair," he said.

"This? This is called wash and wear."

"It's lovely. It's very delicate."

He reached toward her again and caressed her cheek,

225

stroking his fingers along her chin. Her cheeks quivered and she pulled back.

"Mitch, no, we can't. You're married and I'm . . ."

"You're . . . ?"

"I'm sort of attached."

She swung her head away, but he could feel she was ready. Only her idea of propriety kept her from joining him. He moved swiftly, taking her face in his hands and kissing her, his tongue searching her lips, pressing for an opening. Her face fell to his shoulder.

"No, Mitch, no, this isn't right, please understand . . ."

He kissed her harder, his tongue diving deep into her mouth and his hand grazing her leg. He felt no stirring of arousal, no passion, but was compelled to continue, to bring her to him. His mouth, his body, his hands— these were only weapons to be used against . . .

She was Jill.

You are a soldier, a soldier

in the delta, the cool air . . . soldiers running . . .

Her body pressed against him and he called on his sex to serve him. He felt himself stiffen, blood coursing in his thighs. Jill's breathing grew deep and moist. He peeled her blouse from her shoulders. His hand played across her breasts and her small pale nipples. He reached behind him and hooked his finger around the lamp's chain, putting them in darkness.

"Mitch, please, stop," she whispered, but with no conviction. Her hand crept down his leg, passing slowly over his hardness, drawing lines up his thighs.

He stood and shucked his tie with one yank, then his shirt and pants. He tucked his hand in her skirt and slid it down her legs. A sudden charge seized him as his hands circled her hips and his tongue licked her belly. She parted her legs. With his hand and mouth he pulsed back and forth.

Still he felt no passion. He would bring her to a frenzy. He would send her into flights of ecstasy, to the edge of consciousness.

Between her legs sweat flowed like honey and dripped onto his face. His closed eyes fixed on a red sun filling a white unending sky, a flag, a banner, as she tried momentarily to resist, her legs offering pressure. He frothed, drenching her, and she opened wider. His fingers worked their way inside, and she slid under him, moaning.

He picked her up and carried her into the shadowed bedroom. He laid her down on the quilt, flowered in boughs of purple and shafts of green. From his suitcase he removed his black robe and wrapped it around him.

"Mitch?"

He did not answer her, but tugged with his foot the other case, narrow and long, to the side of the bed. In her fever, and in the darkness, she could not see him, only a black outline against the mirror.

He knelt beside her, taking one nipple in his hand, the other in his mouth. Her head swayed beneath him. His sucking spread a milky film on her skin, and at a guiding touch from his hand, a grasp of her buttocks, she slid closer, moving in and out against his leg. His hands eased down her chest, and he pressed her mound of fur, two fingers parting her lips, the other hand cupping her thigh and massaging to her rhythm. She sought him out now, pulling him, encouraging him, but he withheld himself.

He wanted her very high. He wanted her screaming.

She pulled at him again and reached between his legs. Her fingers encircled his hardness, rubbing her moistness into his flesh.

She whimpered a soft cry. "Mitch, now."

And still he waited while

a light in the sky, a canopy of white

shot through him. Not passion, not arousal. It was the memory he felt, the memory he saw, the memory in his blood that drove him on.

She swept him on top of her, urging him into her. By steps he eased between her legs, thrusting slowly. She was wet and hungry, welcoming him readily. He arched his back above her, pointing down, pressing down, pushing down, sliding up.

"Oh. Oh my God, ah, ah . . ."

227

She soared. She moaned. She took her pleasure. Her hands slapped against his naked, hairless flesh in the rhythm of her gasps. Let her have her pleasure.

He reached down beside the bed and snapped the clasp on the narrow case. His hand groped for the shaft of steel. He had the sword in his hand, cold metal, and worked his way to its hilt, to the handle of the sword of the family of Goto. It slipped from its velvet bonds.

She looked up at him, eyes wide, still moaning. But her passion was nearly spent, she had stopped moving, and she caught the glint of metal above her head.

"No! No! Mitch! What . . . what . . . ?"

She had seen the sword. She tried to squirm from under him.

"Stop! No!"

He aimed the gleaming tip for her neck, but she rolled her head away. The sword hit the pillow, plunged into the bed. Feathers fluttered up in a cloudy burst. He jabbed again, nicking her hand, and she screamed in pain.

She threw him from her body and leapt away. He chased her through the half-lit darkness. She ran to the front door, tried to open it, but the chain was on, and with a single furious kick he forced it closed. She was cornered now. She lunged at him desperately, screaming a shrill, guttural cry. Her flailing arms struck the hilt of the sword, and Mitzu's grasp on the weapon faltered. The blade nicked his ear and blood trickled down his neck.

"Mitch, what are you doing? Stop, stop, oh God, stop. Help! Help!"

He must end her screaming.

I am a soldier.

He grabbed a handful of her hair and she fell prone to the floor, pulling him down with her. She started to crawl toward the couch, escaping from him. He clamped a hand on her leg and slashed the sword at her, but she darted away. Mitzu's robe caught on the table leg and snagged. The sacred fabric ripped. Uncle Tadashi's robe, the robe of the warrior.

Jill picked up a lamp and threw it at him with all her might. The base of the lamp missed his head by inches, and porcelain shattered across the floor.

She must die. She must die now.

She ran into the bathroom and barricaded herself in with the straw hamper, sitting against the sink and pushing with her legs. She shouted toward the ventilating duct, hoping someone would hear.

She must die for the insult to the blood of Nagata.

Mitzu raised his left leg, tightened his muscles, and threw his weight into the door. In the crack of splintering wood it opened, shards flying in all directions. She was crouching in terror, her eyes beseeching him.

He drove the sword into her arm, but her screaming continued. Blood spurted onto the tiles, a pool of red against white becoming a wide circle, a dark red sun. She leapt up and ran past him, and he heard her clawing at the lock of the front door.

The screams had come echoing through Ralph Sheed's bathroom air vent. Having come in ten minutes before from a State Department dinner, he was nursing a premature hangover in his kitchen, directly above Jill's apartment. Who in God's name was screeching like that? You never heard noises in this corner of the building, because almost everyone was single and nobody had children. Sounds like it's below me, Sheed thought.

He walked down the back steps and put his ear to the door of 6A. Not a sound. The screams again. They were coming from Jill Britten's apartment. He had met her several times in the elevator, and she had watered his plants when he was in Mexico last winter. He was about to bang on the door when the door opened and she stumbled toward him in a blur, blood dripping from her hands.

"Jesus, Jill, what the—"

A black figure flew past him in a flash, and somewhere he thought he saw a blade. And then he realized Jill Britten was unconscious in his arms.

The ambulance arrived before Alex and Toby did. Alex ordered the city sealed. Find the car. Stop every Japanese man you see.

As they screeched into the driveway of the emergency room of Georgetown Medical Center, Alex saw Roger Alford's pink Firebird coming around the corner behind them. How could he explain this to Burt? How could any of them explain this stupid and fundamental miscalculation? Try on the facts like a suit of clothes, Alex thought to himself. If Burt had gotten the letter, why had Jill been Nagata's victim? The clothes didn't fit.

Burt jumped out of the Firebird and met Alex at the door.

"Is she . . . alive?"

Alex nodded. "They just wheeled her into an operating room. Burt, I'm sorry, we never even thought—"

Burt hugged Alex and whispered, "Don't, please, don't start blaming yourself."

The vestibule running alongside the emergency room, with its ugly green chairs and bright overhead lights, was eerie and depressing. A woman with bleached red hair in curlers and a bandage taped over her nostrils sat on a nearby couch reading *The Daily World*.

"She's lost a great deal of blood," the nurse on duty told them ten minutes later. "She's going to be in surgery for a while. I can't tell you how long."

For half an hour Burt paced the narrow hallway, lost in his thoughts. The general had not been at home when Burt called, and the Pentagon denied any knowledge of his whereabouts, keeping arm's length from a retired officer who was making political news. But the night desk officer, at Burt's furious insistence, was able to find the general at the home of one of the Joint Chiefs' senior political analysts in Chevy Chase.

Alex sat in a phone booth at the end of the wall, watching Burt pace, and talking with Toby Morrison. The blue Chevrolet, Toby said, had been seen by a District policeman twenty minutes before the ambulance got there, but the report hadn't reached the Bureau until half an hour later. Now the car had vanished into the night like a ghost.

"Toby, that isn't possible."

"Alex, we're *trying*. We have enough cops on the highways. If he uses the highways. He can't get on a train, and it's too late for him to take a plane. He has to lie low. We'll find him."

Alex considered for a moment the possibility of Nagata's getting out of the metropolitan area. Not likely, but he had somehow driven in without being spotted, and he could conceivably drive out just as easily. There were too many roads to cover, and he could slip through the net.

Alex said, "What's the closest American General plant?"

"There's a reactor in Maine, and then Toms River in New Jersey, and Brock Point in Connecticut."

"I want a riot team ready to fly to New York tonight, and Maine alerted. Is there anywhere else?"

Toby shuffled papers at the other end of the line. "American General did some secondary steam work at the Con Ed plants, but the closest full installation, aside from Jersey and Brock Point, is outside of Columbus. Hell, he can't get to Ohio fast enough, can he?"

"No. I'll see you in an hour, maybe two."

"Alex, we'll have to leave from Dulles. Or get National's noise regulations suspended."

"Get 'em suspended, Tobe. And wait for me."

He hung up and pulled a cigarette from his pocket. As he stood to go outside the general came toward him through the emergency room door. The Great Man, Alex thought. Alex didn't actively dislike the general, but there was no love lost between them either. The general was in uniform, including his peaked cap, which hung over his eyes at a rakish angle. Sitting near the entryway now was a disheveled-looking man in dirty white coveralls. His son had been in a motorcycle accident and had been in surgery for four hours. The man stood up when the general passed him, and then, without a word, sat down. Burt went rushing to his father.

"Hello, Dad." Tears were forming in the corners of Burt's eyes.

"Hello, Burt, how is she?"

"She's in surgery. That's all we know."

"Well, by God, where's the head resident here? Where's the top man in—"

"Dad, stop it. We'll have to wait."

The general was awkwardly holding his son, his arms stiffly hanging over Burt's shoulders.

"General," Alex said, nodding his head. "Why don't you sit down. Can I get you some coffee? There's a sandwich machine in the lobby."

The general declined and Burt loosened himself from his father's grasp. Alex pulled three chairs into a circle and told the General about the threatening letter, reciting the Bureau's efforts to find the sender.

"Burt, you should have told me."

"Frankly, Dad, I didn't think you'd be interested."

The general blanched, obviously stung by his son's tone, and Alex, hoping to quell the animosities, continued with the story. He concluded with the discovery of the victims' fathers in the *Post* photograph. General Britten, for once in his life, was speechless. For fully a minute they sat with their heads hung down.

"I knew Dick Farrell's boy was a priest," the general finally said. "And Elmer Bly showed me a picture of his little granddaughter. What was the girl's name?"

"Charlotte Kirkaby," Alex said.

"That's right," the general said. "She was married right out of college. I didn't make it to the wedding. It's awful. It's tragic. Her husband died of cancer, a year or so ago. That poor little girl is going to grow up without parents." He paused, his face a grim visage of sadness. "And you say it all started with this photograph in the paper. So in a way it's my fault."

"No, Dad," Burt said, "it doesn't have anything to do with you. You can't be responsible for every madman on the planet."

Alex sympathized with Burt's sharp response. To the general, all events reflected back on him. But Alex knew that the general was never going to change. He was the true existentialist. He believed the world would end with his own death.

Alex was exhausted by the telling of his story, and in exhaustion felt bereft of either emotion or involvement. For the past two hours he had been thoroughly in control of himself, a consequence of habit. But he had limits, and anguish, grief, and fear welled up in him like a river bursting its banks. He looked at Burt and the general, locked in their angry shells, and without a word stepped out into the damp night. The city was very quiet. Washington was a town without much public night life, except in the ghetto, and all parties took place in private. Alex leaned against the building and lit a cigarette.

She could die, he thought. She was the only woman he had ever truly loved, and she was going to die.

The general came through the door and in the mild breeze cupped his hands and lit a cigar.

"Can't smoke in there," he said, clearing his throat. "He won't talk to me, Alex. He won't drop this political stuff and talk to me."

Oh God, Alex thought, spare me. Don't get me caught in these family fights.

"He's just upset, George. It's not the right time."

Alex felt his eyes swelling, a prelude to tears. Don't cry, you simpering jerk, it won't do any good.

The general put a hand on his shoulder, and Alex couldn't control himself. The tears trickled out onto his cheeks, first a few drops, and then a sluicing current.

"Pray with me, Alex," the general said.

"I'm praying."

"I mean out loud," the general said.

"It's not my style, George," Alex said, trying to stop his tears.

Don't die, he implored her. Don't die.

* * *

They had been waiting in silence for an hour. Alex was mulling over the police report, wondering how Mitzu Nagata had been able to get into Jill's apartment. And what was she doing at home? She had been in the library every night this week. And why had she been completely nude when she stumbled into Ralph Sheed's arms?

Just past two o'clock, a doctor came toward them. He had unruly long brown hair, a pale face, and a slight build. He looked so much like a teenager, Alex thought, that had it not been for the stethoscope around his neck it would have been hard to accept him as a doctor. He introduced himself as Jon Apted.

"She's going to be all right, gentlemen," the doctor said. "She's out of the recovery room, but she's still sedated. It's going to be a half hour or so before she comes out of it. Why don't you go in and wait? I'm sure she'll want somebody there when she wakes up."

The woman who was reading *The Daily World* approached Alex. Her red hair gave her the look of a scarecrow.

"Light?"

Alex flicked his lighter and held up a flame.

"Thanks," she said, turning to go out the door. Then she stopped and turned back to Burt. "You're a congressman, aren't you? I heard the nurse."

"Yes, I am," Burt said.

"You're making a fine mess of this country," she said, her voice a snarl. "All of you."

Burt ignored her, spinning on his heels and following Alex, the general, and the doctor to the elevator. They rode up in silence, and then followed the doctor to Jill's room.

Her face was so gray Alex gagged. The backs of her palms were bruised black and blue from the intravenous needles. Swaths of white cotton cover her arm.

Burt went to her side and brushed strands of tangled hair from her forehead. The sight of his sister thoroughly unnerved him.

"She's never been in the hosptial," he said weakly. "Not since the day she was born."

The doctor said, "She may come to, and then fade out again. That happens with anesthesia."

Alex had walked to the other side of the bed. He reached under the sheet and took her hand. Her flesh was cold.

"My God," he said.

Burt held her other hand. Her fingers clasped suddenly around his.

"She's waking up," Burt said.

"I doubt it," the doctor said with a smile.

Her voice came out as a croak. "Burt," she said. Her eyes opened for a fraction of an instant and then closed again.

"She *is*," Burt said excitedly. "Look."

Her finger seemed to be tracing a circle on his open palm. Alex, the general, and the doctor watched as she drew the circle again and again, her finger marking slow revolutions.

"What is it?" Alex asked.

Her finger continued marking the circle, this time crossing it with a line down the middle. Her eyes opened again. Her finger moved back up the line, then drew a diagonal to one side, and then another in the opposite direction. Her eyes closed.

"Alex, it's the *peace* sign. It's the old antiwar sign."

Her eyes opened, she sucked in air, and then her eyes closed.

"What does it mean?" Alex asked, punching his palm with his fist like a frustrated football coach.

Burt walked over to the general, who was standing at the foot of the bed. "Dad, stay here. I'll be right back. I think I know what it is."

Alex followed him out the door.

The D.C. police were still dusting Jill's apartment for fingerprints when Alex and Burt arrived. Alex flashed his FBI identification. Burt immediately went to the filing cabinet in the bedroom where he had

235

installed Jill's telephone answering machine. The machine wasn't there.

"It must have gotten ripped out in the fight," he said. "It has to be here somewhere."

He found the machine of the floor behind Jill's desk. Turning it upside down, he held the bottom up to show Alex.

"It was my old machine," he said. "I put the peace sticker on it, gave it to Jill when Marge bought a new one."

He set the machine on the desk, plugged it in, and pushed the playback button.

"Hi, Jill, it's Alvin. There's a departmental meeting next Thursday. Could you bring the syllabus for the inquiry courses? Talk to you tomorrow. Bye."

Alex said, "I tried to call her tonight. It wasn't on."

A few seconds of dial tone played on the tape, and then there was a click.

"Jill, it's Terry. I can't find those Friedrich essays. I think Karen Sacks has my copy. You might try Doug Dowling at his cabin. Or I'll call him when he gets back. And I tried your sashimi recipe. It was the hit of the party. Love ya'. Bye."

Another pause, another click.

"It's Mitzu, Jill. I'll probably get in around seven-thirty. I can't wait to see you."

Burt's jaw dropped, and he and Alex sat staring at each other as once again the tape clicked and a dial tone droned on.

27

MITZU HAD thought this would be the easiest part, when all his preparations led him to a single predetermined moment. He had expected to meet his fate eagerly. But his throat was constricted, and as he turned the steering wheel he watched the blue veins on the back of his hand throb in the sunlight. The hair on his skin stood up in the currents of air that blew through the car, and he saw them as signs of his own mortality.

There is a time to die, he said to himself. You are a soldier.

Three miles from Crescent Park he stopped at a roadside diner. It was a bunker-like building of concrete blocks with a faded Coca-Cola sign above the door, its red paint now worn by weather to pale mauve.

"A Coke," he said to the young girl behind the counter. She looked as though she hadn't heard him.

"Large or small," she said.

"Small."

She pushed a plastic cover down onto a stack of conical cups and dipped the cup below the counter into a tub of crushed ice. She stared at him the entire time as she held the cup under the dispenser, her eyes wide. Her face, Mitzu thought, was full of innocence and wonder.

"Will that be all?" she asked, placing the cup on the counter.

"That's it," he said.

She reached out for his dollar bill, taking it by the corner as though she was afraid to touch him. Still staring, she hit the keys of the cash register. She slid his change toward him and, slinking backward, leaned against the Coke dispenser.

"We don't get your kind in here much," she said. "You from around here?"

"No, I'm visiting," he said.

"Yeah? Somebody in town?"

"No, Crescent Park, the nuclear plant."

"Oh yeah?" she said, her face brightening. "You work down there?"

"No, I work for the company that built it."

"Oh yeah, where you from?"

"San Francisco."

"Yeah? Is it nice? Is it like on 'Streets of San Francisco,' like on the show?"

"Yes, it is," he said. "It's a beautiful city."

On a makeshift pair of shelf brackets above the Coke dispenser a radio played. ". . . and in continuing ceremonies to Tokyo the Prime Minister laid flowers at the memorial to those who died in the bombing of Hiroshima. This week Japan marks the thirty-fifth anniversary of the dropping of the atomic bomb. We'll have a special report on how the younger generation of Japan, born after the war, feels about the bomb. This is the CBS Radio Network."

The girl looked at Mitzu, who was staring at the radio.

"You Japanese?"

"No, I'm Chinese," he said.

"Oh."

He swallowed the last of his Coke, stepped into the hot afternoon sun, and headed for his car.

Hank Robbins listened to the two men and tried his best to take seriously what they were saying. Travis Webb sat impassively behind his desk.

"Hey, he's not crazy," Hank told them. "He's the only goddamned salesman I ever met from those companies who knows how these plants run. He was just here the day before yesterday and—"

Alex interrupted. "He was here the day before yesterday?"

"Yeah, he had an appointment for yesterday, but he

came early. He said the company just wanted us to know they were available when we needed their help."

Alex turned to Roger Alford and, in as unalarming a tone as possible, said, "Call Krieger in Connecticut and see if he's been there."

Alford left Travis Webb's office and perched on a desk in the anteroom. Alex watched him through the doorway picking up the phone.

"Hey, look, Mr. Burgess, what's wrong with this guy? I mean, what are you expecting him to do?"

"Mr. Robbins, listen carefully, please. Nagata may come back here. Maybe today, maybe tomorrow, maybe never. But if he does, I want you to pretend there's nothing wrong. Do you think you can do that?"

Robbins looked at the ashtray on Webb's desk. It was company issue, a brown glass thing in a leatherette-covered holder. Cigarette butts overflowed onto the desk.

"Hey, you know, you smoke a lot."

"I know," Alex said straightforwardly, disguising his impatience. "What did you do when he was here?"

"Well, you see, I've been having a helluva week. I got two control room men out sick, I got a transmission line burnt out and damn near dropped us into scram, and then my security chief tells me five solenoids are out at the control room entry doors, and . . . hold on, did you have anything to do with NRC calling a security alert?"

Alex looked at his watch. "Yes, we did. You were telling me what you did when Nagata was here."

"Yeah, well, I showed him my trouble spots. He showed me some refinements in the system. He's gonna send an engineer to work with my people."

"Specifically, Mr. Robbins. What *specifically* did you talk about?"

"The security systems and the fail-safe cutouts for the reactor, and the checkpoints to the control room."

Security, control room. It added up.

Alex figured he ought to tell Robbins everything. "Mr. Robbins—"

"Hank, call me Hank."

"Hank, I think Nagata may try to take over this plant and blow it up."

"He can't blow it up," Robbins said. "It won't blow up."

"If he dumps core water, Hank, what would happen?"

"Nobody's that dumb," Robbins said.

"If he *were* that dumb, what would happen?"

"You'd have radioactive clouds from here to Delaware."

"Then we understand each other," Alex said. "He's not that dumb, but he's that crazy. And he's dangerous. He's already killed three people."

And come close, Alex thought, to killing four. Alex was still wondering about the message on Jill's machine. He had thought of almost nothing else since he arrived in New York.

Roger Alford was hanging up the telephone in the anteroom to Webb's office. Alex saw that Robbins had retained his composure, but at the same time he detected a change in the room's emotional temperature. Robbins was getting the message.

"Mr. Burgess, if he's already killed three people and he's coming here, don't you think I ought to tell my men? We ought to get some help."

"We've got some," Alex said, standing as Roger entered.

"*Nada*," Alford said. "They haven't heard from him. His appointment wasn't until tomorrow anyway."

"What about Section Six?"

"They're on the way," Alford said, popping a stick of chewing gum into his mouth. "Be here in ten, maybe fifteen minutes."

"And the troopers?"

"In the woods. They'll let us know who approaches the gate. They're on our frequency." Alford turned to Travis Webb. "Mr. Webb, I briefed your men at the gate."

"They're good men," Travis Webb said.

Hank Robbins was beginning to sweat profusely. "Is it a little hot in here?" he asked.

"A little," Alex said, although the office was comfortably cool. "Now, Hank, when he comes, you're going to go out to the gate to pick him up, just like you usually do. And then you're going to bring him in here. Okay? You think you can do that?"

"Sure, uh, I guess, uh, will he try to kill *me?*"

"No, Hank, I don't think he will. Excuse me for a second, will you?"

He pulled Roger Alford out into the hall. "Rog, when Section Six gets here put two of them opposite the gate just inside the restraining wall, five in the bushes, and four inside the door to the plant. If it looks at all risky, if there's a chance he'll run for the money, they can take him down. But I want him alive."

"You're sure he'll show," Alford said.

"Ten to one," Alex said.

"Five bucks," Alford said. "You're on."

"Yellow Ford van up Crescent Park road," the voice squawked in Travis Webb's office. "Male driver behind the wheel. New Jersey plates. No other passengers visible."

The faces turned away from the radio console. Hank Robbins heaved a sigh of relief.

"That's my control room supervisor," Robbins said.

Roger Alford picked up his walkie-talkie. "Section Six, yellow van approaching gate. Not our man. Repeat, *not* our man. Alford."

"Check," came the reply.

"Maybe he's going to Connecticut," Robbins said.

"Maybe," Alex said. He picked up his coffee cup and walked to the tinted windows facing the main plant buildings. The containment vessel was just visible around the corner. Low privet bushes growing as a single long hedge fronted the entryway, and Alex stared to see if he could locate the Section Six men who were undoubtedly right behind them. They must be flat on their bellies. Tough fuckers. He thought he saw one of the hedges shimmy in the breeze, but there was no evidence of a man there. Beyond the hedges was a long open walkway to the plant itself, flanked by two kiosks decorated with bulletin boards, an attempt by the plant workers' wives to make the place more homey. The facade of the plant itself was unbroken by doorways or windows. It was a sheer sheet of gray marbled brick. The trap was set, ready for its quarry.

But it was the quarry who set the trap, Alex thought. It's his trap. It seemed impossible that Nagata couldn't know they were here. He had warned them. Alex remembered now that when the letter first arrived, he had assumed the man was not interested in being stopped. Which was, up to a point, correct. He had not wanted to be stopped too soon. I missed the most obvious point, Alex thought. He wanted us to chase him, but only reach him in the end. He knew that eventually we would find out who he was, and then trace him to a nuclear plant.

Alex lit a Lucky, walked to the coffee percolator, and filled his cup. Robbins, he noticed, was sweating more than ever. He was not going to be capable of meeting Nagata at the gate and convincing him to come into this building. Nagata would instantly smell his fear.

"White two-door sedan," the radio squawked. "New Jersey plates. Female driver behind the wheel. No passengers visible."

"Sally Kelleher," Travis Webb said. "Night shift secretary. She's due at four, but she's always early."

The phone message, Alex thought. He wouldn't have left the phone message if he didn't want to be caught.

"Section Six," Roger Alford said into his walkie-talkie. "White two-door sedan approaching gate. Not our man. Repeat, *not* our man."

"Check," came the reply.

Alex said, "Did you talk to Connecticut, Rog?"

"Yep," Alford said. "*Nada.*" He turned to Robbins. "Are you expecting anybody else? Is that all of them?"

"Sam Hochman's due at four," Robbins said. "He'll be right on time. Sam's never early."

Alford shot a short glance in Alex's direction, his implied concern obviously evident.

242

Alex turned to Robbins. "What kind of car does Hochman drive?" he asked gravely.

Robbins looked from Alford to Alex, and suddenly he, too, was aware of the danger.

"A new Rabbit," Robbins said. "What color is it, Travis? It's blue, isn't it?"

"Blue," Travis Webb said.

Roger Alford reached again for the walkie-talkie. "Hollie, if a blue Rabbit, male driver, comes your way, get him off the road and keep him there."

"I read you," came the reply.

Alex reached over Webb's desk for the walkie-talkie. "Hollister, don't stop him if there are any other cars coming up at the same time."

"I read you," Hollister said. "You want to keep him out of the cross."

"Right," Alex said, thinking there wouldn't be any crossfire.

It was ten minutes to four. Travis Webb stood up and strapped on his gun, a police revolver similar to the FBI standard issue.

"Mr. Webb," Alex said, "we'd like you to stay inside."

"We're on alert, sir," Webb said. "That means I'm supposed to hit every station every two hours."

"Mr. Webb, please, our men can handle everything," Alex said as politely as he could. "We don't want you to take a chance getting hurt."

Travis Webb sat down, clearly displeased. But he did not bother to unstrap his gun.

"Blue Chevrolet," the police radio squawked. "Up Crescent Park road. New York rental plates. Oriental male behind wheel. No other passengers visible."

"That's him," Alex said.

Roger Alford barked into his walkie-talkie. "Section Six, blue Chevrolet approaching gate. This is our man. Reapeat, this *is* our man."

"Check," came the reply.

Before Alford had finished, the police radio was squawking again. "Blue Volkswagen, New Jersey plates.

243

White male behind wheel. No other passengers visible. Now on Crescent Park road behind Chevrolet."

There was silence in Travis Webb's office. Hank Robbins gave Alex a pleading look, asking for help.

"Hank, just be cool. There's nothing wrong. Let your man park as usual and you escort Nagata over here. Do you know what you're going to say?"

"Yes, sir," Hank Robbins said, his breathing deep and irregular. "I have to get us security passes. He'll remember that we needed 'em."

Alex touched Robbins' hand. "Relax, Hank. You'll do just fine."

The intercom buzzer sounded and Robbins answered the call.

"Yes, let him through. I'll be right out."

Robbins set down the phone. Alex saw that Robbins' hands were steady. They had been shaking five minutes earlier.

"Good luck, Hank."

"Yeah," Robbins said dourly. "Thanks."

It happened very fast, and only later would Alex be able to reconstruct the precise sequence of events. From the window he watched Robbins walk toward the gate. As the steel frame slid open on its tracks and the blue Chevrolet pulled forward, Robbins stopped in front of the plant. Behind the Chevrolet the blue Rabbit sailed through the gate, its occupant waving to the guard on duty.

Roger Alford perched next to Alex near the window, walkie-talkie in hand. To Alford it seemed that Alex was giving all his attention to the unlit Lucky dangling from his lips. Alex was thinking of all the times he had waited for someone like this. The foggy night in Atlanta when two German terrorists were scheduled to rendezvous with a stockbroker who funneled their money through American banks, and who had been fingered by an alert post office clerk from a "Wanted" circular. The afternoon in New York when two Puerto Rican FALN terrorists were captured trying to plant a strip of plastique and a timer in a wastebasket in a Chase Manhattan bank. Now, outside, the Chevy was parking on the macadam directly in front of the privet hedges. But the Volkswagen had also stopped instead of continuing past to the parking lot at the rear of the security building.

"I coulda told you," Travis Webb said.

"Section Six," Alford said, "watch out for driver of the Volks."

Alex, into the walkie-talkie: "I want Nagata alive."

Nagata stepped from his car and was walking toward Robbins, who was feigning surprise. Nagata carried a long case in his hands.

"Section Six, he might be armed."

Sam Hochman, a squat balding man in his fifties, had left his car engine running and had come around to talk to Robbins. Robbins made an introduction. Nagata and Hochman shook hands. Robbins turned to steer Nagata toward the security building.

"Something's wrong," Alex said. "Nagata's not moving."

Nagata must have sensed Hank Robbins' tension, for he whirled around and grabbed Sam Hochman, pulling him against his chest. One of the walkie-talkies behind the hedges was open to transmit, and Alex heard a voice: "Mr. Robbins, come here immediately or I'll kill this man." Nagata had slid a sword from the case in his hand, and was pressing the blade against Sam Hochman's neck.

"Section Six, stay down," Alford said.

Nagata's voice could still be heard. "Hank, stand behind me and follow me into the plant. If you move away from my back, I'll kill this man. Stop! Don't go in that direction."

Hank Robbins did as he was told. He moved behind Mitzu Nagata, making a human sandwich.

Smart, Alex thought. We can't touch him.

"Section Six, stay down," Alford said. "If he sees you he's liable to slit that guy's throat. He's going into the plant. Section Six, scatter. Don't let him see you."

The men in the bushes, the men on the other side of the restraining wall, and the men in the security office watched mutely as Mitzu Nagata, with Hank Robbins against his back and Sam Hochman held tight to his chest, took short jerky steps into the main power plant.

Travis Webb picked up his phone. "Scram the plant. Get off the grid. Scram the plant. Do it now!"

With Robbins behind him and Sam Hochman in front, Mitzu slid quickly down the industrial gray hallway. At the end a guard was waiting, manning a swing-away gate at the top of a flight of steps.

"Move," Mitzu said. "Or I'll kill this man."

"Let him through," Hochman squeaked, feeling the sword's blade at his throat.

They descended slowly. On the third step Hank Robbins stopped.

"Stay right behind me, Hank," Mitzu said flatly. "I want to feel you against me. If I don't, I'll kill this man."

It was not the same voice Robbins had heard two days earlier. There was no easygoing charm, no buoyancy. But neither, oddly, was the voice angry or harsh. It was lonely and disembodied. Hank did not believe that Mitzu Nagata would kill anyone today.

But he obeyed the order. He stood close to Mitzu, step by step.

"If they shoot me in the back," Mitzu said, "I will still have time to cut his throat."

I'm right behind you, Hank thought. I'm right behind you and I'm not going anywhere else.

"Can you tell me why you're doing this?"

"Honor," Mitzu said. "Duty."

They were at the bottom of the steps. Mitzu glanced to his left. Robbins saw the shadow of a man disappear at the far end of the hallway.

"Come out," Mitzu said. "Drop your weapon, please."

He says *please*, Hank thought. He has a knife at Sam's neck and he's polite.

The man at the end of the hall moved into the light

and tossed his pistol onto the floor. The thud echoed up the hall.

"Come this way," Mitzu said.

The man started to walk. When he was halfway to them, Mitzu called out.

"Stop. Lie down, please, against the wall with your arms out in front of you. If you move, I will kill this man. Please don't get up. I don't want to hurt him, but I am a soldier."

Hank could hardly believe the voice now, so soft, and the behavior, so lucid. A soldier? What did he mean, a soldier? They edged past the man lying on the floor and continued to the first of three checkpoints leading to the control room. Above them was an enclosed gallery through which visitors passed on tours of the plant. Mitzu looked up.

"There's nobody there," Hank said.

Mitzu pulled Sam Hochman toward the wall. Hank Robbins moved with them. Mitzu opened a panel in the wall and picked up a telephone.

"Those above us will please stand up or I will kill this man."

Roger Alford's face rose into view beyond the Lucite windows. Hank looked up, and was suddenly terrified for Sam Hochman's life. It was easy to see the others hiding.

"All of you please stand up now. Please."

Alex's face appeared above the panels next to Alford. All around the glass gallery the faces rose into view, the entire Section Six squad, Travis Webb and three plant guards, and several New Jersey state troopers.

"We are going into the control room now," Mitzu said. "If you interfere I will kill this man." He hung up the phone. "Hank, your card, please."

"Mr. Nagata, uh, Mitch, it won't work. The solenoids are still down. I told you the other day."

Mitzu turned around to face Robbins, still holding the sword at Sam Hochman's throat.

"Why are you lying, Hank?"

"No, Mr. Nagata, uh, Mitch, I'm not." He reached

into his pocket. His hand was shaking uncontrollably. Christ, which pocket did I put the card in? Save me, I hope I didn't leave it in the office. He felt in his other pocket, and pulled out a white plastic card that activated the gate in front of them.

"Here," Robbins said, his voice quavering. "You can try it yourself. Don't hurt Sam, Mr. Nagata. You don't want to hurt Sam."

Mitzu smiled, an incomprehensibly indulgent smile, the smile of a deaf and dumb mute.

"No," Mitzu said. "I won't hurt him."

He inserted the white card into the slot. The gate did not open.

Mitzu whispered into Sam Hochman's ear. "What's your name?"

"Hochman," Sam said. "Sam Hochman."

"Mr. Hochman, I am very well trained in the art of the sword. If you do not do as I tell you, I will cut your head off. This isn't your time to die. Do as I tell you."

Sam swallowed hard. Hank could see that his cheeks were flushed. "Okay, whatever you say, whatever you want me to do."

"I am going to let you go, but don't run. Understand?"

"Right, I won't run."

Mitzu released Sam from his grip.

"It is my time to die," Mitzu said. "Please help me. Ask the men inside to open the door."

Sam Hochman leaned toward the speaker on the wall.

"It's Sam Hochman. Open the checkpoints."

No voice came back.

"Tell them I'm going to kill you."

"He's gonna kill me," Sam Hochman said.

Ten seconds went by, perhaps twenty. The gate did not open. Mitzu picked up the telephone that connected to the gallery above.

"If you do not instruct the men inside to open the control room gates, I will kill both of these men. Watch."

He lashed with the sword and sliced Hank Robbins'

shirt down the front, removing only the buttons. In the gallery above, Alex and Roger saw the demonstration.

"I can do what I promise," Mitzu said. "I can kill both men quickly. Now order the men to open the door."

The checkpoint gate hummed, then flew open.

"Go through the gate, Hank. You, too, Mr. Hochman."

The voice was changing now. It wasn't soft, and it wasn't polite either. It was cracking a little, sounding crazy.

He followed them through the three checkpoints. When they reached the control room door, they stopped.

"Open the door, Hank," Mitzu said. "Open it slowly and push it the whole way back."

"Yes, sir," Hank Robbins said.

He pushed the door open. The control room personnel stood in a row against the far wall. Hank glanced to his left at the control board. The plant had been scrammed. They were off the power grid. He saw Mitzu look at the control board, too, and Robbins knew that Mitzu could interpret the flashing lights.

Mitzu laid the blade of the sword across Hank Robbins' chest.

"You will all get out, now."

The nine men did not move.

"Get *out*, for Chrissakes," Hank shouted.

The nine men filed through the door, looking over their shoulders as they fled.

"You, too," Mitzu said to Robbins and Hochman.

Sam Hochman darted through the door and ran down the hallway.

"The sword," Hank Robbins said. It was still on his stomach.

Mitzu pulled the sword away.

"You know it's been scrammed," Robbins said, completely without fear. He knew Nagata wasn't interested in hurting him. "You know this plant better than I do. It'll take an hour to recycle it. By then they'll get you."

"Yes, I know," Mitzu said. "It's my time to die. Go, leave, please."

Up above, in the gallery above the control room,

Alex watched the two men talking. Sam Hochman was on his way through the door.

"What are they gabbing about?" Alex said. "Why the hell is Robbins talking to him?"

As Alex spoke, Hank Robbins backed out through the control room door. Alex leaned toward Travis Webb.

"The plant's off the grid, right?"

"That's right," Webb said. "We have about forty-five minutes to get him out of there before water recycles to the core. You better call for reinforcements, and fast."

They looked down. Mitzu Nagata was kneeling in the center of the room. He had taken off his jacket and shirt, which were on the floor in a pile. He held the handle of the sword in both hands, aiming at his own chest.

Alex said, "What in God's name is he doing now?"

Roger Alford turned his head away and fell back. Alex heard him retching, and then the others. The smell of vomit filled the air.

Mitzu plunged the sword into his abdomen. He pulled the blade upward, enacting *seppuku*, the samurai ritual of disembowelment. A grimace creased his face. He leaned forward onto the sword, twisting it, cutting through the tough flesh of his stomach. This is my death, he thought, this is my time to die. I am a soldier, dying for my Emperor. I am valorous and serene.

The pain stung more fiercely now. He looked down at his own flowing blood. A blinding anguish rose in his body like a flame. He felt as if his flesh were on fire. He pulled harder on the sword with all his remaining strength. The rising pain grew worse, but he did not cry out. Can I still be alive? His stomach opened. He felt light-headed. His blood was spilling in a torrent, pouring onto the floor. I am a soldier. There is a time to die. Am I alive? Should I not be dead? His knees slipped, spreading wider in the pool of blood.

His head fell to his chest, and he was dead.

28

THE CORRIDORS were dim. Blue light beamed down in murky circles. In the distance dishes rattled and a door creaked open and closed. At the nurse's station two interns discussed an orchiectomy performed that afternoon, and a nurse worked the crossword puzzle in the Baltimore *Sun*. The hospital was settling in for the night.

Alex trooped down the hall from the elevator, his jacket slung over his arm. He was weary—the last shuttle out of La Guardia had not departed until nearly ten. His mind was a jumble of unanswered questions—about Jill, about himself, about whether they would continue together.

In the solarium Burt was asleep on a couch, curled up and twisted like a rag doll. His briefcase was open on the floor amid copies of committee testimony and bills. Alex touched his shoulders and shook him.

"I'm back, Burt. Wake up."

Burt rubbed his eyes with his fingertips. He stood and threw his arms around Alex.

"You poor son of a bitch, how are you?"

"I'm okay. How's Jill?"

"She's up waiting for you, I think. Alex, be gentle with her. She's brokenhearted. She's afraid she's going to lose you."

They walked down the hall together, Burt with an arm around Alex's shoulders.

"I'll leave you two alone," Burt said.

"No, come on in. We talked it all out this morning, and I'm not up for any postmortems now."

She was sitting in bed, reading, when they entered.

"Oh, Alex, I'm so sorry. I can't tell you how sorry I am."

He went to her and hugged her tight against him.

"Alex, I wish I'd told you about him. On the phone this morning I didn't have the words to say what I meant. I just wanted to tell you that he was the first love affair I ever had and I . . . I . . ."

The speech had come fast, and now she was about to cry.

"Let it rest awhile," Alex said. "Did you get my message from Hollister?"

"About the baby," Jill said. "He told us. And about the report from the doctor in San Francisco. You know, I think Mitch in his madness was only doing what he had to do. What he thought was right."

"Jill, don't say that," Burt blurted out in exasperation. "He was a murderer."

"You don't understand. His family is descended from thousands of years of warriors. He spent his whole life trying to get away from that. You know the robe he was wearing? It was a symbol. He couldn't get away from his own history."

"Jill, I—"

"No, Burt, listen. You have to see how a man could crack apart, how he could believe everything his family stood for had been taken away from him. The minute I heard about the baby I knew. He told me the baby was fine. He needed to get back to something he'd lost. Alex, tell him you see what I mean."

Alex was so happy to see her alive, to know that the voice on the telephone had not been an illusion, that he wanted to agree with her.

"I suppose I do," he said.

"Well, I don't," Burt said. "I don't see it at all."

Alex slid his arm around Jill. He would wait to hear more about why she had invited Mitzu to her apartment. There wasn't much point in bringing it up now.

"He tried to kill me," she said. "And he killed the others. But it's almost as if *he* didn't do it, as if he were caught up in something mystical and too powerful for him. That's why he wore the robe. That's why he didn't get a gun. That's why he used the swords. He was going

252

back into time. It's as if he were . . . I don't know, an instrument of history."

"That's a romantic idea," Alex said. "What he was, was an instrument of murder."

Jill pulled away from both of them, staring down at the notes she had been taking. She would have to write about Mitzu Nagata someday, and about Hiroshima. She held up the book she had been reading. On the cover was a photograph of a mushroom cloud.

"He was a murderer," she said. "But ask yourselves why. And ask yourselves what were we all?"

GREAT ADVENTURES IN READING

☐ **CAITLYN McGREGOR** 14413 $2.95
  by Kitt Brown
  The story of a woman of the American frontier with a dream to build a homestead in the wilds of Kentucky.

☐ **HELLBORN** 14414 $2.50
  by Gary Brandner
  A novel of demonic terror and possession. A terrifying demon chooses his bride and a horrifying method to possess her.

☐ **FORBIDDEN WINE** 14419 $2.95
  by Fiona Harrowe
  Set in the fourteenth century, this is the tale of a woman trapped by passion and bound by a love she could never have.

☐ **LOVER'S CHOICE** 14420 $2.25
  by Cynthia Blair
  A tale for young adults about two beautiful but very different sisters who learn to accept themselves as women and like each other as friends.

☐ **THE UNINVITED GUEST** 14421 $2.50
  by Barbara Kennedy
  The perfection of Dan Griswold's Florida citrus empire is marred when a dead body floats ashore during his granddaughter's wedding reception.

Buy them at your local bookstore or use this handy coupon for ordering.

COLUMBIA BOOK SERVICE
32275 Mally Road, P.O. Box FB, Madison Heights, MI 48071

Please send me the books I have checked above. Orders for less than 5 books must include 75¢ for the first book and 25¢ for each additional book to cover postage and handling. Orders for 5 books or more postage is FREE. Send check or money order only. Allow 3-4 weeks for delivery.

Cost $_____ Name_____

Sales tax*_____ Address_____

Postage _____ City_____

Total $_____ State_____ Zip_____

*The government requires us to collect sales tax in all states except AK, DE, MT, NH and OR.

Prices and availability subject to change without notice.

8200

JOHN D. MacDONALD

The Travis McGee Series

Follow the quests of Travis McGee, amiable and incurable tilter at
conformity, boat-bum Quixote, hopeless sucker for starving kit-
tens, women in distress, and large, loose sums of money.

☐ THE DEEP BLUE GOOD-BY	14176	$2.25
☐ NIGHTMARE IN PINK	14259	$2.25
☐ A PURPLE PLACE FOR DYING	14219	$2.25
☐ THE QUICK RED FOX	14264	$2.25
☐ A DEADLY SHADE OF GOLD	14221	$2.50
☐ BRIGHT ORANGE FOR THE SHROUD	14243	$2.50
☐ DARKER THAN AMBER	14162	$2.50
☐ ONE FEARFUL YELLOW EYE	14146	$2.50
☐ PALE GRAY FOR GUILT	14148	$2.50
☐ THE GIRL IN THE PLAIN BROWN WRAPPER	14256	$2.25
☐ DRESS HER IN INDIGO	14170	$2.50
☐ THE LONG LAVENDER LOOK	13834	$2.50
☐ A TAN AND SANDY SILENCE	14220	$2.50
☐ THE SCARLET RUSE	13952	$2.50
☐ THE TURQUOISE LAMENT	14200	$2.25
☐ THE DREADFUL LEMON SKY	14148	$2.25
☐ THE EMPTY COPPER SEA	14149	$2.25
☐ THE GREEN RIPPER	14345	$2.50

Buy them at your local bookstore or use this handy coupon for ordering.

COLUMBIA BOOK SERVICE, CBS Publications
32275 Mally Road, P.O. Box FB, Madison Heights, MI 48071

Please send me the books I have checked above. Orders for less than 5 books
must include 75¢ for the first book and 25¢ for each additional book to cover
postage and handling. Orders for 5 books or more postage is FREE. Send check
or money order only. Allow 3–4 weeks for delivery.

Cost $_____   Name _____

Sales tax*_____   Address _____

Postage_____   City _____

Total $_____   State _____ Zip _____

*The government requires us to collect sales tax in all states except AK, DE,
MT, NH and OR.
Prices and availability subject to change without notice.
8193

CLASSIC BESTSELLERS
from FAWCETT BOOKS